MW00770732

WEAVING DREAMS IN OAXACA

(wah-HAH-kah)

A NOVEL

May you weave your own beautiful dreams—

KAREN SAMUELSON

Karen Samuelson

Lucia Press

WEAVING DREAMS IN OAXACA

Copyright © 2023 Karen Samuelson

All rights reserved. This book or any portion thereof may not be reproduced or used in any manner whatsoever without the express written permission of the author, except for the use of brief quotations embodied in critical articles or book reviews.

This book is a work of fiction. References to real people, events, establishments, organizations, or locales are intended only to provide a sense of authenticity, and are used fictitiously. All other characters, and all incidents and dialogue, are drawn from the author's imagination and are not to be construed as real.

A glossary of Spanish/French terms is provided in the back of the book.

FIRST EDITION

Identifiers: ISBN 979-8-218-12713-8

Interior Design by Word-2-Kindle
Cover design by Karen Samuelson and Amy Calkins
Map art by Alana Ambrose
Author photo by Earl Christie

To adopted children everywhere and their families,
including mine:
My husband and son, my own true loves.

Two roads diverged in a wood, and I—
I took the one less traveled by,
And that has made all the difference.
--Robert Frost

PUEBLA
VERACRUZ
GULF OF MEXICO
OAXACA
LACHATAO
BENITO JUÁREZ
OAXACA
SANTA ANA
XOXOCOTLÁN
JUCHITÁN
GULF OF TEHUANTEPEC
PACIFIC OCEAN

Chapter One

FRANCESCA
New York City ~ August

SHIMMERING VIOLET

Francesca Shannon, Frankie, a lead in the dance company NYC Moves, has never approached the West Village studio in such a state. Her stomach is a wreck. She pauses outside the entrance to look at the poster of last year's spring performance where she's midair in a grand jeté wearing a shimmering violet slip. Smashing, she thinks. Frankie loves the contrast with her coppery-brown skin and is grateful to the photographer who captured this stunning moment, her best self.

As she walks up the narrow flight of wooden stairs, sheened with age, today she notices every grain and scar. God, you'd think I'd have better stamina for these things, she berates herself. At the threshold to the second floor, Frankie tucks her unruly auburn hair into a silvery headscarf and unshoulders her dance bag.

She is at once transported by familiar sounds of feet tapping out hip-hop, jazz rhythms and whispered landings in ballet: all live, beat-to-beat sculpting. A colleague's voice counts out the time to a jazz routine in Studio A. Snatches of Curtis Mayfield come from Studio B. She pauses and tears fill her eyes; she hadn't expected to cry so soon. This is the place where she's grown from a girl into a woman. It is home, at times more so than it was living with her mother. Is that all about to change?

Her imagined conversation with Raoul, the Director, has been haunting her waking and sleeping, like a dull headache. At age sixty-six, his chiseled face, lined but beautiful, falls into a scowl when she interrupts his phone call, but Frankie can't wait anymore. She knows he and the other dancers have noticed her drop in weight from one-hundred and twenty-five to one-hundred and nineteen pounds. At five-feet nine, it's tipped the balance from thin to skinny, not a good look on her, and she doesn't blame them for wondering. Yet, she's not going to tell all. She wants to speak with Raoul privately.

Immersed in a heated phone call, he hits the off button with vigor. This is not the moment Frankie was hoping for. She enters his office and closes the door. Her hands are shaking so badly, she clasps them behind her. Although Frankie's rehearsed this conversation ad nauseum over the past three months, her stomach does a sickening nose dive.

"Yes, Frankie, what is it?" Raoul stands up as if he has someplace else to go making her even more nervous.

She plunges in with an ungainly staccato. "Raoul, I need a break." Her heart is thrusting itself against her breastbone. She pauses and breathes deeply the way she's been trained to make it through a rigorous dance piece. "I need some time to think things through, to decide if I want to stay with the company. There's so much travelling, and rehearsals are twenty-four seven." Frankie pauses. "I'm thinking about having a family, Raoul, and for me, the two don't mix." She breathes slowly, her pulse beginning to regulate. "I was dragged to a new neighborhood in Brooklyn every three years as a kid, and that was bad enough, never mind hauling a kid through Europe while on tour. Plus, as you're well aware, I'm thirty-two."

Raoul's jaw drops onto his Gucci crucifix and gets stuck there for a few seconds. "Oh my God, Frankie, you've got to be kidding! You could probably dance up until your forties in some capacity. And I don't need to tell you about all the prima donnas literally waiting in the wings." Raoul holds out his hands in disbelief. "We're in New York City, the Big Apple, the juicy one everyone wants to tear into." Frankie backs up to the door and unable to stop the tears, covers her face with her hands.

"Oh my." He comes around from his desk and opens his arms. "Come here Frankie, come give Raoul a hug. Okay, that's better; don't make me cry too." Frankie cries in his arms, aware of the strong muscles enclosing her. "How long do you think you'll need?"

Looking into the gray-green eyes she can get lost in, Frankie says, "Three months. I want to leave the country and get a fresh perspective."

"I knew something was up dearest; we all did. You've lost weight and have been acting prickly and that's not like you. And this is not coming at a great time, but it's never easy in the arts, is it? Okay sweetie, three months. That's all I can give. That means a decision before the New Year, before casting and rehearsals for the spring performance."

Raoul scans Frankie up and down. When he touches her cheek, it feels like he's looking into her soul. "I think you are right now exhausted, Francesca. Dancing is in your blood. It's who you are. You just need some time to rest all those lovely muscles. And children? Shouldn't there be a limit to all this breeding?"

Raoul laughs, but Frankie knows he finds children annoying. "Okay, go figure things out, but let's talk first. Let's have a drink together." He tilts his head. "And I know the breakup with David was a nightmare. It was a while ago, but is that a part of all this?"

Frankie hesitates, "Yes. There's lots to sort out."

But Raoul doesn't know the whole story, the reason David felt betrayed and why he vanished. No one in the company knew she was pregnant last year. Certainly, no one knew about the abortion, or that her weight loss wasn't just about David, but the unexpected avalanche of grief and doubt that toppled her appetite for life. Only Paula, her best friend from high school, has been privy to all this. Thank God for Paula's Buddhist compassion, her listening and not judging, their precious friendship.

Frankie chose not to tell her mother she was pregnant for the same reason she didn't tell David. Their personalities are too big and could have swayed her one way or the other.

She's not proud of this vulnerability. But, Frankie knows that as a lawyer, David has uncanny skills of persuasion; and her mother, she's certain, would have said anything to keep her performing. Motherhood and dance; they're on her terms.

Raoul tears up as he wipes Frankie's cheek. "We'll all really miss you this season. I'll miss you *so* much."

Frankie grabs a Kleenex off his desk and blows her nose. "Me too. But first, I'm going to take one last class, the Master Class with Juliette. She's come all the way from Paris, and I've been wanting to study with her for over a year."

"Yes, you do that, and don't forget how good it feels and how few people on this planet can move the way professional dancers can, the way you can Frankie. It's a gift. You've worked so hard to be the spectacular dancer you are, the fouetté queen. Don't give it up now." Raoul looks truly distressed.

Frankie nods and tries to smile. "I know Raoul, but of all people, you know these gifts come at a cost. I wasn't counting before, but now I need to think things through."

Raoul opens the door. "I'll call you tomorrow about having that drink."

She looks back at his beloved face. "Thanks Raoul," and she gives him another hug.

Juliette in Studio C has just begun the warm-up. Frankie learns the quirky jazz routine with ease but feels no soul, only muscle. She cuts out early, something she's never done in twenty-four years of classes and hurries off to the changing room. Her body feels leaden, but the top of her head is light, like it's going to spin out of the room and split her in two. She peels off her top and tights, the cloth and sweat clinging to her skin like a lover and wonders if it's really possible she could have performed her last dance with NYC Moves. A gripping sensation in her gut keels her over and she holds her belly. When David left it was more like a full body slam and ensuing six-month ache. The post-abortion was pure panic and self-doubt. But this!

Frankie throws on her street clothes, foregoing make-up and hair. She doesn't want to see anyone from the company. On 7th Avenue, trying to cross the honking chaotic street, Frankie fights a monstrous urge to run back up the studio stairs and cry her heart out in Raoul's arms. She waits on the sidewalk in a limbo of agony for two full sets of lights: green/yellow/red/; green/yellow/red, not caring if people think she's crazy. Finally, Frankie forces herself to race to the other side. She's played her hand. The scene is shot. There is no take two.

Chapter Two

Oaxaca, Mexico ~ Early September

A MONKEY AND A PARACHUTE

Resting her head on the plane's window, Frankie longs to ride on the weightless ease of the cottony clouds. Today, as it often does, flying makes her feel tender and reflective. She thinks about the Brooklyn dance studios where she studied ballet, jazz, modern and improvisation and the parade of teachers that began at age seven. Dancing has always fed her soul like nothing else. Music, playing her body like an instrument of finely-tuned nerves and muscles, is her perfect partner. And Frankie, extending, releasing, collapsing and leaping, loses herself in the interplay of gravity and space. She has finessed a high axel turn like no other dancer in her company, and critics portray her as "poetry in motion".

She remembers, at age fourteen, the rush of being accepted into Brooklyn's High School for the Performing Arts. Her mother, Patricia Shannon, Tricia, was there every step of the way, driving her to school and classes in the bleak deep-freeze of January. To this day, her mother always sits in the front row and claps the loudest and longest. Frankie finds her mother proud, loving, and annoying beyond measure.

Frankie's also learned to endure the gritty underbelly of professional dancing: muscle wrenching workouts, torn ligaments, physical therapy, mountains of ice packs, and pain meds, but at this moment, aloft over Mexico, she is happily pain free.

Frankie latches her seatbelt and closes her eyes as they prepare for the descent. In a half-hour she'll be on the ground in Oaxaca, one of the southernmost states in Mexico. This trip, an arrow shot deep into the heart of another culture, puts a vast enough distance between her and the Big Apple. A painter friend from Soho couldn't stop talking about the light and architecture and general vibe of the city. She said it was surrounded by Indigenous pueblos with amazing artisans and folk art. Frankie is excited about exploring, brushing up on her Spanish, and looking for a place to volunteer with children. She hopes spending time with them will help her organically come to the right decision about the "if" and "when" of motherhood.

No one, except Paula and Raoul, knows the questions she's struggling with, not even her mother, especially not her mother, who would have proclaimed her opinion as if it were truth. Still, Frankie doesn't like lying to her. She's told her mom that she and several dancers from NYC Moves are collaborating with a Oaxacan dance troupe this fall. Oh well, sometimes a little fiction is necessary to move forward with real life.

Frankie stops herself from asking the woman next to her if she could keep her annoying elbow on her side of the arm rest. Paula, in her gentle way, has made her see that frankness is something she should work on toning down. Frankie doesn't mean to offend: she's just being honest. At times, she blames her mother for her lack of filters, but she will add Paula's suggestion to her Oaxacan to-do list.

Frankie smooths her pants along her thighs, and for the third time, checks to make sure her passport, three pairs of glasses and wallet are still in her carry-on bag. During this flight, she's become painfully aware that her regrets and a life-altering decision have been in a holding pattern for too long, weighing on her shoulders like an undeployed parachute. She's tired of this freefall and prays it will open soon revealing the best place to land.

Frankie reapplies her cherry-blossom lipstick, adjusts her earrings, and sits up straighter. Wanting answers but trying not to obsess reminds her of the one meditation class she went to with Paula. The Buddhist monk began the session with, "Whatever you do, don't think about the monkey." Well, this monkey is crawling all over Frankie and whooping in her ear as the plane descends into the Oaxacan Valley.

Chapter Three

PROFESSOR MACDONALD
April (that same year) – Amherst, Massachusetts

SPIDERS

Daniel MacDonald, Ph.D. is known to his students as Professor Mac. He heads into the Arts and Humanities building at the University of Massachusetts main campus in Amherst. The name MacDonald and a light Boston accent are the only Irish things about him with skin more olive than his Italian mother, coal-black hair and beautiful cocoa-brown eyes that make many an undergrad's heart flutter. He enters the classroom and dumps his folders and computer on the desk.

"Okay folks, listen up. Remember to get your immunization cards in to me by Monday. The trip to Guatemala is in just two weeks, and I'm very excited about visiting Tikal together. As you know, it's the most famous of Maya ruins, and pre-Columbian Maya culture is my favorite subject. *And*, what's "Mayan" is yours."

A group groan is punctuated by real laughter from a tattooed thin brunette in the front row, Adriana, who habitually taps her glittery fingernails on the desk.

"Okay illustrious crew, please get into your groups from yesterday. I'm going to pass out your weekly brain crunchers. And 'No, Sam, that is not a cereal'" elicits another groan as students move into their groups.

Professor Mac has the enviable ability to focus on each student so they feel like the only person in the room, and they love him for it. He orchestrates lively discussions in his field of pre-Columbian History and Culture focusing on Mexico and Central America, his areas of expertise. On weekends, Mac plays with a jazz-funk band, his musicality and skills on the keyboard adding to his charisma. Riffs constantly run through his head: riffs he hums out loud, often unknowingly.

After class, Mac heads to the Student Center Cafe to grab some lunch and gets into the salad bar line. At five-feet eight inches with a zest for the entire food pyramid and sitting for hours correcting papers, he has to watch what he eats. Vegetable gardening is a hobby, but it's not particularly aerobic and leads right back to the refrigerator.

"Hi Professor Mac! Sounds like someone's happy today. Is that an original song? Does your group play that?"

Mac turns around. "Oh, hi Adriana. I guess I was humming." Embarrassed at being heard, he sets that aside. For Mac, students are a sacrosanct group, and teaching is more a calling than a job. Last year, he and his wife, Deanna, took in two students fall semester because they couldn't afford housing. He has to admit though, the way Adriana can go on and on does at times make him want to seek shelter.

"I'm so excited about our field trip! I've been googling articles about Tikal every night. You know, I've never been out of the United States before." As Adriana speaks, she gets closer and closer. Mac isn't fully comfortable with the skimpy tight clothes of most undergrads and would appreciate more barriers between all their lovely exposed skin and him.

"Well, as your first trip abroad, it must be exciting. I hope visiting the ruins will make what I've been teaching come alive." And despite himself, he feels a tingle of excitement when Adriana momentarily puts her hand on his forearm, a ring on each finger.

"I'm sure it will, but I'm so nervous about the shots. I'm a needle-phobe, but I'll make myself do it for the trip."

"You'll do fine. It's all very quick. And full disclosure, I'm an arachnophobe."

"Oh, that's a thing about spiders, right?"

"Yes. Terrified of them." Mac pays for his salad. "Well, off to get some coffee."

"Okay, but wow, you haven't made one pun yet." Adriana gives him a conspiring smirk.

"I'll come up with one for Friday."

"See ya, Professor. Bye-bye. Later."

Mac heads to the coffee section to grab an espresso. He watches as Adriana, staring at the army-green kale, abruptly switches to the burger and fries line, and he fears she has a crush on him. Mac finds her an inquisitive, bright student, who's no longer annoying now that he knows how to juke her verbiage and carry the day's topic into the end zone.

And, she appreciates his word-play when others groan. If it weren't about her, she'd appreciate his current football metaphor, especially since most would guess he's never carried a football anywhere, never mind the end zone.

Mac walks across the quad to an old brick Greek Revival structure with two white columns. His third-floor office has a bird's eye view of the quad. The windows rattle in the Northeast winter winds, and in the summer, are open to the drone of bees and lawn mowers. This building must be last on the list for green renovations, he figures.

Mac closes his office door and puts down his salad and espresso next to a picture of Deanna, his wife, small and blonde, with light brown eyes. She's a little plump and Mac loves her that way. He thinks of her as cherubic and revels in her softness and curves. He also loves her razor-sharp mind and acerbic wit which is anything but angelic. With a doctorate in epidemiology, she's a principal scientist at Bionomic Labs in Greenfield, researching infant respiratory diseases and their relationship to climate change.

Deanna views the world through the lens of a scientist. For that reason, Mac is hesitant to tell her about an unusual dream he had last night that has stuck with him all morning. He was somewhere in the woods sitting in a circle of people, and there was fog or smoke swirling around them. They were chanting in a language he didn't understand, yet he was drawn to them and felt a part of the group. Maybe he'd had too much wine at dinner, or it could have been the melatonin. He read someplace it can give people weird dreams.

***

At home that evening, Mac corrects papers and has dinner alone as Deanna is working late at the lab. They live in a small pale-green Victorian house in Montague, Massachusetts, a tiny New England town with a manicured common and spired white church. Twenty-minutes due north of Amherst and fifteen-minutes south of Greenfield, it's in perfect commuting distance for both.

Two hours later, as he's turning out the bedroom light, Mac hears Deanna come home. Lately, he's been craving more of a sexual connection and tonight it's all he can think about. When she climbs into bed, he pulls her close and knows she can feel his desire. "I'm sorry Mac," she speaks into his chest. "I'm so pooped, but let's plan a time on the weekend."

So much for spontaneity, Mac thinks. "Fine. You let me know when." He turns away but the ache continues and sleep eludes him. Maybe the countless hours and constant stress at the lab is why they haven't had sex lately? Then he wonders if he's manly enough, acquiescing to Deanna about not having children and how to spend vacations. She always seems so sure of things. Is his passivity a turn-off?

Their first summer together, she made it clear she didn't want children. She explained that as a Catholic, her life's purpose is to ease the suffering of children, and those children she considers family. Besides, she said, "The planet's choking itself to death with people."

It sounded noble at the time, so Mac brushed aside any reservations. He fell more and more into her orbit, and the following February, on Valentine's Day, asked her to marry him. He was vaguely aware of the danger in acquiescing, but he did and does truly love her. He respects her dedication and intelligence, and depends on her understanding and support.

Mac rolls onto his back and tries to remember the last time they made love. It takes a few moments, but the images emerge; he recalls the softness and scent of her skin no one else sees and touches. He has to admit though, lately he's tired of being his own best friend in that department and hopes she'll want to be intimate before the trip to Tikal. Mac would love her to join him, but her research always seems to be at a crucial phase, and that's just how it is.

Mac fluffs up his pillow, feels Pumpkin, their overweight orange tabby, jump up to sleep at the foot of the bed, and an hour later succumbs to the darkness and Pumpkin's rhythmic purring.

Chapter Four

Tikal, Guatemala (April, two weeks later)

COPAL

Mac, with incipient joy, looks around the wooden table at his class of twelve: young men, women, and gender-fluids of various races, an ethnic and economically diverse group. This is why he loves teaching at a large state university. He wouldn't trade it for the Ivy Leaguers any day. And this trip to the Yucatán Peninsula in Guatemala is a thrill, his first time travelling with students to Tikal, a key to understanding pre-Columbian culture. They're in Flores, an island in Lake Petén Itzá in the northeast of Guatemala. Yesterday they spent the day touring locally and resting up for their pre-dawn excursion.

At 2 a.m., Mac accompanies them to the only restaurant open at this hour. They order plates of tortillas, fried eggs and black beans. As the sleepy students eat, they mumble together softly or listen to music on earbuds. He reminds them that the shuttle bus will leave in twenty minutes. Adriana sits across from Mac and stares when he's not looking. Mac, oblivious, dunks a tortilla into his egg yolk.

Under starlight, they shuffle on cobblestone streets to the bus. The air, with moisture from the fog settled over the lake, is warm and palpable. It's too dark for the students to see that the bus is painted in bright primary colors, but Mac knows from his previous visits to Central America. He stands outside the bus and watches as each student climbs up and says "Hola" or nods to the driver. A statue of El Virgen de Guadalupe is bolted to the dash and a picture of Jesus dangles from the mirror. Music plays even at this dreamy hour, a band with a prominent horn section, but the volume is not raised yet, thank God. Each bus driver is their own DJ and proud interior decorator of their motorized shrine, a tribute to Catholic saints and Indigenous gods that bless and protect their journeys.

Once they're under way, Mac stands up and faces his class. "Okay, my illustrious ones, I know you'd prefer to sleep and I get it, but let's go over a few things before entering the realm of the Ancient Maya." A few students groan but Adriana is wide awake.

"We have an hour and a half ride to the Petén Jungle in the Tikal National Forest and our ETA is thirty minutes prior to sunrise. Get ready to see one of the largest cities the Maya ever built. Let's review a few facts so you'll have them fresh in your mind, then you can rest. As you've learned, the Maya were sophisticated mathematicians, architects, and astronomers with their own observatories. They worshipped their celestial gods by building temples aligned with the risings and settings of the sun and moon.

Where do we get much of our knowledge of their culture and mythology?"

Adriana's hand shoots up. "The Popul Vuh."

"Exactly! And what does the Popol Vuh tell us about the hero twins who defeated the Lords of Death?... Yes, Nico?"

"They went to the underworld and came back with their slain father's head, which is kind of cool but gross, and then since they were heroes, they put the twins in the sky as the sun and the moon."

"Yes, very good, and the temples, constructed to highlight their movements, created celestial light shows to entertain and appease the gods. Who remembers the name of the moon goddess?" Mac looks around. "Rachid?"

"Ixchel."

"Bingo! What an impressive crew. And they're still unearthing the history and secrets of the Maya. Don't forget, after flourishing from 700 BC to 900 AD, they mysteriously disappeared, like Atlantis and dinosaurs." Mac pauses. "Wow, pretty eloquent for 3 a.m. Okay, back to sleep."

Kids nod off as the bus travels the smooth highway. The entrance bracelets Mac ordered are already on their wrists as they'll enter Tikal before the majority of the morning workers. Mac closes his eyes and hums quietly, tapping his feet, as a riff arises from this country's feel and sounds. In the bus headlights, the flat green land flies past. In one hour, the jungle canopies in the north will emerge like the waves of a vast green ocean.

***

Julio, their guide, accustomed to getting up early, greets the class with gusto. He leads the way on the twenty-minute walk to Temple IV, warning the drowsy students to watch their steps over roots as large as limbs. Mac has already checked that everyone has their requisite water bottles, bug spray and sunscreen for the later solar onslaught of a normal jungle day. Julio leads them to the largest known pyramid of the Maya world, Temple IV, facing east and rising to two-hundred and two feet. He shines a giant flashlight for safe footing; trekking at this angle is not for the faint of heart or sleepy. They carefully climb the wooden stairs, erected so visitors don't have to attempt the original, very narrow steep stone steps. At the top of the stairs, they land on the temple's limestone platform, a base for the summit shrine with its giant roof comb in Petén style. The students and Mac sit on the ancient stone blocks, knee to knee, waiting.

Within minutes, a fanlight of iridescent spokes begins to pierce the dark and spread over the horizon, the jungle's natural wake up call. Spider monkeys begin to squeal as howler monkeys screech. Toucans chirp at nearby birds who squawk and trill. The verdant undergrowth stretches itself awake with small movements. Here, above the jungle canopy, they have a soaring quetzal's view. Mac feels the hairs on his arms rise, and even Adriana is awestruck into silence. Light threads itself through the green canopy and grows, orchestrating a symphony of color and sound. Yes, Mac thinks. This is precisely why people spend hours on a plane, sleep on lumpy mattresses and arise at an ungodly hour. This is what "awesome" truly means. In his students' eyes he sees the reflected sunrise as they honor these ineffable moments with a holy silence.

Shafts of light play along other temple tops and walls. Mac is transfixed. He hears the screeching of what sounds to him like the howler monkeys, but then feels the pull of an unprecedented sensation catapulting his consciousness. Their screeching becomes a screaming crowd as the jungle below opens up into a field. Men are running in and out of shafts of light after what looks like a rubber ball. They wear helmets and hip pads and have marvelous hair arrangements. These short men are bronzed and muscled in ways Mac hasn't seen in his time. He intuitively knows the rules of the game and wants to run and join them. Copal incense wafts around the crowd as the spectators jump to their feet screaming and pumping fists into the air.

Suddenly, and again without volition, Mac is back on the stone pyramid stair with his students, the screaming fans silenced. He looks around to see if anyone else appears as stunned as he feels; the students all looked mesmerized, but in a relaxed way. Adriana notices him looking and smiles.

The smell of copal has unleashed a memory of childhood dreams; he was a player, just like those men on the field. He drew pictures of them, and when he showed his parents, they commented on his drawing ability and exceptional imagination. But by the time Mac was ten, the dreams had stopped and were forgotten until this moment. He wonders what happened to his drawings.

After another few minutes, the wondrous light show is complete, and the sun twin is in the sky merely doing his day job. The guide begins to tell them the history of the Maya, but Mac, for the first time in his life, has a hard time paying attention to talk about rain and corn gods, stelae and hieroglyphics. What out-of-body experience just happened, he wonders. Was that a trance? A parallel universe? He considers perhaps he's spent too much time studying the pre-Columbian world and is now experiencing time warps. And what about those dreams as a kid?

It's already getting warmer, but Mac is sweating from more than the temperature. Is he becoming unglued from jet lag? No, Tikal is only two hours earlier. Mac takes deep breaths to center himself. He tries to chalk the experience up to a sometimes-overactive imagination.

Julio leads the group down the stairs, as Mac takes up the rear, watching his steps carefully and listening to jungle sounds that are eerily familiar.

Chapter Five

A STRANGER'S COLOGNE

Frankie makes her way back from a huge outdoor market across town from her apartment in Jalatlaco, one of the many neighborhoods in Oaxaca. In her smooth, long lines of elegant clothes and big hoop earrings, she moves with a grace people notice.

As she walks through the zócalo, the central plaza, a signature of Hispanic cities and towns, she stops in front of its beautiful colonial church, La Catedral de Nuestra Señora de la Asunción. Frankie read the books her artist friend gave her about Mexican history and learned how the ornate facades hide the Spanish Conquistadores' heinous past when churches were often erected on stolen holy ground on top of Indigenous temples. It makes her look at the graceful arches and columns with more discernment. Never having been a great student, she loves this experience of learning about the world by seeing and touching it.

Crossing over Calle Benito Juárez, she turns left towards Jalatlaco, but the sky opens up with a sudden afternoon downpour typical towards the end of the rainy season. El Saguaro, a corner restaurant, signals a welcoming refuge with courtyard twinkle lights and waving palms. Frankie tucks herself behind a corner table next to a terra cotta planter and orders a café con leche. Strands of lights, like long-legged ballerinas, are draped along the restaurant walls. As she sips her coffee, she looks into the mirror across the room; in this lighting her auburn hair looks chestnut, her hazel eyes black and her edges softer, more relaxed. She loves the effect... incognito in Oaxaca, a chica instead of a shiksa as some of her friends back home call her.

A young man and woman who look to be in their early twenties sit at the table next to her. Frankie admires the young woman's gorgeous white embroidered blouse and covets her glossy black cascade of hair. Being a dancer, Frankie notices people's bodies and sees the young man is lithe with a masculine shadow of a beard and a striking profile. He wears black jeans and a light-blue cotton shirt. Their skin is a lovely amber, the color of dark honey. Frankie's has a more bronzed tone with a light splash of freckles over her cheekbones. She knows her color is from the Jamaican father she's never met, since her mom is a strawberry-blonde with alabaster skin and ocean blue eyes.

Frankie opens the book she bought written in Spanish in the hopes of reviving her once advanced-level fluency. As she flattens it out, she notices the shape of her fingernails. Usually, weekly manicures deter her from using them as worry beads, but on this trip, she's given up and places one hand under her thigh to hide the nubs. She'd like another coffee and feels impatient at the waiter's lackluster pace, but instead takes the opportunity to cultivate patience. Paula would be so proud.

Frankie becomes absorbed in reading about the complex lives and love relationship between Diego Rivera, the Mexican muralist, and Frida Kahlo, the painter. She knew they were socialists, but didn't know Rivera slept with Frida's sister, splintering apart their marriage. She also learned that Frida's mother was a Tehuana, a Zapotec woman from the Isthmus of Tehuantepec, which is what inspired Frida's brilliant clothing. Frankie notices her self-portraits displayed on shirts, calendars and books all over Oaxaca. She loves her bold look. As she reads about the personal tragedy and pain Frida incorporated into her unblinking art, Frankie appreciates her as a woman who lived life true to her core. Frida died in 1954, but Frankie wishes they could have met and imagines their becoming acquaintances.

A "Buenas tardes" pulls her away from her Frida fantasy. "Excuse me, por favor, la crema?" The man from the next table is standing in front of her pointing to the creamer.

"Of course." But, before Frankie can hand him the tiny pitcher, he extends his hand. Oh shit, she thinks. I don't want to talk, but I can't be the rude Americana. She shakes his hand, smiles and makes a mental note to tell Paula how polite she's become. The man continues standing there after taking the creamer.

Frankie's barely able to get out a "No hablo español" even though she speaks fairly well, when he interrupts.

"Ah, no problema. I speak English. I have studied English with Americans who visit here, and I thought you looked like una Americana."

Damn, I was hoping I could pass for French, or at least generic European, but I have to credit him for not saying gringa. His girlfriend smiles at her as if she understands English as well. Though annoyed at having her solitude interrupted, Frankie now notices an aroma of spiced tomatoes wafting across the terra cotta tiles from the kitchen. It mixes with the wet ancient cobblestone streets and the not-so-subtle fragrance of this stranger's cologne.

"Is this your first time in Oaxaca?"

"Yes. I arrived a few days ago."

The young man looks at the woman at his table who nods, and he says, "Well then, why don't you join us? We are from Santa Ana del Valle, a pueblo thirty-five or so kilometers southeast of the city, but we know Oaxaca very well."

Oh no, tour guides looking for a customer? She wonders.

"Also, would you like to try with us some mezcal…our local drink…do you know it? It's alcohol from the maguey cactus. People compare it to tequila, but it's different, a little smoky, delicious!"

Here we go, she thinks, a tour guide and liquor salesman. Frankie looks at the woman who says, "Si, venga," and pats the chair next to her.

Okay, it's getting hard to refuse a little friendliness and mezcal on a lazy, rainy Wednesday afternoon in a place where she knows absolutely no one. I just hope this isn't some kind of con. Thought like a true New Yorker, Frankie notes, smiling to herself and them at the same time. She gathers her belongings and arranges them precisely in her bag, surprisingly grateful for a little company.

Somewhere between the coconut and almond mezcals, Frankie loses track of time and any muscle tension she's been carrying. She's no longer self-conscious about her fingernails and uses her hands expressively to punctuate her speaking. She learns that Enrique and Raquel are celebrating the opening of a garage on Highway 190 where Enrique just landed a job as a mechanic.

"And at night I DJ right here," Enrique says. He spreads his arms expansively as if he owns the place. "It turns into a dance club. You should come sometime."

"Yes, that sounds like fun. I could definitely improve my salsa."

"Aha! I am a master teacher of the art of salsa." With a flair, he snaps his fingers in the air. "I give classes at nine and the dancing begins at ten."

Raquel nods with enthusiasm. "Si, he is fantástico. You should really come."

The mezcals magically appear from the bar and Frankie notices no money has exchanged hands. They ask Frankie about her life, and although it's not their fault, she feels self-protective not wanting her cover, her anonymity, compromised. After another mezcal though, she thinks, what the hell.

"I'm a professional dancer in New York City, and I'm down here sorting out a few things." Frankie almost says, I'm on a break but knows no dancer can take a break as there's always the fear you won't be able to come back. She silently reminds herself to find a gym and personal trainer by the end of the week. She crosses her legs, sits up straighter and looks at each of them. "I'm at a kind of crossroad."

"A dancer, si? De veras?" Enrique tilts his head towards Raquel. "Then you can teach Raquel and me some moves. But crossroad, what is this?"

Frankie has to admit Enrique is becoming more guapo with every question and toss of mezcal, and Raquel doesn't seem jealous like the Latinas in the telenovelas. Frankie realizes that's a stereotype but the thought materializes anyway. At least she didn't say it aloud. She imagines Paula's smile like a blessing.

Raquel explains before Frankie can. "A crossroad is a time when you have an important decision to make." She crosses her index fingers in an "X" to demonstrate. "So, you need to choose which way to go. It's like me. Should I apply to medical school in Guadalajara or finish my nursing degree and work here in Oaxaca?"

Frankie leans closer. "Your English is really good. I wish I could speak Spanish that well." Raquel smiles beatifically.

Enrique holds Raquel's gaze and nods a solemn, yes. "This crossroad is something I understand completamente."

Frankie thinks maybe Raquel wants Enrique to pop the big question, or maybe she wants him to support her idea of going to medical school. In any case, something's up.

"You're ambitious, Raquel. Med school's tough. I was never very good at school."

"Yes, I am. I want to help Indigenous people in pueblos like where we come from. Western medical care isn't easily available, and there's some suspicion of medicine other than traditional healing. That's valid too, but there are other ways. I was lucky. I got a scholarship to study nursing at the Autonomous University of Oaxaca."

"Impressive."

Enrique adds, "Very. Only two scholarships each year for twelve pueblos."

"I'm not great at weaving which many people in my village do; they're beautiful artisans, but I don't have that temperament or talent. I had to find another way."

Enrique looks at Frankie. "Raquel's a brain. She was the smartest kid in Santa Ana. Tenth grade was enough for me." Raquel's cell phone rings and she excuses herself leaving Frankie alone with Enrique. Oh God, Frankie thinks, is this a ploy? Part of the sales/con scheme? Get the gringa drunk and leave her with the telenovela star? Frankie leans back but the quick movement makes her dizzy.

"I really need to get going. I'll ask for the check."

"No worries, Francesca. You're our guest. No need to pay."

"Thank you, Enrique, that's very kind. I'll at least leave the tip then." Frankie puts down a generous tip and gets up as gracefully as she can.

"Oh, let me give you a lift on my motorcycle. It's a little bumpy, but I'd be happy to do this."

"What about Raquel?"

"I'll come back for her. Soon." Frankie lets go of feeling like she needs answers to everything right away, and something loosens up inside. I can look at this crossroad as an adventure, not a burden, and still have fun while I figure things out. No grasping. Go with the flow. Let things evolve. Paula would be so proud of me, that little Buddha. As she and Enrique are leaving the bar, he turns to the bartender.

"Hasta luego, Gregorio." Gregorio looks to be in his mid-thirties. He's lighter-skinned than Enrique and taller with brown wavy hair and blue eyes.

Gregorio winks. "Adiós, guapo." Frankie agrees that Enrique's handsome but is surprised to hear it from the bartender.

"I'll be back to get Raquel in a bit."

"I'll be waiting," Gregorio shouts out with a kind of *come and get me* attitude.

Outside, Frankie gratefully leans on the restaurant wall and notices the rain has stopped. The buildings are washed clean, and the late afternoon light is golden on the yellow-stoned municipal buildings. She looks at Enrique. "Are you okay to drive?"

"Of course not, Francesca, my American friend," he smiles mischievously, "but it's more fun this way, and it's only a few blocks." Frankie's penchant for control is rendered useless by his enchanting smile and the alcohol. She laughs. Frankie's long harbored a motorcycle-mama fantasy: riding naked holding onto a handsome dude with the wind caressing her skin and hair. This is as close as she'll ever get. She would never risk riding a motorcycle or even a scooter in NYC. Dancers in casts need not apply. But here, in this moment, she chooses a thrill. Who is this woman in Oaxaca?

As Enrique and Frankie turn the corner of the building and head to the parking lot, Frankie thinks, what could go wrong in a few blocks? She hops on the back of the motorcycle which barely accommodates her leggy frame. It's a heady ride hanging onto Enrique's taut waist. The shops and restaurants fly by. When a street opens to the east, she can see the low-slung Sierra Madres embracing the Oaxacan valley. They cruise into Jalatlaco, and Frankie tells Enrique to stop at the smaller zócalo there called El Llano, or plain. She's not going to let this guy know where she lives. She's not that drunk. Trying to make a dignified exit off the bike, she is a dancer after all, she visualizes a tour jeté which gives her enough momentum to land on her feet, not squarely, but at least upright.

Enrique looks back and yells, "I'll call you soon." Oh dear, did I give him my number? Oh yes, something about his uncle and kids and an orphanage and children's center nearby. Oh God, I must have blabbed more than I thought.

Frankie waves goodbye, and feeling light as a sparrow, sings a silly ditty forming in her head. "Mañana iguana, si! Muchacha borracha, si!" Oops, she trips over a cobblestone but rights herself quickly, hoping no one has noticed. She remembers the last time she drank this much; it was at Sanzibar's on 15th Street five years ago on her 27th birthday, the night she met David. Paula's astrologer friend was right, at least about meeting him. Frankie brushes the air to shoo away uncomfortable memories. Her thoughts float back to Enrique. This fun-loving guy has his beautiful and brilliant girlfriend and a flirty bartender blowing kisses and calling him handsome... hmmm.

She resumes singing. "I must be loca y moca; muchacha borracha; mango y tango!" Inspired, Frankie does a little tango step through the black iron gate to her apartment next to the main house.

Her private haven has tiled floors, pine furniture and bright cushions. She's already decorated the refrigerator with pictures of Paula, her mom and the dance company, as well as *The Four Agreements.* They're excerpted from a book of the same name by Don Miguel Ruiz, a Mexican author. The book was last year's birthday gift from Paula, chosen to help Frankie launch her self-improvement plan. *Do Your Best - Be Impeccable With Your Words - Don't Make Assumptions - Don't Take Anything Personally.* She hasn't exactly followed them this afternoon but is still feeling unusually good about herself. She realizes just getting out of New York City has been transformative, like shedding a winter coat for fabric that breathes.

Frankie opens the sliding glass door in the bedroom to the patio, her favorite space. Old bird cages are full of yellow impatiens tumbling onto the brick floor, and fuchsia bougainvillea flings itself over the patio wall like a diva. She drinks in the colors.

In a corner is a blue-striped hammock she manages to climb into without spilling out the other side. For the rest of the afternoon, Frankie enjoys a mezcal-induced siesta with lovely erotic undertones.

Chapter Six

LA AMERICANA

Enrique returns to El Saguaro after dropping off Frankie, la Americana. He plans to contact her in a few days since she wants to volunteer with children and may be able to help out his uncle, Tío Pepe.

He goes in through the back entrance. Gregorio is bringing out a case of beer from the walk-in cooler with a bar towel draped over one shoulder. He shuts the door with the back of his foot, puts the case down on a table and they embrace without a word. Enrique puts his hands in Gregorio's back jean pockets. Gregorio sighs, rests his head on Enrique's shoulder for a moment and then backs up to look him in the eye.

"You're not going to try that gringa thing again, are you?"

Enrique smiles and jumps back like a puppy. He knows he sometimes annoys Gregorio who's twelve years his senior and a serious painter. At first, Enrique worried their educational differences might be a problem, but in the year they've been together, he knows Gregorio has come to respect him and appreciate his curious mind. Gregorio's taught Enrique about art and music and the world writ large and seems to enjoy his role as guide and mentor.

"Look, mi amor, our last attempt with a gringa was disastrous. Please don't involve that poor girl."

Enrique says coyly, "Maybe I wasn't even thinking about it." He takes the bar towel off Gregorio's shoulder, tosses it around his neck and pulls him closer. Gregorio puts a finger on Enrique's lip to stop his attempt at a kiss.

"Then why did you invite her to your table?"

"I thought I could talk her into a tour on my bike, you know to the typical places: El Tule, Teotitlán del Valle, and even Santa Ana, but then she talked about wanting to volunteer at an orphanage or children's center, someplace where she could spend time with children. And she's not a poor girl, believe me. She's a professional dancer from New York City on a break."

"A real professional? An artist? Or some pole dancer in a dive bar?"

"No, de veras. It's true. She's with a dance company and says she has no time to spend with children there and wants to give back, so I told her about Tío Pepe's place in Santa Cruz Xoxocotlán, and I got her number."

"Hey, can someone get a drink here?" They hear Raquel calling from the bar.

"I have to go. Raquel has classes in the morning and tomorrow's my first day at the garage." Enrique pulls him close with the towel and Gregorio kisses him softly on the lips.

"You know, mi vida, in the long run it would be easier to just be honest with your father, abuela and Teresa."

"Oh sure, and then Teresa won't ever let me near Miguel. Do we have to go over this again?"

"Fine, you torment me. I torment you, but all this pretending is its own torment." Then Gregorio kisses him harder. Enrique turns to leave.

"Tell Raquel I'll meet her out back in the parking lot. Oh, and just so you know, I do think la Americana would make the perfect novia." He smiles playfully. Gregorio looks like he's going to say something but just shakes his head and walks back to the bar.

Chapter Seven

IT TAKES A VILLAGE

Two days after the mezcal madness at El Saguaro, Frankie's cell phone wakes her.

"Hola, gringa Francesca," says Enrique. "Do you want to see Santa Ana del Valle, mi pueblo bonito?"

"Enrique?" Dear God, he sounds as chipper as her mother in the morning. She looks at her clock. "Oh my God! It's only 7 a.m." She waits for Enrique to acknowledge the early hour, but nothing. Maybe it's cultural, maybe just personal, and then the concept of "stretching" rescues her. Does it really matter?

"Francesca, I am close by to your neighborhood." Frankie sits up, brushes a hand through her hair, and thinks, what the hell, he's just one of those energetic people, probably up at 5. "I'm going to visit Teresa and my son Miguel. I don't think I mentioned them before. She was my girlfriend, my novia. We broke up a few years ago, but we're still friends, and I like to spend as much time as I can with my son."

"Wow, you've got lots going on." She conjures up Raquel sitting at the bar and Gregorio blowing a kiss.

"And Uncle Pepe, my dad's brother, is visiting for lunch. I thought you'd want to meet him. He's the Director of Nuestros Niños que Necesitan Ayuda y Amor, or Our Children in Need of Help and Love, also known as NNAA. It's the children's place we talked about. He said he'd love to talk with you about volunteering, especially since you speak Spanish." Frankie gets out of bed and talks while taking off her pajamas. She can do this—spontaneity, adventure and kids!

"Great!" she says. "I'll be at the Llano, on the corner by Avenida Benito Juárez, in ten minutes."

"Bueno!" He hangs up. Frankie wonders if this is the development of a friendship or a tour she should pay for? Something like this would be more comfortably clear in the U.S. Time to fully embrace the *go with it* attitude. At El Saguaro, he did mention giving tours as a part-time gig, along with his work at the garage and being a DJ, and he's also a dad! Goodness, Enrique has the stamina of a professional dancer!

Frankie throws on the capris she wore yesterday, finds her favorite jersey and grabs a sweater in case it's windy. She brushes her teeth, applies a bit of eyeliner, but foregoes the lipstick. She doesn't know how they dress in Santa Ana and doesn't want to stand out, even though everything about her screams Americana apparently. She deftly threads a yellow scarf through her hair to keep it off her face.

***

Being on the motorcycle is electric and the wind heavenly as Frankie hangs onto Enrique. This intimacy causes her a twinge of awkwardness she didn't have when drunk, but his comfort-level and energy are contagious. She gets caught up in the novelty of every tienda and side street they pass, and soon they're climbing up the foothills into the countryside.

They arrive in Santa Ana and Enrique parks the bike at the town plaza. He takes Frankie on a tour of the small, but ornate church, La Iglesia de Santa Ana del Valle, adorned with a gilded altarpiece and statues. Close by is a community historical museum called Shan-Dany where local archeological finds are exhibited and kept, not sold to larger museums. Frankie soaks in Enrique's practiced and knowledgeable lectures.

After the tour, in the town's only comedor, they drink coffee and eat chilaquíles. Frankie loves the lightly fried corn tortillas with cheese and cream, especially with salsa verde, a green chili sauce. When it's time for the check, Enrique insists on paying, but Frankie feels awkward.

"Enrique, please let me know your fee for today. I know giving tours is also your work."

"No problema, Francesca." For some reason he calls her Francesca instead of Frankie. "You will maybe help my Tío Pepe, so I will help you."

"Well, I'm going to at least pay for gas and breakfast." She thrusts thirty dollars into his top pocket. When he starts to speak, she says, "No, no, no, no."

Enrique shrugs and winks. "Thank you. I like the bossy women." He gets up. "Okay, let's walk down the hill to Teresa's. You'll love the view."

True to his gregarious nature, Enrique makes their morning walk entertaining by introducing her to every Santa Ana resident they pass. Frankie is humbled and happy to be included in this way. Does he do this with all the tourists, she wonders? As they near Teresa's house, Frankie sees a young woman coming out the front door with a woven bag slung over her shoulder and a small boy by her side. She lights up when she sees Enrique.

"Teresa! Miguelito!" Enrique yells and the adorable three-year old runs towards them. Enrique swoops Miguel up in a bear hug and gives Teresa a peck on the cheek.

"Teresa, this is Francesca. I'm giving her the Santa Ana del Valle tour. She's from the States, from New York City."

"Mucho gusto, Francesca," she says and extends her hand.

"Igualmente."

Enrique swings Miguel around. "I know this isn't my day with Miguel, but I wanted to say hi." Teresa smiles.

Frankie notices how her lovely smile complements a calm, unhurried presence.

"That's nice. Walk with us then. Venga. Tía Panuela and Ana Maria are watching Miguel while I work at el Mercado de Artesanías."

As Miguel zigzags up the road swiping a stick back and forth at imaginary foes, Enrique touches Frankie's arm. "You should see the market with their beautiful weavings. Santa Ana del Valle is famous, especially for its rugs, like Teotitlán del Valle, and Teresa's a master weaver."

Teresa smiles. "Si, come by the market. Always someone is working on the pedal-loom. You will see wool with all colors natural from las plantas y insectos. We weave by hand. Come."

"I'd love to." Frankie thinks it sounds intriguing but wonders if she'll be expected to make a large purchase as part of the tour, then tries not to get ahead of herself. One of *The Four Agreements* comes to mind. *Don't Make Assumptions.* And, not for the first time, she wonders if she needs to work on trusting people more.

Frankie lags behind allowing them to walk together as a family as they move up past the plaza and down a dirt side street. Again, she wonders about Enrique's sexuality, and if he is straight, does Teresa know about Raquel? Is she jealous? In NYC, she had excellent gaydar, but in another culture, she knows she could be misinterpreting signs. She reminds herself again about assumptions.

Miguel's aunt and cousin greet him with kisses and sweep him inside the house. As beautiful as Frankie finds this to witness, it also stirs up longing and envy. Since David's out of my life, could I possibly do family in a different way like this? What about adopting as a single mom? Artificial insemination? Would Paula help? My mother, once she got over herself? But wouldn't a family with two parents be better? And could I leave a child behind for weeks when I went on tour? Frankie's torrent of questions brings on a headache and she loosens her scarf. It's okay. This is why I came to Oaxaca, to figure this out. She's stopped walking without realizing it, and Teresa and Enrique, ahead by twenty feet, turn around.

"Are you okay Francesca?" asks Enrique. "Do you need some water? The road is dusty."

"I'll buy some at the comedor. No worries."

"Bueno. We are close by to there."

She catches up, then lags slightly behind. Even though Miguel doesn't have Enrique living at home with him, she sees the unity to their arrangement and certainly love. Then again, this is a different culture. In this pueblo, there literally is an extended family and village helping raise Miguel. Back home, she'd have to create her own, but where would she start? Most of the dancers she knows don't have children. Frankie considers putting her mother in charge, her capable day-care director mother. Oh, I really am confused! she thinks.

The three of them reach the town plaza and step inside el Mercado de Artesanías, a single-story building with a white interior, the perfect backdrop for the brilliantly-colored rugs, table runners, and tablecloths hung on the walls and from the ceiling. Frankie and other tourists take time to admire the works of art: the rainbow of colors in signature Zapotec designs and the woven depictions of trees and birds.

Women in knee-length cotton dresses with smock-aprons sell smaller woven items on tables: handbags, coasters, placemats and smaller rugs. Teresa explains that many weavers here have clients in the Southwestern U.S. or sell in the bigger markets in Tlacolula and Teotitlán del Valle.

Frankie peruses the tables for gifts for Paula, Raoul, her mom, and three of her closest dancer friends, Tina, Audrey and Phillipe. After purchasing woven bags and placemats, she buys a medium-sized rug for her apartment in New York, content that with what she's bought, she's contributed to the community and will have a lovely memento of Santa Ana.

After saying their good-byes to Teresa, Enrique and Frankie ride north on his bike to his house a mile and a half away. She's looking forward to meeting his father, grandmother, and Uncle Pepe and having lunch together. She's already worked up an appetite and is hoping Uncle Pepe will like her.

Chapter Eight

SCORPIONS AND A JAGUAR

After spending all day in Tikal, Mac and the students are back at the hotel. As the students nap, Mac is busy sketching pictures of his unexpected foray into a pre-Columbian Maya sporting event. He often draws or doodles when thinking about problems or working his way through a difficult piece of music. He's pleased at the detail he's rendering and can almost smell the copal.

That evening after dinner, once the students are off to their rooms, he calls Deanna and is instantly soothed by her voice. "Mac, I was getting worried since I hadn't heard from you."

"Oh, sweetie." At a loss for how to explain his mystifying experience, he looks around the room. "Oh… it was a spider. I was doing battle with an arachnid hovering between me and the cell phone."

She laughs. "As long as it isn't a scorpion."

"Scorpion? They have those down here?"

"Yes Mac, just shake out your shoes before you put them on."

"Thanks Deanna!"

"You'll be fine. They're hardly ever fatal. Just don't startle one, and definitely shake out your shoes." Mac looks with suspicion at his shoes under the nightstand and moves further back on the bed.

They talk about their days, Mac avoiding the most important part, but when Deanna says, "Sweet dreams my wandering professor," Mac interrupts.

"Wait a minute, honey. I need to tell you something. The oddest thing happened." Mac explains his out-of-body experience as best he can; moments of silence follow.

"You're just overtired Mac. You have a lot of responsibility with all those kids and it's probably getting to you. And you do have quite an imagination."

"That's all true, but this felt different."

"I'm sure things will feel better in the morning. You know how that is. Love you. Get some sleep."

"Love you more."

The call ends, and Mac thinks, I don't know. I think this is going to feel just as strange in the morning. He lies back on the thin uneven mattress, listening for the footfalls of spiders and longing for the arms of sleep to rescue him. Deanna was right about the responsibility. He knows his students are taking advantage of the drinking age. He's heard the music and hooting and imagines there's a continual waterfall of mezcal and margaritas they're diving into. Hopefully, no one's getting pregnant. Maybe Deanna's right and it was all his imagination.

It isn't until dawn that Mac finally enters the depths of REM sleep, but his subconscious state is soon lured into a very different realm.

***

Hot steamy vapor smelling like eucalyptus and something he can't place rises around him in what looks like a sweat lodge. He's able to breathe alright if he inhales slowly. He's sitting in a hazy circle with five figures who are chanting in a language he doesn't recognize. Meditatively, each person stands up and walks one behind the other. Mac follows and ducks through a low opening to find himself outside of a circular palm hut next to a grotto with cobalt-blue water. Pillows of mist float everywhere. The three-quarter moon, reflected on the water, ripples the faces of three men and two women; they look Indigenous but not necessarily Maya. The men wear white cloths wrapped around their loins and the women, white tunics. Each immerses themselves in the cold grotto water, creating steam that spirals into the darkness. Mac copies them in this midnight baptism. They step out onto a path of moonlight, sweat and water mingled, reflecting each to the other like beacons. Mac shakes himself off like a wet dog and follows as they form a circle on the ground between the hut and grotto.

After some moments of silence, a man sitting at the furthest end of the circle, lean and brown with long silvery hair begins playing a drum between his crossed legs. He repeats an ancient rhythmic pattern. Everyone closes their eyes and Mac follows. The rhythm is meditative and transportive. Mac, no longer aware of his body or time, feels diffused in a sense of lightness and liberation. When he opens his eyes, an animal has appeared by each person. The drummer has a beautiful marble-skinned snake languidly wrapped around his neck. A bear floats above a man who looks like a Native American with regal features like they're carved of rock; he reminds Mac of Sitting Bull, the Sioux leader. There's a woman to his right with a raven perched on her left shoulder. Compact and exuding an earthy strength, her long black hair matches the raven's sheen. A tall Black man with broad shoulders has a beautiful multi-colored quetzal resting on his forearm. The other woman sits erect; wavy golden hair cascades over her sharp bones. A monkey, perched on her shoulders, circles its arms on top of her head, like a halo. The animals feel omniscient. Mac wonders if he has one and turns to look. The liquid green eyes of a sleek black jaguar shine back. Mac intuits a fierce loyalty from the jaguar he's never experienced in life. He senses his animal is trying to communicate something and twists closer.

Mac awakens, suspended over the edge of the bed, tangled and damp in mosquito netting. It takes him a few seconds to realize where he is. He wonders, is this sweat or grotto water? He lays back to let the enigmatic images wash over him. They remind him of that odd dream he had last spring before going to Tikal. As Mac becomes more alert, he starts to think, but the more he thinks, the more he questions his sanity which sends him rushing to the mirror. He looks deeply into the reflection of his eyes for so long he feels like he's being sucked into a tunnel. Who am I? Who are those people and animals? Why was *I* there, wherever *there* was.

Mac wonders if the hallucinogenic drug the Maya sometimes use in ritual ceremonies hasn't infiltrated the drinking water. Then he remembers he's only been drinking bottled water. After a few minutes, he starts to calm down. As his anxiety wanes, the amazing visual aspects of his dream become more intriguing than disturbing, and the eyes of the jaguar more enticing.

He straightens out the covers and mosquito netting and settles onto the mattress. He is comforted by the fact they'll leave for Massachusetts in two days. For the most part, it's been a great trip, but he's looking forward to getting home and being with Deanna. He'll finish up the spring semester in two weeks and teach only one course in the summer when he'll have time to reflect on and explore what these experiences might mean. In the fall, he'll happily be on sabbatical.

Chapter Nine

Montague, Massachusetts (August)

THUNDERCLOUDS

It's been over four months since the Tikal trip. On a late August afternoon, Mac is reading in his study in Montague. A wall of windows overlooks a brook and field studded with oaks and maples on the cusp of autumn's fiery explosion.

He's grateful his sabbatical will give him plenty of time to research in his field, but especially to continue to dig deep into the unusual experiences that have continued from time to time since Tikal. In his research, Mac has settled on the topic of shamanism and Indigenous healing circles. He was familiar with some facets of shamanism from his field of study but is now aware of its worldwide scope beginning ages before the European conquests.

Mac understands that these people in his vision-dreams, as he thinks of them, are healers with spirit animals to guide and protect them, and they operate outside of our known space and time. He's considering studying this fall with a renowned shaman who gives workshops in nearby Vermont. He shares his experiences with Deanna sparingly, as her usual response is to roll her eyes and say, "What an imagination you have, Mac!"

He wonders, why him, given his fear of blood and spiders. As an academic, he prefers books and maps and artifacts. But these mysterious vision-dreams touch on something deep inside. He wishes Deanna were more open instead of walling him off outside her western-based medical monolith.

While he's musing, thunderclouds blossom from the stifling heat that collides with a cold front heading south from Canada. The air quickens and the room darkens. Mac loves the quirky changes in New England weather and its four seasons, but fall, this upcoming one, is his favorite. Feeling more alive in the brisk autumn air, he'll zip up his corduroy jacket and roam the woods suffused with yellow, gold, and cardinal-red leaves. He looks forward to picking apples with Deanna. They'll make pies for neighbors' potlucks and he loves the woodstove smoke that scents the air. Autumn winds whisper that anything's possible, and for Mac right now, this is especially true.

Conversely, this late muggy summer afternoon is draining. The comfy tweed couch tempts him from his desk. He lies back and Pumpkin jumps up, settling on his chest and purring in his ear. Sleep seduces and gently nudges Mac over the edge.

It begins as usual with a circle. This time they're inside sand dunes scented with beach-roses, a crystalline ocean breathing nearby. Each person communes with their animal and shares healing information telepathically. Sometimes it's about specific cases and other times about healing modalities they're introducing into the world through practitioners.

When done, all except Xanu, the head shaman, get up and start along a footpath towards the sea. Mac hears a message in his mind to stay back and turns to the silver-haired elder and kneels before him. The shaman reaches his right hand and places it on Mac's right shoulder, then places his left on Max's left, making an X, a crossroad. His eyes are a green-brown hazel with gold flecks. His hands exude warmth, and Mac understands directly that they're bonded by a shared energy.

"Mac, you are an old soul and have roots with ancestors long ago in Mexico with the Olmecs, Maya and Zapotecs. Your past is calling and will be revealed to you soon. May your past, too, be a part of your future. Remember, I am always here for you."

Mac wakes and sits up, his shoulders still warm from Xanu's hands, and he feels charged with purpose. He finds it curious that Xanu is pointing him to Mexico, a center of pre-Columbian culture so dear to him. But roots? Maybe he's referring to a past life. As he said, I'm an old soul.

When Mac hears Deanna come in the front door and walk into the kitchen, it brings him back to the present moment.

"Yum! I smell something good!" He hears a pot lid lifted and placed back. "Pesto! Oh, my favorite! Did you use veggies from the garden?"

Mac gently puts Pumpkin aside to join Deanna. He loves making her happy with his cooking. The proud owner of a green thumb, dirt and plants are his Zen place like when he plays the keyboards. He's made a salad with homegrown green leafy lettuce and cherry tomatoes and bought fresh parmesan and mini-raviolis, her favorite pasta.

Deanna grins. "Wow! "I'm starving!" She puts down her brown leather bag and puts her arms around his neck. "You're the best." Mac kisses the top of her head.

"Yes, just for you, my sweet," but inside he's nervous at the thought of trying to explain his "conversation" with Xanu. Deanna's skeptical his vision-dreams have any intrinsic meaning. She says it's all brain chemistry and that the purpose of night dreams is to sort through our conscious chaos. She is a credentialled scientist after all, with a life dedicated to what can be seen, measured and manipulated. She's suggested Mac see a therapist, but he knows this isn't a mental health issue. Xanu's reference to Mexico has directed his compass, but how can he begin to explain this to Deanna? Mac's stomach flutters so much it diminishes his appetite, no small feat.

Deanna sets the table. "Red or white?"

"There's a cold chardonnay in the fridge." Deanna pours two chilled glasses and they have a lovely meal, catching up on her current experiment and Mac's research for a new course he's creating on pre-Columbian healing. He doesn't use the word "shamanism" with present company, but all this withholding does not sit well with him. Could the slippery slope of deception open up to a chasm in our marriage, he wonders. Or am I just being over the top? Don't all relationships survive because of small deceptions? His black panther comes to mind, and Mac feels the steadying force of his green eyes.

"Deanna, after dinner, why don't we go for a walk along the stream while it's still light out?"

***

They walk through a fallow field to get to the stream and follow it into the woods. Nudged forward by the wine and his desire to be authentic, Mac plunges into an avalanche of words.

Deanna listens through to the end, then stops short. "But I thought you were working on your new course?" Deanna's wearied expression makes Mac cringe inside. "Really Mac, why don't you speak with a professional? There are so many psychologists around here."

Mac speaks carefully. "They're not ordinary dreams, Deanna. Look, I can tell you're exhausted; we can talk tomorrow."

"But we're talking now, Mac. Can you explain more about this message and a possible trip to Mexico?"

"That I have roots there and maybe things for me to learn. It could be part of my sabbatical work."

"But who gave you this message? One of the phantom healers?" Deanna shakes her head. "I've tried to be patient, but what is happening to you, Mac? And I'm not the only one who's worried. Did you see the look on your parents' faces last Sunday at dinner when you told them about your Tikal experience?"

"They're not stories, Deanna. I've told you they're experiences. I think of them as vision-dreams."

"Oh, my God! Visions? Was the Virgin Mary there too?"

"That's not funny, Deanna."

"None of this is funny." With a smoldering look, she turns back towards the house, picking up her pace. Mac hurries to keep up. Deanna talks into the wind without looking back. "I don't know what to do with these conversations. And, what upsets me the most, is that you act like this is all normal."

Once in the kitchen, Deanna flings the refrigerator door open. "God, I hope we have more wine." She looks at Mac. "If not, maybe you could make some out of water because I can't do this without drugs which it sounds like you're on." Deanna leans back against the counter, crosses her arms and catches her breath. "Instead of getting help, Mac, it's like you want to go deeper, but it's totally weird stuff."

"To you, but what if I *do* want to learn more? Why are your beliefs more real than my phantoms as you call them? Look at the Trinity, a three-Gods-in-one bargain. What's the proof there? And since you brought it up, turning water into wine, all those Christian miracles, are they any less weird than shamanism?"

"For one, I thought we shared those beliefs, and Christ *was* a historical figure who lived and breathed as a human."

"Fine, I'll give you that, but he was pretty magical. And, I do share most of your beliefs, but none of it negates shamans being connected to a higher power."

"But why does it interest you so much when you live in one of the most advanced areas in the world in medicine and science?"

"The vision-dreams, Deanna! They're fascinating and involve me personally. And, *clearly* there's more than one way of understanding the world."

Exasperated, Mac heads out the screen door.

Deanna yells, "Mac, please!"

But he's already striding across the field heading towards the stream.

***

Mac returns within the half-hour and stands silently at the doorway to the dining room. He can see Deanna, chardonnay in hand, standing by the study window. She's watching a hawk circle over the field as a small bird, protecting its nest, charges and disturbs its flight. Deanna massages her temple then sits on the couch next to Pumpkin. He sprawls onto her lap and she pets him. Hopefully, she's soothing both of them, Mac thinks.

Mac knows patience has never been Deanna's strong suit, so he lets her be and starts cleaning up the kitchen. She's admitted before she's a bit of a control freak, and Mac feels sorry for upsetting her world, but she could try to be more understanding. Instead of judging him, she could be more objectively curious about his experiences, even if she's not comfortable with them. Isn't that part of love? Stretching enough to make room for the other?

Chapter Ten

CHOCOLATE SAUCE

An undeclared truce, like the cool fall weather, settles over the house. It is both an impasse and a respite, unsustainable but temporarily keeping the peace. Relationships can stand only so much discord before there are cracks, a leaning towards breakage, entropy. But Mac and Deanna are trying, they really are.

Today is Mac's parents' forty-second anniversary and they're coming over to celebrate. Deanna's roasting a chicken with potatoes and vegetables, and Mac is cutting up fruit for dessert crêpes with a top-secret chocolate sauce he devised over decades of a blissful addiction. He used it to seduce Deanna and it clearly worked, but that was then.

Deanna slips up behind Mac and puts her arms around his ribs, her head resting on his back. "Sweetheart, please don't get mad, but is it possible to not bring up the dreams, I mean vision-dreams again? It's not like you're booked for Mexico or anything, and it *is* your parents' special day."

Mac stops mid-stir, turns and hugs Deanna then bends to kiss her lips. "Not to worry. No problema mi amor." He smiles to himself and thinks maybe his chocolate sauce is still working.

***

The four are seated at the table, with Mac's mom, Sophia to his right. Her hair is a silky salt and pepper color, pulled back in a loose bun. She's a pretty woman who's kept herself in shape with yoga and swimming. Joseph, his dad, sits across from him. He's having some problems with high blood pressure and has ostensibly been on a diet, but is just as robust as ever. He has a commanding presence and delightful Irish wit. Mac holds a plate of vegetables out to his mom, but instead of taking them, she stares at Mac. He puts the plate back down, and she puts a hand on his forearm.

"Daniel, are you having any more of those dreams?" Her eyes fill up.

Mac's stomach tightens and he glances at Deanna. "Mom, we're not going to talk about that. Today we're celebrating your anniversary." Mac raises his glass but only Deanna reciprocates.

His dad is looking at his mom. "Sophia, I thought we were going to wait until after dinner?" Looking shaky, Sophia puts her head in her hands.

"Oh my God, mom. What is it?" Deanna comes around and puts her arms around her and says softly, "It's okay. Mac's okay. He really is." Deanna looks at Mac and her father-in-law with confusion and concern.

Sophia sips from her water glass. "There's something we need to talk about. Once Deanna mentioned Mexico, that was it."

Mac looks at Deanna. "You told them about Mexico?"

"Just briefly, an update."

"So, I can't talk about my life, but you can?"

"Well, we've all been concerned."

"So, my family talks behind my back?"

Joseph intervenes. "That's enough. Daniel, there's something your mother and I need to tell you."

"Oh God, is one of you sick?"

"No son. No, thank God. Daniel, after your mother and I got married, we tried to conceive, for many years. We went to doctors. Your mom had a condition that made chances mighty slim. There was nothing then like there is now with all these egg donations and implantation what-have-yous. Your mother was under a lot of pressure. You know the Italians. The constant 'When are you two gonna have a kid?'"

Sophia puts a silencing hand on Joseph's arm. "I couldn't get pregnant, Mac, and my sisters, all four of them were having kids, even my two younger ones. At first, I was happy for them, of course, but as time went by, it got harder: baby showers, baptisms, first communions, birthday parties. I had to act like the happy sister, smiling all the time, but inside I was miserable."

Joseph intervenes. "I never felt it was a problem, but those Italians, it's like an eleventh commandment for God's sake. 'You must bear children. Whenever possible, many.'" He gently places his hand on Sophia's arm. "Your mom took it to heart."

"Yes, because I so desperately wanted a child."

Mac looks at them. "So, where did *I* come from? Am I like a *surrogate* child?"

Joseph tries a soothing voice. "We're getting to that."

The calmer he is, the tenser Mac feels. "But I've seen my baby pictures. I saw pictures of mom pregnant."

"Yes, because she wanted people to *think* she was pregnant."

"Joseph, *stop*. I need to tell this." Sophia leans forward and folds her hands prayerlike on the table. "I pretended to be pregnant. You were adopted, sweetie. The best thing in our life we ever did." She can't stop her tears. "Right Joseph?"

"Adopted? Me?" Mac unconsciously shakes his head in the negative as the words slowly make themselves understood.

"Mac's adopted?" Deanna bites her lip and reaches over to Mac, but he's already standing.

"Why didn't you tell me before?" He starts pacing. "So, who are my real parents?"

Joseph winces. "We are, Mac. You're asking about your biological parents."

"Sorry, I don't know the correct lingo."

Sophia says, "I know this is hard. I know. Sweetie, please sit down."

"I can't sit right now."

She looks up at him like an injured bird. "It was you with your dreams and now Oaxaca."

Mac interrupts, "But I never mentioned Oaxaca."

"Yes, but the dream about Mexico was a message from God to finally tell you the truth." She takes a deep breath. "Your biological mother is from Oaxaca, Mexico but we don't know who the father is. It didn't say on your birth certificate. The thing is, my family doesn't know. No one does. They thought I delivered you at Brigham and Women's Hospital in Boston. I'm so sorry. I was desperate then, and now I'm so ashamed." Joseph gets up and puts his hand on Mac's shoulder, but Mac shrugs him off.

"Not now, dad." He looks down at his hands. "I thought this skin was Italian, but I guess not. God! I need some air."

Sophia jumps up and implores him with hands on heart. "Wait! Mac, please! I love you more than I could love anyone."

Mac looks at them. "I know you do. You and dad. I never doubted your love. Ever. But I never thought I'd have to doubt your words." Mac grabs the sweater from the back of his chair and flees.

Sophia covers her face with her hands as Joseph's blue eyes brim over. Deanna retreats to the study and watches as Mac crosses the field and disappears into the woods.

Chapter Eleven

NIÑOS Y NOVIOS

Enrique's introduction to Uncle Pepe was a success. Frankie's on her second week as a volunteer at NNAA, or Niños de Amor as she sometimes likes to call it. It's in Santa Cruz Xoxocotlán, a small city three miles south of Oaxaca proper, and easily accessed by bus. She's just begun her lunch break at a picnic table by the playground and hears Enrique's motorcycle coming up the road. He makes short, frequent visits between his two jobs, sometimes to do repairs and other times to play with the kids. He really is a good person, Frankie thinks.

She gestures him over. "Come. Are you hungry? I have tortillas, cheese, salsa and avocado."

Enrique grins, "Seguro, I'm always hungry." He sits down across from Frankie. The table, set under the shade of a giant Pochote tree, provides a full view of the children. The older ones, who go to a nearby school for the morning session, have just returned. After they eat, they'll change out of their school uniforms and join the younger kids on the playground. Enrique explains that in Mexico, students are required to wear uniforms, but many can't afford them, so NNAA provides those as well.

Yelling and laughter come from all directions: the monkey bars, soccer field and a well-worn tire swing. Behind the picnic table is a one-story dormitory. The yellow-painted walls are the backdrop for a colorful mural with larger than life, eight-foot farmers and artisans from nearby pueblos. They till the soil, weave, make pottery, and carve wood. Frankie loves looking at the art. She loves the entire Oaxacan area with all the bright buildings in tangerine, red, and blue, and thinks New York City could take a lesson from its more expressive southern neighbor.

"Enrique, thanks for recommending I talk to Gregorio. The trainer he connected me with is great. I'm at the gym early six days a week, and it's much cheaper than in New York."

"I am happy for that. And La Reforma is close to Jalatlaco."

"Yes, I can walk there."

Raquel comes around the dormitory in a simple lavender dress and Frankie finds her annoyingly stunning with no make-up, earthy yet elegant. At the same time, the erect way she carries herself says, *I may be lovely, but don't mess with me.*

"Hola, hermanita!" Enrique yells. Frankie's mind does a double-take.

"What? Did you just say hermanita? That means little sister, right? *Your* little sister?"

"Si, muy bueno, Frankie. You are almost bilingual." He laughs.

"Your sister? Really?"

"De veras. She's my younger sister but she can be bossy like my mother was." Enrique says that loud enough for Raquel to hear.

"That's only because you haven't grown up yet," she rebuts.

"Oh my God, I thought you two were novios!"

Raquel sits down and grimaces. "Eww. I thought we told you when we first met at El Saguaro's?"

"No, but now I see the resemblance. It's funny what we notice or not depending on the context. I just made an assumption, something I'm trying not to do."

"Trust me," Raquel says, rolling her eyes, "I'm not Enrique's type." Enrique gives his sister a *that's not very funny* look and turns back to Frankie.

"Tío Pepe says you're great with the kids. He loves having you here. And it really helps you speak Spanish. Lots of foreigners want to volunteer but without the language, it's much harder."

Raquel nods in agreement. "Are you liking it?"

"So much."

"Uncle Pepe says even Julio came out of his room for the dance class."

"He did, and he has great musical sense. I think he's just shy."

"Yes, he's quiet. His mom passed away when he was six. For a few years, his only living relative, his aunt, who lives in Los Angeles, was trying to bring him there, but she had her own problems with money and immigration. Now he's twelve and resigned to living here. Older kids are much harder to place. Most people want an infant." Without thinking, Enrique, Raquel and Frankie turn to watch Julio who's sitting on the other side of the playground watching a soccer game.

"These kids are amazing. I'm already getting attached."

Raquel opens a container of cantaloupe and offers it to Frankie and Enrique. She looks closely at Frankie. "Just be careful if you start to fall in love because some of these kids are up for adoption, and they sniff out sentiment like treats to a starving dog. They're aching for a home and family." Raquel tilts her head and raises her eyebrows at Frankie, but she looks away. She hasn't shared her "family or dance?" question with them.

Enrique devours half the cantaloupe and talks between bites. "I'm not sure love and careful can be used in the same sentence."

"Well, sometimes es necesario hermano, especially with children. Only half the kids here are up for adoption; the others return home at night, probably to a crowded cement house with a dirt floor and not a lot of food, but at least they get meals here and love there. Well, love here too, of course."

"Kind of like our home." Enrique jokes. Raquel makes a disparaging clicking sound with her teeth.

"We have plenty, more than enough compared to these kids!"

"Cálmate, hermana; it was a joke. You can be too serious." Raquel ignores Enrique and looks at Frankie.

"Most of the kids here are Triques. They're the poorest and most oppressed Indigenous group in Oaxaca."

"Now you sound like a textbook." A grinning dusty boy runs over and hangs onto Enrique's neck and begs him to play soccer. Enrique leaps up.

Raquel moves closer to Frankie. They watch Enrique pass the ball. "As you can see, my brother's still got a lot of kid in him."

"Yes, I love his energy."

Raquel takes a bite of her tortilla with shredded chicken and cheese. "God, I am so hungry. I came here after class to drop off desks papá made for the kids. My dad's a great carpenter, but Uncle Pepe can barely change a light bulb, so my family helps him." Raquel takes another bite.

"So, you're studying nursing?"

"Yes, at the University in Oaxaca."

"Wow! That's exciting. Did Enrique tell you he gave me a tour of Santa Ana? It's so pretty. I love your church with all the gold paint and statues, and the weavings at the market are amazing!"

"Yes, it's a special place. Enrique said you met Teresa and Miguel?"

Frankie nods and smiles when she thinks about their sweet family. "Teresa seems like a really good mom and she's so talented. You said you don't like to weave?"

"Oh, I tried. I'm just no good at it. What I really love is biology. I was always capturing small mammals and insects as a kid and studying them. I used to torture Enrique, put them in his clothes and bed. My mom made me stop."

"Oh, Enrique told me about your mom. I'm so sorry."

"Yes, it's very sad. Five years ago, she died of cervical cancer which, as you know, can easily be prevented. That's one reason I decided to study medicine, so that doesn't happen to other Indigenous and poor women. I was seventeen when I made that promise to God and myself."

"That's really admirable Raquel. Hmm… and I was seventeen when I made a promise to my dance company and Raoul, my boss who acts like God."

Raquel smiles. "We both know what commitment is then." She looks over at Enrique still playing soccer. "Enrique took our mom's dying really hard. They were very close, even closer than me and my mom. Are you close with your mom?"

"In some ways, yes. I'm an only child with no father as a little girl, so it was just the two of us. We moved around a lot in Brooklyn. It's a borough, a huge neighborhood of New York City." Frankie doesn't feel like sharing that her mom is wonderful but pushy and hard-working but stubborn. That she was a hippie who dropped out of college to work in daycare because she got pregnant with Frankie and ended up staying. She doesn't mention the step-father who came to live with them when she was twelve who smoked too much dope and only really cared about Tricia. Frankie often felt the two would be happier if she disappeared. So, she basically did. She disappeared into the world of dance and found family there. As Frankie's lost in thought, Raquel waits for more information and in the awkward silence brushes flies away from her food.

"Do you see your mom a lot?"

"Um, I haven't seen her in a while. You know, I've been here and all. But yeah, she comes to all my shows. And she texts me every few days." Frankie's not going to say to someone who's lost their mother that she sometimes wishes hers would move to a different time zone.

"In my family, it was just me and Enrique, and as much as we argue, I love my brother."

"I can see that. I always wanted a sibling, but my stepfather didn't want kids. My mom met him when I was twelve, and he barely tolerated me, so it's probably good they didn't have any."

In talking about her mother, Frankie gets ambushed by guilt for lying, for pretending she's in Oaxaca doing a collaborative dance project. Like Hydra, the Greek multi-headed monster, the deception grows with each text. In order to keep the story straight, Frankie records her own myth-making. Yellow post-its full of white lies frame the refrigerator.

Enrique bounces back to the table. "Are you two talking about me?"

"It's not always about you, hermano."

Enrique smirks, "It often is." Raquel bats at him like he's an annoying insect. Behind Enrique trails Esme, a six-year-old with long silken black hair and chestnut-brown eyes. She was playing on the swings; at her heels is three-year old Leonel, her shadow. Esme tentatively puts her hand on Frankie's forearm.

"Would you braid my hair later, Frankie? Like on Monday?"

Frankie brushes Esme's hair off her face. "Of course. At the beginning of quiet time come find me in the office." Esme keeps hanging onto Frankie's arm, so Leonel climbs onto the picnic table and taps Frankie's shoulder. Frankie turns to look at him and feigns surprise.

"Leo!"

He giggles. Raquel is watching the three of them. Frankie can feel it. Esme lets go and runs off to the monkey bars and her shadow follows.

Enrique says, "Esme's a sweet girl. I don't think she has a family."

"Neither does Leonel," Raquel adds.

Frankie's surprised. "It's hard to imagine such adorable children not having a home." Frankie pauses. "I guess that was a stupid thing to say."

"Yes," Raquel is quick to agree. "Cute shouldn't have anything to do with it."

"So, they don't go home at night?"

Raquel offers, "No. Tugs on the heartstrings, doesn't it?" Frankie nods.

"How couldn't it?" Enrique chimes in. The three are quiet for a moment. Frankie notices Julio is no longer outside and wonders if he's in his room alone.

Enrique disrupts their contemplative mood. "Oh, Frankie, I just remembered something my Tío Pepe would like you to do. He doesn't speak much English and is leaving for a few days. I would do it, but on the phone not everyone can understand my beautiful English." He shrugs in faked disbelief. "And my sister is too important and busy for these things." He smiles playfully at Raquel. "Could you call back some guy from the States, a professor? He studies pre-Columbian culture. Sometimes our number gets mixed up with one for an art history museum in Xochimilco."

"Sure, just write down his number and the name and address of the museum. I'd be happy to speak with him."

"Si, cómo no. I'll leave it at the front desk." Then he looks at Raquel, his foot tapping under the table like morse code. "There is one other thing. Ok Francesca, I'm just going to go with this cause you're cool. You're from New York City, so…" Raquel's eyes widen as Enrique expels the breath he's been holding. "Are you cool with gay guys?"

"Oh, not again Enrique!" Raquel gets up abruptly knocking over the cantaloupe container. "You really think this is a good idea? One runaway bride wasn't enough? How much did that cost you?"

Frankie practically spits out the limonada she's drinking looking from one to the other. "Well, now I'm dying to hear. And Enrique, just so we're clear, many of the professional dancers I work with are gay men. My boss is a flamer which he'd be the first to admit, and I adore him."

"Well, here is not New York City and it can be un problema, you know, with some people. In the Catholic Church, some of the priests are okay, but after our mom died, our papá got too mad at his Catholic God for taking her and became an Evangelical convert. Now he's married to the Bible. He reads it like every night, his new best friend. So, el problema is, I'm gay and I have a boyfriend, and right now I still live with my father."

"It's Gregorio, isn't it?"

"How do you know this?" He looks at Raquel accusingly.

She shrugs. "It wasn't me."

"I didn't know for sure. I was confused because I thought you were with Raquel, but I have noticed the way Gregorio looks at you and teases you."

"Yes, he can be a tease, but the thing is, I love him very much. I want to live with him, but I need an alibi."

Raquel interrupts. "Is all this really necessary?"

"Can I speak boca grande?"

Raquel pushes at him. "Don't call me a big mouth."

"Here would be the plan: we become novios, girlfriend and boyfriend, pretend of course, then I move into Oaxaca to live with you, but really with Gregorio, and you said you have to go back to New York by late December, si? So, my gringa novia has to go back to work and will visit later. So, I am covered."

Raquel interrupts again. "Live in Oaxaca? What about dad and abuela? And you think dad will give you his blessings to live together without being married? And to a gringa?" Raquel turns to Frankie, "Sorry, no offense."

"Argh, Raquel. Enough! Oaxaca's not that far, and you'll be around. Did you think I was going to live in Santa Ana forever? And living with a woman will be much easier for dad to hear than the truth." Enrique turns back to Frankie, "Then when you go back to New York, we have a long-distance relationship. I have money saved for to pay someone to do this." Frankie doesn't know what to say.

Raquel moves closer to him and softens her tone. "Enrique, seriously, I think you should just tell dad. It's time."

"What about Miguel? You think Teresa's going to let me spend time with him if I am un homosexual? She's religious too."

"Yes, but she's not a fanatic. She'd never prevent Miguel from being with you. She wouldn't hurt him that way."

Frankie looks at Enrique. "So, Teresa doesn't know you're gay?"

Raquel jumps in first. "No, and he'd be doing her a favor. She's been wanting to marry him for years."

"I wish I could marry to Teresa. Everything would be easier."

"Well, you can't, and la pobresita needs to know the truth. Do *I* have to tell her?"

"Don't you dare."

Frankie shifts back on the bench and hugs her knees to her chest. "Well, this is getting complicated." She tries to lighten things up. "Like a telenovela!" Then she wonders if that was politically incorrect. God, this being sensitive is harder work than she thought, but Raquel laughs sarcastically.

"Enrique is the drama queen of telenovelas."

Enrique pleads with his intense brown eyes. "Please, don't listen to her Frankie. You wouldn't even have to do anything."

"Well, I don't actually have a real novio at the moment, but…"

"Yes, and you love children. You understand I can't lose my son."

"Stop saying that, Enrique. You don't know it's true. Teresa's not like that." Raquel's voice has a whiny pitch.

"I don't want to chance it." Enrique stands up and kicks the dirt. "You know what people will say. And you forget how miserable my life was. You were too busy torturing animals."

"I never tortured them. Everyone's miserable sometime."

"But they don't get tied up to a tree. Do you know how long I sat in the dark before Tío Pepe found me?"

"People grow up. No one's going to disrespect you now."

Frankie tucks some loose hair into her scarf. "So, let me get this straight. We'd have to pretend we're dating so people will believe we're together?"

"Si, you would have to pretend to like me, you know, in a romantic way, like a true novia."

Raquel groans, "Good luck pulling the wool out of dad's eyes."

Frankie laughs. "I hope not! You mean pulling the wool *over* his eyes."

"Oh yes, now I remember. I'm studying idioms. Forgive me."

Enrique digs, "Maybe study harder."

Raquel makes a "phhht" sound.

Frankie looks at Enrique. "You are pretty handsome. It might not be such a hardship. No seriously, I need to think about this. I came here to get clarity about my life, not complicate it. I mean I understand your need, Enrique, I really do, but I don't know if it fits into my life right now." She looks at Raquel. "And clearly Raquel doesn't think this is a good idea."

He tosses his head towards his sister. "This isn't about her."

"Oh, like what you decide doesn't affect me?"

Raquel stands up and wipes crumbs off her shorts. "I'm sure there's another way to work it out. It may not be perfect, but…."

Enrique interrupts, "But you get to have everything perfect. Right? The perfect student, the perfect daughter."

"You know that's not true. Mom certainly didn't think I was perfect, and papá just assumes I'll stay in Santa Ana. I can feel it. And then what about medical school? I'm expected to help with Abuela Florencia and she'll probably live to one-hundred and ten. Everyone has problemas Enrique."

"Oh, I see now. You want me there so you can leave."

Raquel pleads. "Why don't you at least try talking to him?"

"For the same reasons you don't talk to him about medical school."

"That's different."

"Is it?"

Frankie shifts her gaze towards the mural. She wishes she weren't in the middle of this. "I'm going to get the kids." She stands up. "It's arts and crafts time."

Enrique stands to face her. "I'm sorry, Francesca. I didn't mean it to be like this. We'll talk later, yes?"

"Yes, we can always talk, of course."

Enrique gives Raquel a disappointed shake of his head. "I'm helping Uncle move some furniture, then I'm going. And from now on, stay out of my business, okay?"

Without a word, Raquel turns towards the office in a lavender whirl as Frankie heads to the dormitorios.

Chapter Twelve

Oaxaca, late-September

A RED SOX BASEBALL CAP

It took Frankie only a few days to make the decision to be Enrique's "novia," and now they've been "together" for three weeks. Having agreed to do this feels aligned with her newfound spirit of adventure. Since coming to Oaxaca, knowing Raquel and Enrique has been grounding. She really likes them both although Enrique is decidedly more fun. El Saguaro feels like their place and the connection to Niños de Amor is invaluable. Frankie notices that as she's becoming more open, unexpected opportunities are popping up. Back in NYC, who could have imagined her doing something as spontaneous and audacious as being a faux-novia?

While the niños are having their homework help and quiet time, Frankie looks over the handwritten list of invitees to the upcoming annual October fundraiser. She told Uncle Pepe she'd organize it into an Excel spreadsheet with their contact information. She's also going to suggest having the kids perform a dance recital that she'll choreograph to add to the evening's appeal.

If she were in NYC, she'd be in rehearsals day and night. As she daydreams about last spring's choreography, her muscles automatically tense and flex. She's landing in her mind when Enrique's motorcycle pulls up outside the Center. The joy of imagined dance is replaced by a yearning that makes her throat ache and she swallows the longing.

"Hola, mi amor!" Enrique yells, with an exuberant entrance. He's hoping Uncle Pepe will hear. He speaks more softly, "I'm going to los dormitorios to fix window screens. The kids are getting bites at night, but he's useless with these things." Enrique heads out through the back of the office.

Frankie doesn't know why everyone has to constantly say that. She really likes his Uncle Pepe. She goes back to working on the list, and when Enrique returns, like method actors, they stay in character and make a game of flirting. But Frankie is distracted by a handsome stranger in a Red Sox baseball cap who's just come into the office.

Enrique kisses her lightly on the lips, then yells, "Adíos mi amor, mas tarde." Frankie knows he wants to make certain Uncle Pepe is aware they're novios, and as he spins around, Uncle Pepe comes through the front door. Enrique's face lights up, and Frankie, distracted by this waiting stranger, has to force herself to focus her attention on Enrique. His strategy is that Uncle Pepe will report back to Enrique's father about his new novia. Enrique's assured Frankie that like all old men, over cups of coffee or Coronas, the brothers love to gossip.

"Gracias, sobrino! Excelente."

Enrique smiles. "De nada. I am always happy to help you Tío." He jaunts off, and the three of them watch him go. The waiting man observes all this with great politeness and patience, but Frankie can see he's anxious. He's been taking off and putting on his baseball cap and humming intermittently. At first, he looked out the window watching the kids play, then focused on Enrique, and now he's looking out the window again. Frankie can see beyond him to the playground; Esme's screeching on the swing with joyous terror as she swoops skyward. Frankie's impulse is to run out and tell her to slow down. Leonel's next to her pumping his legs like crazy but not getting far, and Julio's dribbling a basketball with two of the older kids. Frankie's happy to see he's joining in more.

The man turns from the window. "Excuse me, my name's Professor Daniel MacDonald. I called a few weeks ago, and I know you left me a message, but I didn't really understand. It was a reference to a museum. Anyhow, I decided it would be better to do this in person." He looks quizzically at Frankie, "You speak English, right?"

"Yes, I'm from New York."

"I thought you looked American."

"Thanks, I guess. I'd prefer a less obvious persona." She smiles. "My name's Francesca. I've been in Oaxaca for six weeks and I volunteer here a few days a week." They extend hands at the same time. "Happy to meet you."

"I'm happy to meet you too. I'm Daniel MacDonald, but please just call me Mac."

"And call me Frankie. Where do you teach?"

"UMass in Amherst. I'm on sabbatical this semester." Frankie notes the incongruity between his Irish name, Boston accent and his dark eyes and cocoa-brown coloring.

"With an Irish-sounding name like MacDonald I'd expect a few freckles."

Mac looks taken aback and she fears that was probably too unfiltered. She hopes she hasn't somehow offended him. "Funny enough, there's a reason for that." He pauses so long she's not sure he's going to explain. "Well, I'm adopted. I just found out. And this is the orphanage I lived in before I was placed with a family."

"Wow! You *just* found out?"

"Well, a few weeks ago."

Frankie wants to say, *holy shit! That's a mind fuck*, but remembers her resolve. "That must be ah… interesting. I mean wow, must have been a surprise, right?" Frankie thinks what a stupid thing to say. Maybe blunt is better.

"Yes, it's quite a story. My parents just told me. Maybe I'll have the chance to explain it all another time, but right now I'm pretty anxious to locate my birth records. I want to get in touch with my biological family."

Tío Pepe enters the office and Frankie introduces them. "Tío Pepe, meet Professor MacDonald from the United States, from Massachusetts, and Professor, meet Señor Pepe Algazon, the Director of Nuestros Niños que Necesitan Ayuda y Amor. More easily remembered as NNAA, or as I sometimes call it, 'Niños de Amor'."

"Mucho gusto, Professor." Uncle Pepe extends his hand.

Mac shakes it. "Yes, si, mucho gusto, Señor."

Mac pulls a piece of paper from his back pocket which he refers to intermittently as he annihilates the pronunciation and lyricism of Spanish with a rugged Boston accent. Frankie tries not to wince as Mac asks Uncle Pepe for help. "Ah, por favor, puedes ayudarme?" She bites her lip as he explains he's looking for his biological family. "Estoy buscando mi familia biológica..."

When Mac finishes, thinking he comprehends Spanish better than he does, Tío Pepe launches into his native language with questions about birth dates and his adoptive family. A few words are hard to understand even for Frankie.

Mac spins his cap around in his hand. He looks at Frankie and shrugs. "I have no idea what he just said."

Frankie smiles warmly. "I can see that. Look, why don't you two go slowly and I'll try to interpret." She says the same to Tío Pepe in Spanish. He nods and speaks.

Frankie translates. "It turns out that since there were no computers here when you were born, Señor Pepe will have to go through all the boxes of files in the storeroom, and he doesn't have time today or tomorrow. You could come back on Friday." Frankie sees Mac's face fall and asks Tío Pepe some questions in Spanish and he responds.

"Mac, you and I can go through the files. I'm happy to help. Right now, the kids are on a supervised break."

Mac, relieved, breathes in. "Thank you. That would be great." This awesome adventure of helping Mac uncover his biological family is giving Frankie goosebumps.

Tío Pepe looks out the side window to the parking lot. "Ah, Raquel is coming. She can help too."

Frankie feels an irrational sense of propriety over Mac. Is it because they're both Americans, or does she want to be the only one to share in his personal mission? Or is it because Raquel brings with her both brains and beauty?

He twirls his cap one more time. "Shall we?"

Uncle Pepe explains the situation to Raquel, and she follows them into the backroom mouthing "muy guapo" to Frankie which annoys her. He's obviously handsome, but she shrugs noncommittally. She has to admit, though, she's already checked out his ring finger, and he unfortunately wears a wedding band handsomely. She thinks he could drop a few pounds and would probably not be comfortable in a New York City night club dancing until three in the morning. Frankie again tells herself not to make assumptions and reminds herself why she's here in Oaxaca.

She can't help it. She compares every man, single or married to her ex-boyfriend, David, a successful lawyer, comfortable in his own skin with everyone, like a mayor. She has to admit his confidence was a draw and wonders what that says about her. Lost in memories, she trips on a tile and smacks into the professor. So much for graceful first impressions.

Raquel says, "Let's each take a set of shelves. I think some boxes are organized by the adoptive name, but some are by birth year." They choose different areas of the room and spend forty-five minutes poring through files. Frankie's perspiring and her neck is starting to itch.

Raquel interrupts, "I'm sorry, I have to leave in a few minutes to get back to class. I just came by to drop off some paint for Uncle Pepe." She looks at Mac. "But I'd really love to help you find your biological family. It's one of my favorite parts of helping out here."

"Me too!" Frankie adds and Raquel gives her an odd look.

Five minutes later, Raquel squeaks like a dog's toy. "*Here*! It's hopefully in this box. It's got lots of folders from your birth year." She dumps the box in Mac's arms. "Got to run. Good luck!" Raquel flashes a smile and is gone.

Mac stands like a toy soldier. Frankie isn't unhappy to see her go and Mac is oblivious. He starts searching the files.

"Do you want me to help you look through some of those?"

"No, that's okay." Frankie starts in on another box. A few minutes later, Mac, looking like he might cry, says, "I can't believe this!" He hugs a folder to his chest.

Frankie feels so unexpectedly happy that she bites her thumbnail instead of lunging to hug this stranger.

"Could you make me a copy? Then I can relax in my B&B and read it carefully. I don't know why, but I'm so nervous."

"Of course you are. I can only imagine. But it's kind of exciting too, right?" He nods.

"Here, let me take the folder. I'll meet you out front in a minute." Mac hands it over like a newborn and leaves to wait in the lobby. When Frankie hands him the copy, Mac looks slightly dazed but happy.

"I don't know how to thank you and Raquel." He makes a slight bow. "I'm really grateful."

Frankie smiles and watches him walk away. When he reaches the door, she blurts out, "Ah, if you feel like a bite to eat later, after you've read your file of course, we could meet up. El Saguaro's a good place." As she's suggesting this, she's wondering where the hell this is coming from. She wouldn't normally do something like this in NYC, not so soon after meeting someone. Mac looks surprised and she tenses, thinking, oh boy, no filters. She grabs the edge of the counter wanting to duck down and disappear.

He smiles. "That'd be nice. I'd love the company, especially today. I'm staying near the zócalo. Where's El Cigarro?"

Frankie laughs, "It's El Saguaro. That's the name of a cactus."

"Oh dear. Lots to learn." He pulls a card out of his wallet. "Here. This has my cell on it. Let's talk later. Around six?"

"Great. Sounds great."

The sound of Mac's car recedes. It takes Frankie a while to stop feeling stunned. Okay, so I asked a guy out. Not really. He's married, so it's a dinner thing, not a date which makes it more relaxed. This whole trip is an experiment. I'm stretching everything here, not just my body.

Then she does stretch. First, her arms to the sky, then out to her sides, and she twists side to side to work out the knots and kinks. She does a perfect double-pirouette for no reason. Frankie usually relishes the early afternoon quiet out here a few blocks from the highway, but after that rush of camaraderie, it's a lonely kind of quiet. Frankie notices the leaf silhouettes dancing behind half-drawn blinds and the studio comes to mind. She imagines Raoul instructing as the dancers practice at the bar with sunlight warming the wood floor. Frankie, full of deep longing, feels she can almost touch home.

The dormitorio bells abruptly bring her back to the Center, and Frankie's longing is replaced with images from yesterday morning: the warmth of Esme's arm around her neck, Leonel's hand in hers, and Mariela's soft palm pressing her cheek, all three smelling of the same laundry soap. So powerful this visceral, animal-to-animal contact. Like being cozy with your cousins in a sleeping bag, like puppies in a litter, bonded and safe.

But Frankie wonders where all these good feelings will lead. Will she ever see these kids after the fall? Is this really helping her figure out if she wants motherhood? Frankie concedes to total confusion and decides to try one of Paula's counsels about acceptance: breathe into your problem with its discomfort; breathe and let it be; don't judge or run away. Watch your thoughts float; don't chase them. Frankie takes a deep breath and then another and another, and the following moments stretch out like a cat, paw by paw. She feels herself soften as her questions recede and children's voices and earth-colored footsteps pad their way closer.

Chapter Thirteen

SECRETOS

Sitting on the patio drinking a Dos Equis, Mac is thrumming with excitement as he calls Deanna. From the second-floor of the hilltop B&B, he has a postcard view of red-tiled roofs diminishing as the road descends to a cross street. The steeples of Santo Domingo rise like sentinels against a blue sky, the weather is glorious, and Mac couldn't be happier. That is, until Deanna talks first about a revealing new study they're doing instead of asking him about his quest. He learns she's heading into another long night at the lab, but as she speaks her voice is lively instead of tired. "But enough," she says. "Tell me your news!"

Finally! Mac thinks. "Didn't you get my text with the picture of my original birth certificate?"

"I'm sorry Mac. Today was so hectic, I never checked my phone, but I'll do it when we hang up. So, tell me, what is your birth name? And where were you born? Tell me everything."

And so, Mac tells her what he's learned. By the time they hang up, he's really missing Deanna. He wants to hold onto her tightly, smell her hair and be reassured at the outset of this journey that whatever he finds, home as he knows it, will still be home. Home including his parents and Deanna's family. He worries about the potentiality of dueling loyalties but douses that thought with his last few sips of Dos Equis.

Minutes later, he's walking across terra cotta tiles through the B&B's courtyard hosting a fountain of spouting frogs and potted ferns the size of VW Beetles. It's cool and peaceful. On the street, he passes a tienda selling traditional clothes, ropa típica, and staring back are Frida Kahlo's uni-browed eyes on a t-shirt. He reminds himself to find Deanna something special to bring back, maybe a pretty silver necklace with inlaid turquoise, but not the t-shirt. Not her style.

Mac's happy his B&B is just a few blocks from the zócalo. As he passes through, he pauses to listen to a marimba band and feels a pang for his keyboard. The zócalo is surrounded by stone buildings with columns and arches with restaurants underneath. Happy patrons are chatting and eating. He's grateful he won't be dining alone, on this day of all days. He hums the music he just heard as he follows Frankie's directions to the street, Miguel Hidalgo. In a yellow cotton shirt, he revels in the early evening warmth and notices the waning sunlight on the Cantera stone of La Catedral. He makes a mental note to stop there on his way back and explore the interior. What possible treasures and artifacts will he find? The aesthetics and history in every cornerstone in Oaxaca call to him.

Mac likes the vibe he felt from Frankie today. She and Raquel were really helpful. It would have taken days for him to go through all those records by himself. In a way that surprised him, the process felt good as he realized how many people like him are adopted, and NNAA is just one small orphanage in one country. He's now a member of a bigger family of adoptees. He remembers when Raquel found the box with the right year, he felt like a kid at Christmas.

And God, is Raquel beautiful, but a bit intimidating, like being confronted with a live piece of art. Frankie is attractive too, in her own way, and is warm and friendly. What a beautiful smile and wild hair. Had she known that guy she kissed at the orphanage from a previous trip? She's been here a month or so and already has a boyfriend? I guess that's possible. She doesn't seem flaky though. I'm sure she too has her story, and it was friendly of her to suggest dinner.

The real Frankie interrupts his thoughts as he notices her waving from the restaurant patio. Mac waves back, happy to see a newly familiar face in a city full of strangers. Feelings can get magnified when you travel alone, and Mac is deeply appreciative at that moment.

As Mac crosses the patio and sits down across from Frankie, he smiles looking at her top. "I love your shirt."

"Oh thanks, yeah. I don't usually do pictures, but I think Frida's pretty amazing. So?"

Frankie hunches her shoulders and opens her hands practically bouncing in her seat. "So, who are you? What did you find out?"

Mac sits back delighted. He takes a piece of paper from his back pocket. "I read through all the paperwork, but I can barely remember my birth name there are so many parts to it." Mac straightens out the paper on the table and reads. "Apparently, I, Daniel Joseph MacDonald was born Rafael Alonso Alvarez Garcia Cocijo at 2:10 AM on August 15, 1982 in Hospital La Reforma in Oaxaca. There was a note in my file saying I am of Zapotec heritage on my mother's side, but my father is unknown."

"Wow! You're part Zapotec?"

"Yes, I can't believe it. I have Indigenous blood. It's like a transfusion!"

Their waiter appears.

"I'd like a chardonnay please." Frankie looks at Mac, "A drink?" He hesitates. "Oh, I shouldn't assume other people drink. Blame it on my Irish heritage, and possible insensitivity." She makes a silly face.

Mac laughs. "No problem. I'm half…" Mac pauses. The waiter is being patient. "Ah… a Dos Equis, por favor." The waiter leaves. "I was just going to say, I'm half Irish, but I'm not, am I? I'm not Irish at all."

Frankie makes a disappointed face. "Extremely doubtful. Maybe you have the soul of an Irishman?"

"I suppose at this point anything's possible. When you're told your whole life you're half-Italian and half-Irish, well, it's how I've come to identify, but who am I really? Hispanic and Indigenous? American? A mongrel?"

"Yeah, it must feel kind of crazy, like how would I feel if my mom said, 'Your father wasn't really Jamaican. He was Moroccan.' I mean, my whole life I've felt connected to

Jamaicans, but I don't know why. Kinship? Or maybe I've just imagined it."

"Speaking of other cultures, I'm hoping your boyfriend, I mean novio, is okay with us having dinner. He didn't look like un machista, but I'd hate to have to defend your honor with a duel or something." Mac is smiling but Frankie startles a bit at the word "boyfriend", then laughs out loud at Mac's melodrama. When Enrique's not around, it's easy for her to forget they're "novios".

"Enrique? Oh, he's Uncle Pepe's nephew. Remember Señor Algazon, Director of NNAA?"

Mac nods attentively. "Of course."

"Enrique helps him out with repairs and maintenance and spends time with the kids. Oh, and he's very cool. He understands men and women can be friends. So, not a problem." Frankie thinks she's gone on too long. Gratefully, their drinks arrive.

Mac lifts his glass of beer. "To new friendships."

Frankie clicks her wine glass back. "Yes, and to new beginnings. New roots." They click again.

"Thanks for being my interpreter with Señor Algazon. Not speaking the language is a huge deficit. Yesterday I signed up for classes at Proyecto Lingüístico. It's on Avenida Juárez." Mac takes a sip of his Dos Equis. "I studied Spanish for a few years in high school, but I'll never catch up in time for finding my family."

"If you need someone to do more interpreting, I'm happy to. It'd be fun." Frankie casually tosses this out aware that with his good looks and charm, if she's not playing with fire, she's at least holding a box of matches.

"That would be great! I'm thinking of going to the home address in the paperwork on Thursday. I'd like to sightsee for a day or two before I start looking. Once I start, I won't be able to focus on anything else, and I want to get a sense of Oaxaca and its history. I teach pre-Columbian art and culture, so I'm smack in the center of my wheelhouse."

"Well, I can show you around Oaxaca proper, what I know of it, if you'd like. And you'll definitely want to check out Mitla. Great ruins I hear. Your line of work. You could be my tour guide." Jesus. Now I've lit a match, Frankie thinks.

"Sounds like a plan." Mac takes his last sip of Dos Equis. "I have a rental car."

Frankie fights the urge to go to the ladies' room to reapply her lipstick. She knows the mauve shimmer goes well with this royal blue dress. Let it go, she tells herself. Stretch. With that word, she's at the dance studio, her leg on the barre as she pliés low, then up on toe reaching taller, her arms extended at a right angle. When the waitress comes over to take their order, Frankie blinks away the image.

Without hesitation, she orders chicken enchiladas with mole sauce. "It's my favorite. Mole is a famous Oaxacan dish; the sauce has at least a million spices and flavors including chocolate."

"Count me in on anything with chocolate." They order and settle back, then Mac leans forward, "So, we've spent a lot of time on me. Tell me about you. You mentioned your mom is Irish."

"Yes, very. Corn beef and cabbage on Saint Paddy's Day. She doesn't suffer fools and she's stubborn but very loving and loyal." Frankie looks across the street considering the word "pushy" but pauses and looks back. "The truth is, my mom's ambitious. For me. She knows what she wants from my life better than I do." Frankie pauses. "That probably sounded weird."

"It sounds confusing. And your dad? What's he like?"

"Ah, I never really knew him. Besides his being Jamaican, I've been told very little. He was a fling from the late 70's." Frankie puts out her arm. That's where I get my coloring. My mom was a bohemian type. It was a one or two-night stand, a week tops from what I can gather. She won't talk about it. She's not one to share her most private stuff. Is your dad like that?"

Mac looks at her blinking. "My adoptive dad, yes, except when he drinks. Then he belts out songs and talks about everything and gets sentimental. He's great."

"He sounds fun. My mom's not too sentimental. She says, 'Leave the past where it belongs.' She won't even talk about my grandparents except for the fact they're dead and no one got along."

Mac raises his glass. "To uncovering secrets. For both of us."

Frankie clinks his glass. "Salud! What about your mother? Your adoptive mom. What's she like?"

"She's wonderful except for the gigantic lie of omission. It's strange because she's an open and expressive person but clearly hid her feelings from her family. And I always thought they were so close. My mom actually *pretended* that she was pregnant with me. Maybe it has to do with pride, like with your mom, but it's pretty weird."

"That is extreme. No offense." Frankie pauses. "But I think it was different then. Women were more expected to have kids, and it sounds like especially in her family."

"True. But the ripple effect from that lie, wow. I mean, what box do I check on those forms that ask for race and ethnicity? And maybe I have siblings here in Mexico. It would be ironic since I always wanted some. I wonder who I'd be if I had grown up here?"

"Wow! Lots of questions. I get it. Sometimes I think about who I'd be if I hadn't grown up in Brooklyn with the opportunity to study so many different styles of dance."

"Yes, that whole nature or nurture question. I'm lucky my parents had enough money so I could take keyboard lessons and go to college."

"Me too. I mean we never had extra money, but my mom made sure she could pay for my dance classes, and as soon as I was old enough, I worked at the studios." Frankie feels another stab of guilt for the ongoing deceit with her mother. The refrigerator's turning yellow.

Mac finishes his enchilada, wipes his mouth and puts his napkin on the table. "But, besides the big lie, I'm very lucky. My mom's loving and a great cook and my dad's funny.

He's this big guy and people love him. I've felt cherished my whole life."

"You are lucky. I wish I knew my biological dad. I only learned his name from seeing it on my birth certificate. I was seventeen and needed it to apply for a passport. I'll never forget his name: Sanka Roje Joshua Willis. Before then my mom would just say she couldn't remember." Frankie shakes her head. "Can you believe that? And when I told my mom his name, she said, 'Don't get too attached. It's probably fake.' I think he was a small-time drug dealer or something." Frankie's feeling her second glass of wine. "You know, I don't usually talk about my biological dad."

"Oh, I'm sorry. If it's making you uncomfortable, well, we could talk about me again."

Frankie laughs and thinks, God, he's so easy to talk to. "No, talking to you is okay because you get it. My mom made it clear she didn't want to discuss my dad or her parents so I stopped asking. And I had this step-dad from when I was twelve, so then it felt even more taboo to bring up my biological dad. And my stepdad was kind of a loser, a big pot smoker. I think my mom likes strays. You know, what you're doing here in Oaxaca is making me think again about looking up my biological dad. It's really brave you came here."

"Oh no, I'm not brave, not really. I'm afraid of spiders for one. And my wife. Ha!" he says offhandedly. Disappointingly, he doesn't offer anything more about the wife, but says, "This feels more like a birthright, not bravery."

"But it is brave because you don't know who you're going to find or what they're going to be like."

"I guess, if you look at it like that, but the curiosity is overwhelming. I can't imagine not trying to find them. You know, you could look up your dad, or hire someone to do it."

"I might. I sometimes wonder if he likes music and dancing, like me. And Mac, I don't want to give you the wrong impression about my mom. As I've said, she's really been there for me, especially around my dancing."

"She sounds very supportive. So, besides dancing, what do you do?"

Frankie laughs, "Actually, I *am* a dancer, so not much else. It's my work and I love it. I'm with a company called NYC Moves."

Mac whistles. "Now I understand all the classes. And wow! I know that name. You're famous!"

Frankie grins and raises her wine glass. "Not really, but that's what I do."

"Amazing!"

Frankie soaks it in, and undone by Mac's avid attention, ignores the red flag waving *WIFE*. "I'm here taking a season off, like a sabbatical, but I still have to keep in dancing shape. You can lose it so quickly."

Mac pats his belly. "I know, it's hard staying this trim."

"You're fine." She gives him a quirky smile. He must know his handsome face goes a long way past a few extra pounds.

"I admire your discipline."

"It's my job. Just like for any other athlete."

Mac tilts his head. "But why Oaxaca for a dance sabbatical?"

"I needed someplace different, far away from New York, and a friend of mine had lived here and raved about it." Mac waits to hear more, but she doesn't feel like getting into her personal quandary. "So, Mac, besides teaching, what do you do?"

"Well, I'm a musician. I play keyboards in a band, and I write songs."

"Really?" She wants to ask more questions, but the waiter comes over to clear their plates and leave a dessert menu.

Mac looks serious all of a sudden. "Frankie, I have no idea what this search for my family is going to bring. Are you sure you're up for this?"

"Yes, of course." She puts her hand out as if reaching towards his arm but then clasps them together. "This is huge for you. Don't worry about me. I'll be there as a witness and interpreter." She hesitates, "And I hope as a new friend. I love the idea of being part of helping someone find their roots. Family's really important to me too."

"Thank you. I'm grateful for your company. I wish my wife could be here, but she'd be distracted by her research. And at heart, she's a homebody, venturing out of the U.S. only once on our honeymoon trip, to Italy and Ireland of all places."

Frankie thinks, oh God the wife. I did just gush about family, so why shouldn't he talk about his?

"And speaking of travelling, I realize when I felt at home in an Irish pub, I assumed it was because I had Guinness in my blood. In Florence, I felt such ease with the language and art that I knew it must be my Italian genes. But none of that was true. Maybe we're all more connected to other cultures than we think, and it's only our limited perspective of who we are that makes our world smaller than it needs to be."

Frankie nods. "I think you've got something there, Professor." Mac smiles, and Frankie's happy he can take her small joke.

Then she notices Enrique behind the bar with Gregorio. Damn, she thinks. He wasn't supposed to be working tonight. He looks up and startles when he sees Frankie. She makes a *stay away* face, but Enrique, always quick to act, literally hops over the bar.

"Mi amor, Francesca, may I to meet your new friend?" He kisses Frankie on the lips. She wants to hiss, but instead breaks off the kiss quickly.

"This is Mac, Professor MacDonald from near Boston. He came in today when you were leaving. Remember?"

"Ah si. You have the Red Sox hat."

Mac smiles. "Yes, I do and I came to NNAA today to find my birth records. I lived there until I was adopted. Your Uncle Pepe and Raquel and Frankie were very helpful. I'm so grateful." Mac smiles at Frankie.

Enrique extends his hand. "Ah, que bueno and mucho gusto, Señor Mac. Yes, so then you are the one who called. You are Oaxaqueño?"

"Yes, apparently that's true." Mac looks from Enrique to Frankie. "How nice that Frankie volunteers at NNAA."

"Si, the children they are loving her." He looks at Frankie who smiles vapidly.

Gregorio, annoyed, looks on from the bar and waves a dish towel in the air. Enrique delicately waves back, a little fey in Frankie's mind if he's trying to pull off a novio role, but it's all part of his charm.

"Be right there." He turns back to Mac and Frankie. "I have to help. Gregorio called me in. They are short of help, and as you can see, very busy. I hope you enjoyed la comida."

"Delicious. My first mole sauce. A very memorable evening, Enrique, thank you." Mac smiles at him. Frankie smiles too, but inside she's willing him to move on.

"See you later, mi amor." Enrique winks and gracefully hustles back to Gregorio. She wanted to slap the wink off his face and is surprised by her reaction. Why is it that a week ago, this charade was a lark but now feels like a bad joke? But she knows for Enrique, there is nothing remotely funny about it. She's agreed to honor their arrangement and will do so.

Mac insists on paying the bill.

"Thank you, Mac. Next time, my treat."

"Sure thing."

They head out into the promising evening. Live music and children's laughter draw them towards the zócalo. On staging next to La Catedral, a guitarist and three singers perform while dancers from a local pueblo are dressed, ready to go on. Frankie lightly touches Mac's arm. "Let's watch for a few minutes. Last week I saw an amazing Argentinian tango troupe in El Teatro Macedonio Alcala. It's just a few blocks away. I love it here. Art is everywhere!" Frankie feels like spinning around, arms wide open like Julie Andrews in *The Sound of Music,* but she holds back. Instead, she beams a smile at Mac who laughs softly at her joie de vivre.

After a few minutes, he suggests going into La Catedral. "I haven't been inside yet."

"Sure. It's another work of art."

"When do you need to get back to El Cigarro? I mean Saguaro?"

"Oh, I'll stop in on my way home. Enrique will be there until 2 a.m. I can't keep his late hours. Six mornings a week I meet with my trainer at a gym close to Jalatlaco where I live."

"Impressive."

"Not to a dancer. Plus, I run in this park in San Felipe del Agua, not far from Oaxaca. It's in the foothills of the Sierra Madres and is very beautiful if you'd ever like to see it." Frankie watches herself light a second match. There's a reason people play with fire, she thinks.

"Sure, but you sound busy with volunteering and workouts. Then there's Enrique and hopefully being my interpreter." He pauses. "Ah, I'm not exactly a runner."

"We can walk. It's a lovely hike."

"Okay, I would love to, but I want to respect your time." The words "eye candy" suddenly pop into her mind. Paula would not be happy, but she can't help herself.

"No worries," assures Frankie. "I have the time."

Leaving behind the lively sounds of the zócalo, they step into the hushed Catedral Metropolitana de Nuestra Señora de la Asuncion. The enormous arch of the ceiling spans an elaborate baroque altar, and in the solemn atmosphere of murmured prayer, Mac and Frankie become introspective. Mac blesses himself from a font of holy water before they walk up a side aisle, passing worshippers praying in front of small chapels. Each chapel, dedicated to a specific saint, displays their paintings and statues, and votive candles light the way for blessings. In one alcove, a priest is saying Mass for about sixty people.

Frankie whispers, "In the U.S., you would never see this many people on a weeknight in a Catholic church unless it was a funeral."

"Yes. I think most of them are locked during the night."

"I wonder who would go even if they were open? This culture is so devout; you can't separate people's lives from their faith; it's like in everything. Every week there's a small parade, usually with a horn section, celebrating a saint. This is not a quiet country, but it's certainly spiritual."

Mac nods. "Yes, and behind all the Catholic celebrations are beliefs in gods from pre-Columbian times. The Indigenous people figured out how to seamlessly blend the two. Am I sounding too much like a professor?"

Frankie pokes him lightly on his arm. "A little bit, but I love to learn."

They move towards the front of the church where the main altar is adorned with a giant bronze statue of Our Lady of the Assumption with raised arms and three angels by her side. They enter the front pew and Mac kneels and bows his head in prayer. Frankie sits and absorbs the peace and artistry, surprised by Mac's devotion. She wonders what he's praying for.

***

At 2 a.m., after their crazy work night, Enrique joins Gregorio behind the bar.

"All the beers need to be restocked."

"Sure thing." Enrique crosses the room to turn up the music and dances around tables on his way back. When he returns, Gregorio looks glum. "Cómo estás, Gregor? Is your father doing okay?"

"It's not him Enrique, and could you *please* turn that down." Enrique hustles to shut off the music, and silence falls like a stone.

Gregorio wipes down the already clean bar. "I'm sorry Enrique. I don't like this charade, to pretend to be happy for you and a fake novia. It feels childish and we can't sustain it."

Enrique uncharacteristically stops moving and tenses up. "But it's working this time. Frankie's got it down. So, why is it a problem for you?"

Gregorio ignores his question. "Look, why delay the truth? Your father, grandmother and Uncle Pepe love you. Do you really think they'll disown you?"

"Oh my God, are we revisiting this?" Enrique hops up, sits on the bar and crosses his arms. "Yes Gregor, the Bible is clear to them and at least a few vocal others that homosexuals should have their balls toasted and served up in hell. And if Miguel is taken from me, from my life, well, I don't know what I'd do."

Gregorio moves towards Enrique and takes his hand. "That's not what I want and you know it. Just consider coming out. Raquel would back you up. We discussed it last night."

Enrique disengages his hand. "Oh, are you planning my coming out party?"

"Enrique, look, you're a natural at drama, but I have no desire for it."

"But you don't need to do anything." Enrique hops off the bar. "So, what's your solution?"

"I just told you but you don't want to hear it."

"So, I get to risk everything because you're a little uncomfortable?" He turns abruptly accidentally knocking over some dirty glasses by the sink. "I'll clean up in the morning." Gregorio doesn't bother to try and stop Enrique but follows him to the back door. He watches him strap on his helmet and start up the motorcycle.

Gregorio yells, "Be careful!"

Enrique shouts back. “I’m trying! For us!” He backs out of his space and drives off.

Gregorio returns to the bar. He watches as a few couples walk by, arm in arm, then a group of young men cavort their way down the street. Gregorio pours himself some cognac, shuts off the lights and sits at the bar waiting for the darkness and liquor to soothe his nerves.

Chapter Fourteen

RESTLESS IN OAXACA

Frankie, restless after her evening with Mac, gets out of bed at 2 a.m. She makes chamomile tea and peanut butter toast and settles on the couch. The attraction aside, Frankie knows part of her involvement with Mac is to distract her from her own issues, but it's doing the opposite with all this talk of families and adoption.

Working with the kids at NNAA is heartwarming and fun, but she sees now she could volunteer forever and not know what it's really like to be a mother. Maybe I'd be happy at fifty with just a dog? It would be so much easier. She remembers how she panicked last week when Esme had an asthma attack. And what if I'm not happy or there's something wrong with my child? Jeez, I'm sounding like Raoul.

Frankie, thwacked by a sudden rush of homesickness, capitulates and opens up the NYC Moves website. And there they are! She was afraid seeing them would make her too sad, but instead she feels happy, magnetized by their faces and finely-tuned bodies. There's Phillipe and Tina, Audrey and Kylee, Sharina, Yvonne, Joel and Moe. And there's a close-up of her beloved Raoul. She tears up.

Could I give up my spotlight with the company? Frankie has often imagined herself lithe and still dancing into old age like Rita Moreno. Some dancers are done at my age, but I'm lucky. I've never had a serious injury. If I lose my edge though, Raoul won't hesitate to replace me with a younger better dancer. So, why am I here enduring the workouts, muscle burns, high-intensity drills, and stretches without the closeness of my family of dancers? Should I just go back home to figure things out? Arghh!

The tea isn't doing it, so Frankie gets up and pours herself some wine. She moves out to the patio and sits under the stars. How lovely, a city where you can see the night sky! Frankie wishes on the brightest star for an answer to reveal itself. A dream, a message in a bottle, any medium will do.

She considers Mac again. Yes, I enjoy his company. He feels grounded and thoughtful, not as self-focused and wound up as these NYC characters I love so much, in spite of their dramas. Too bad he's married. And why did I ruin things with David and get involved in this novia scheme? Who agrees to such a thing when their own life is so fucked up? I get A's for avoidance and ambivalence. Frankie groans and crawls back into bed at 4 a.m.

Chapter Fifteen

LOS ALEBRIJES

On a Saturday morning, several days, one outing and many texts after their dinner together, Mac is driving his rental car with Frankie in the seat beside him. He's blithely humming to himself.

"That's a nice melody. Did you write that song?"

"Oh God, was I humming again?"

"Yes, what's wrong with humming?"

"Nothing, but I often don't realize I'm doing it. I must be nervous."

"You think? I can't imagine why." Frankie smiles at him and drapes her sweater over her shoulders in the cool morning air. Mac notices.

"I'll turn up the heat if I can find it." He fiddles with some knobs and a heat vent opens.

"Thank you, Mac."

"Well, thank you. I'm so glad you're here; otherwise, I'd have to hire an interpreter, a stranger. But of course, I'm happy to pay you too." That felt awkward, but he felt he should offer.

"No way! You were such a superlative guide at Mitla. All ruins look alike to me, but you made them come alive. I felt like I was right there with the Mayans way back when.

"Ah, 'back when' was 500 to 800 BC, and it was the Zapotecas, possibly some of my ancestors, but no worries, no pop quizzes this morning."

"I am so grateful Doctor Professor MacDonald, Sir." Frankie delivers the sarcasm with another smile.

She really is adorable he thinks. Frankie consults the map in her lap while Mac hums and taps the steering wheel. He doesn't care if Frankie hears him. If he's quiet too long, he might explode.

"It looks like this place is on the northern outskirts of the city. At the end of this road, you want to take a right onto Jacaranda, then we go straight for a few miles. Seriously, how are you doing Mac?"

"I honestly don't know. What are the chances they're still living at the same place thirty-seven years later? Or living at all?"

Frankie screams. "Ah! Look out for that rooster!" Mac swerves. The outskirts have become rural with dirt streets and adobe houses spaced widely enough apart for vegetable gardens.

Frankie looks out the window. "I'm surprised at how poor it is here, not that far from the zócalo with all the fancy restaurants."

"Yes, same old story of economic disparity; it's getting worse everywhere and not surprisingly, but sickeningly, is often related to skin color." Mac pauses and looks at Frankie. "Wow! So, am I now a person of color?"

"Hmm, I think you are, but it's like me. I'm of color but without a personal history. At least you're discovering your roots."

"That's true, but who knows what it will all mean in the end. Impossible to tell."

Frankie looks at the map again. "Sorry to interrupt, but slow down Mac. It's the next right across from the church." They pass a tienda and Mac takes a right. "Number thirty-four can't be too far."

They pull up in front of a building with a large front porch filled with wooden shelves displaying terra cotta jugs and bowls, and black pottery from San Bartolo Coyotepec. A woman, in the front yard in a pastel-green top and sweatpants, is watering pink roses. She looks to be in her fifties and Mac's stomach lurches.

"Oh God, is that my mother?"

Frankie puts her hand gently on his arm. "We'll find out, Mac." They get out of the car. "Hola Señora."

She puts down her watering can. "Hola! Quieren comprar cerámicas?"

"She's asking if we want to buy pottery."

Mac searches the woman's face. Shouldn't he automatically know his own mother? He sputters, "Are you Rosario Garcia Cocijo?"

The woman stares like she's trying to figure something out. God, maybe she knows it's him but doesn't want to meet him. His ears begin to buzz.

Frankie asks, "Es tu nombre Rosario?"

"No, mi nombre es Marta." Mac's heart sinks. She continues in a mix of Spanish and non-fluent English. "My name Marta y I do not know Rosario, pero la familia, si. Venga." She gestures to the porch and they follow her into a large room showcasing more pottery and local artwork. Rainbow-colored piñatas hang from the ceiling.

Through Frankie, Marta explains that the Cocijo family moved back to Santa Catarina Lachatao in the late 1990's. She says the grandmother, la abuela, wanted to go back to the mountains, and she went with her husband and daughter, but the daughter's name was Consuela.

"We buy this from them." She gestures around the store. "Son Zapotecas y la abuela es una curandera." Mac's heart swoop dives with the word *curandera*.

Mac looks at Frankie, "Curandera, that means healer, right?"

"Yes exactly." Mac conjures up Xanu and the circle of healers. Frankie continues to interpret. "Lachatao is part of Pueblos Mancomunados, a group of communal pueblos."

"Frankie, ask if she thinks the family is still there?"

"Probablamente," Marta says.

"Tell her I'm related and I was adopted by an American family." Frankie explains and Marta comes closer looking carefully at Mac's face. She smiles at Frankie.

"Muy guapo."

Frankie laughs. "She says you are very handsome but can't remember exactly what they looked like. She hopes you find them and she wants us to please wait a minute."

Marta goes through the big display room to a smaller back room.

Mac feels emptied out, like a broken piñata. He politely browses the artisan work, but his heart is elsewhere. Frankie joins him and they peruse ceramic painted plates, vases, cups, and alebrijes, the famous hand-carved and painted, fantastical animals made in San Martin. Mac picks up a terra cotta vase with palm-green iguanas and coal-black jaguars. He tries to conjure the presence of his animal spirit, but nothing comes.

He sighs and looks around, "I want to buy some pieces from Marta. Everyone around here looks like they could use some money."

Marta returns holding an old cardboard box and looks at Mac. "Es de tu familia." Frankie interprets the rest. "It's funny but I just couldn't throw it away. I kept thinking they would come back but they never did. It's mainly notebooks and some papers. Please, take it."

Mac extends his arms. "Wow, this is a real gift." He starts to tear up. "Gracias Marta." She nods and pats him on the shoulder. "Frankie, please tell her we're going to shop now." Frankie does, and Mac carefully places the box on the floor.

He spends two-hundred dollars and Marta lights up like the yellow sunflowers painted on the adobe wall behind her. She calculates the receipt by hand on a scrap of paper.

"Que Díos los bendiga."

"She says, 'May God bless us.'" Mac, hands clasped in prayer, makes a slight bow of thanks.

Marta waves as they drive off. On the return trip, Mac no longer hums. “God, I was so charged up this morning. I didn’t anticipate a letdown.”

“Yes, it’s hard to be your own detective when it’s such sensitive stuff.”

“But I need to find this out for myself. I just can’t keep imagining every fifty-something woman in Oaxaca is my biological mother.”

Frankie gives him a wistful look. “Yes, but hard not to.”

Chapter Sixteen

CONFETTI

The following Tuesday, Frankie and Mac meet for dinner at Frankie's favorite restaurant, El Colibrí, which means hummingbird. Neither has mentioned going back to El Saguaro, but Frankie purposely includes Enrique in their conversation from time to time to keep up the pretense. Seated outside on the second-floor balcony overlooking the zócalo, they watch the sun's diminishing rays on La Catedral. Mac reaches inside the pocket of his jacket draped on the back of his chair.

"For you, an interpreter extraordinaire." He really hopes Frankie will like his gift. It's wrapped in white computer paper with a sharpie-drawn bow. "Not so fancy, I'm afraid. It's just a little something since you refuse payment."

Frankie feels a bit shy but does a grand jeté in her mind. Since David walked out two years ago, no man, except Raoul, has bought her anything, and that was a glass of house chardonnay. She unwraps a green frog with pink wings, an alebrije, carved from copal wood. "I love it. It's so playful."

"I'm glad you like it. The frog represents change and renewal...sort of like a good luck charm."

"This is very sweet. Thank you." Frankie hopes its charms will work. She rewraps it carefully and places it in her bag, fixes some loose hair inside her scarf, and wills the candlelight to make her skin glow rather than look sallow. She looks around. "It's so nice to share this place and not be the new kid on the block."

After the sun sets, the Cathedral floodlights, bright like a film set, illuminate tree branches and the church façade with its carved wooden doors. Families stroll in the park and eat street food as marimba notes and voices ascend to their table. Six-foot, zeppelin-shaped balloons, tethered to wrists of six-year-olds, rise and descend like giant confetti.

Frankie's bare arms prickle with the festive air, and the wine has warmed her insides as they linger over enchiladas mole for a second time. Mac is relaxed too and notices how much fun the children are having running around the plaza below.

He puts his fork down. "Watching all these families reminds me of being a little kid at the carnival with my parents." As he glances out at the balloons, Frankie notices he's biting his lower lip. "I'm not someone who usually holds a grudge, but every time I think of my parents, I get upset. Didn't they understand what a life-changer it is to learn as an adult that you're adopted?"

"I totally understand, but from everything else you've said, they seem like good people."

"They are. That's why it's so hard to reconcile. Frankly, I think it's unethical. It's everyone's birthright to know where they come from. I literally pray to be able to forgive them. And now they're talking about coming here to visit, so I have to think of a diplomatic way to say 'no'." Mac pauses. "I'm sorry, I don't want to spoil the mood."

Frankie shrugs. "I don't mind. I was angry for a long time not knowing who my dad was, especially when my friends talked about theirs. I think our parents felt like they were protecting us."

"Us or them?" Mac feels like he might get emotional, so he focuses on eating and lingers over a bite of enchilada. "Mmm… these are even better than at El Saguaro. I've never tasted anything this complex. I can actually pick out the chocolate and cinnamon and maybe cardamom."

"Yes," Frankie sighs, sated. "You know I'm so grateful for this place, for all things Oaxacan. I really needed a break from the craziness of New York City so I could think. I love the pace here, and every day I notice something new."

"Me too, and given my field, every pueblo is calling to me. I'd love to bring my students here. We went on a trip to Tikal that was amazing, and now I imagine sharing all of this with them. They're the best thing about teaching."

"It's wonderful to love something so much, isn't it? That's how I feel about dance."

"I can imagine." The warmth between them gives Mac a rush of happiness and he wants to share his shamanic dreams, his visions. He realizes it's easier to talk to someone who doesn't know you well, and hopefully won't judge. Someone you may never see again except for this brief interlude. Like those quirky spaces in his jazz riffs, you can keep them safe or play to the edges. He notices Frankie watching him. "I have an idea. I do this warm-up exercise with my students where one person talks, for like a minute and the other just listens. It's fun. I have to warn you though, some of my stuff might sound kind of weird. But you seem open."

"Weird? How weird? Fetish weird?" She smiles uncomfortably and wishes she could take back the word "fetish". Why did a sexually-laden word fly out of my mouth? She asks herself. To regain ground, Frankie laughs it off. "Oh, you know, TMI could ruin the evening."

Slightly hurt, Mac sits back. "It's nothing bad, just different, but maybe you wouldn't want to hear it." Mac looks at a table across the room and wonders what that couple is talking about and how they're getting along. "Maybe this isn't such a good idea."

"Oh, no it is. I'm sorry. I didn't mean to be a vibe killer. Look, I'll even go first." Mac looks at her over his napkin as he wipes his lips.

"Okay. I'd love to hear more about your mother, or dancing, or your relationship with Enrique, anything really."

Argh! Frankie tenses up hearing Enrique's name. Why shouldn't she be honest with Mac? He's a genuinely sincere guy. Frankie wipes her mouth too, thinking maybe Mac was signaling she has food on her face. She does tend to eat with gusto. She folds and places her napkin on the table, takes a generous sip of cabernet, and sits up straighter.

"Okay, my big reveal: I'm not just here on a break. I'm here to figure out if I want to stay in the professional dance world or leave it to start a family, and I have until the end of December to make a decision." Mac leans in on his elbow attentive as a dog.

"I was an only child with a loving but intrusive mother and no father until I was twelve when the ne'er-do-well stepfather came on the scene. I always wanted siblings to hang out with and share my mother's attention, but he didn't want any. My happiest memories are sleeping over my cousin's house. There'd be a half-dozen of us on the living room floor sharing sleeping bags, and we'd make popcorn at two in the morning and tell scary stories. Or sleeping over my best friend Sharon's house. She was one of five. It was like being part of a tribe, of something bigger than me and my mom. Home felt lonely after those sleepovers. We couldn't even have a dog or cat because my mom's allergic. Not to mention, we moved every three years into a different rental in Brooklyn. I think my mom has some Tinker blood. I vowed I'd have a big family and lots of pets when I grew up. But, here I am, a professional dancer and far from home trying to figure out my life. I think that was more than a minute."

With a solemn brown-eyed focus, Mac has barely blinked. Frankie feels like she's been seen stepping out of her jeans. "Oh! maybe that was way TMI?" She knows she's blushing but is helpless to stop.

Mac sits back. "No, not at all. It's fascinating. I hope being in Oaxaca will help you figure out whatever will make you happy. We have some parallels. I was an only child too and had tons of cousins, but I always wanted a brother or sister. But now that I know my mom's story, I realize badgering them for a sibling must have felt awful. Hmm… another reason to have told me the truth."

"Family stuff! Yikes! Look, I haven't shared my question about having a family or staying with the dance company with anyone here. It's something I have to figure out on my own."

"No worries. I am a model confidante. You can ask my students." He pauses. "But what about Enrique?"

"Especially not Enrique." Frankie so wants to give up the charade, but says, "I don't want it to be a factor in how things go, you know, to bring up such serious stuff right away. It could scare him off." She laughs offhandedly. "I mean it scares me." Frankie plays with the thin silver bangles she bought last week, then folds her hands together on the table.

Mac is still staring intently, like her mother does, but without the edge. "I understand all that completely. But can I ask a question? Why can't you dance *and* have a family?"

"Not if you're performing in a touring company, at least that's how I look at it. I don't want to be dragging kids around the world. I'm not great at multi-tasking. I like to do each thing really well, but being a perfectionist has its drawbacks. That's not to say I couldn't do gigs like teach or do choreography, but I'm not sure if I'm ready to give up performing."

Mac's voice gets lower and intimate. "So, you're going through some intense stuff too." His eyes are so kind Frankie wants to jump in and swim around. She nods, feeling a lump in her throat and looks down, smoothing out her pants, until she can look up without crying."

"Hey, I think it's your turn, Professor."

Mac calls the waitress over. "Could I have a shot of your almond mescal?" Mac looks at Frankie to see if she wants a drink, but says, "Deanna?" Frankie just stares at him. "Oh God, I'm sorry. I meant Frankie, would you like something?"

"Sure. Same thing." Frankie takes the Deanna-gut-shot with a brave smile.

Mac grimaces. "Sorry. I called you Deanna because after what you just said, I was thinking of her. It's funny because it's related, but the opposite." Mac flustered, puts two hands on the table, but his eyes automatically go to his wedding band. He pulls them back. "Okay, this helps me choose my first reveal: Deanna's been clear from the beginning that she doesn't want children. It was an agreement we made before we got married. Instead, she's dedicated her life to science and helping humanity, especially children."

"Well, that's hard to argue with. But, what about you? Do you want kids?"

"I'm not sure. I was never sure. But looking for my biological family and meeting the kids at NNAA has made me think more about children and the possibility of being a father."

Frankie shakes her head back and forth. "Tough issue to compromise on."

"Exactly. So, as we said before, travelling helps people stretch, right? Sort things out. Well, I have a lot to think about." Mac looks across the balcony to the zócalo then back. "Six months ago, I was settled and happy, and knew who I was, or thought I was, but now?" Mac shrugs.

"Wow. You have got a lot on your plate. My best friend, Paula, who's a Buddhist, is my go-to person. She's always saying we need to embrace uncertainty because that's life; it's not so easy though."

"No, it isn't, and I generally don't like things being up in the air. Music is where I improvise, but my life, I like it planned out. That's what's worked." Mac sips his mezcal. "You said your friend's a Buddhist. What about you?"

"I grew up quasi-Catholic and I listen to what Paula tells me about Buddhism, but I don't really know. I feel like there's some kind of greater power, some force that inspires music and dance that's beyond the physical. What about you, Mac? You seemed pretty comfortable in church."

"I pray and meditate but not usually in a church. For me churches are more historical and cultural rather than religious. I believe in some kind of God or Spirit, but religions come with bloody histories of cultural oppression often used to rationalize living a very exclusionary unspiritual life. Look at the far-right Christians in the U.S. Hardly an empathetic, compassionate lot. They tote guns in one hand, and in the other, hold up the Bible like it's a manifesto."

Frankie shifts in her seat. "True. The truth is, I don't spend a lot of time thinking about spiritual stuff. My dance life is all-consuming, but living in Oaxaca makes me more aware of God and people who have faith." Frankie sees how Mac and a highly educated scientist like Deanna would get along. He's such a deep thinker about everything. Frankie's not at all sure-footed in his academic world like she is on stage and hopes he's not judging her.

Mac, on the other hand, is relieved to be away from all the blathering and jousting in academia. He finds Frankie refreshingly intelligent without the pretense, kind of like his talkative student Adriana, but much more sophisticated.

"Deanna, my wife, she's very religious, very Catholic, but in the best sense. A few years ago, I stopped going to church with her. I know she's not happy about it, but I felt like a hypocrite. I have a spiritual connection with nature and my music. You must feel that, right? As a dancer?"

"Totally. Connection and vitality. For me, music is one of the best things about living, and dancing is magical. There's nothing else like it."

"Amen." Mac raises his glass and they click theirs together. A quiet ensues. Mac checks his watch. "Another reveal?"

Frankie pauses. "I'm really tempted, but sorry, not tonight. I have to get up early to meet my trainer."

"And I respect that, but I'm not going to forget. You owe me one. You already know I'm a recently-aware adoptee, my wife doesn't want children and I hum jazz riffs when

I'm happy and nervous. And that I mentioned," and he puts these word in quotes with his fingers, "some weird things happened."

"Well, the weird things are starting to sound more enticing and mysterious than weird."

"Great! To be continued then, the game of revelations."

"Of course. Like psychological strip poker." Again, she can't believe she said something sexual, but Mac laughs. He flashes her a smile. Is he intentionally flirting, the mezcal talking, or is Mac just being his handsome self? Maybe all three.

Frankie notices again the lovely muscles in his forearms and the silver bracelet shining against his coffee-colored skin. Whoa girl. Back off. Private property. Danger: Rip Tide. The wind shifts and their candle flickers for a moment. Frankie shivers. She can't look him in the eye. His intensity makes her feel like she's the only person in Oaxaca, but his charisma's almost too much, like a sorcerer. She draws her shawl tighter.

This Oaxacan trip in general is turning out to feel far less grounding than she'd planned; instead, she's riding currents like a surfer catching waves. When Frankie has the courage to look up at Mac, he's lost in the floodlights of La Catedral and who knows what else.

Chapter Seventeen

El VIRGEN DE SOLEDAD

On a windy evening in early October, Raquel is kneeling in the last pew of the church in Santa Ana. Raquel recognizes most of those praying, but focuses her attention on El Virgen de Soledad, the Black Madonna. Her statue is across the aisle from the Patron Saint of the pueblo, Santa Ana. Statues of saints with downcast eyes gaze forever at the votive candles and flowers at their feet.

Raquel prays for Enrique, that he comes to peace with who he is, enough to share with his father. Raquel prays that her father be more understanding and find room in his heart for Enrique. Since Enrique met Gregorio, she has done this every evening before going home for dinner. She prays for them and for her, that she has the strength to do the right thing about her life's work; she asks for guidance. If she's going to go to the well-respected medical school, La Universidad Autonoma de Guadalajara, she needs to know there's peace at home between her father and Enrique. Raquel makes the sign of the cross and leaves the gray shadows of the church. Outside a prism of light descending from a passing cloud, blinds her, and she collides with someone.

"Díos mío!" a male voice yells as he jumps back. "Oh, of course, it's my sister, el tornado, bam!"

"Sorry! But this must be divine intervention. I was just praying for you."

"Save it for the sick, Raquel. Why are you talking about me behind my back with Gregorio, criticizing my plans with Frankie?"

"So, this is the thanks I get for praying?"

"Why? So God can make me like other men?"

Raquel flinches. "No! Why are you talking to me like this?"

"Pray for Pedro who made me bleed and the ones who taunt others. They need redemption, not me."

"I know, hermano. Calm down. I pray for peace in our family. Ever since mamá died, we both know things haven't been right."

"Yes, papá is deluded by homophobic Evangelists, and that's not going to change. I can't wait to get away and live in Oaxaca. If not with Gregorio, I'll live in the back of El Saguaro. I don't care anymore. And I'm not losing Miguel! This arrangement with Frankie is working, so please, just leave it alone." Enrique spins around and rushes off.

Raquel feels as diminished as the sound of his scooter being swallowed by the valley. She reminds herself that Enrique is often impetuous. She needs to be patient. Something set him off. Gregorio? Maybe *she* should be the one to explain Enrique's lifestyle to her father and Teresa. She could do it for Enrique and for herself. She so wants things to be settled at home. Raquel shakes her head at Enrique's dramatic exit on his motorcycle and is envious. She looks to the sky and asks God for patience, makes the sign of the cross, and heads up the road to have dinner with her papá and abuela.

***

After literally bumping into Raquel, Enrique rides his bike across town and parks in back of a playground. Wanting to burn off some anger, he begins a two-hour hike to a hilltop overlooking Santa Ana. The hilltop has unexcavated ruins and a panoramic view of the Tlacolula Valley, and Enrique hopes to find a broader perspective there, both literally and figuratively. He feels badly he was rude to Raquel, but going to his father right now is out of the question. The repercussions could be irrevocable, but could Teresa possibly understand? He has to admit Raquel has him thinking more in that direction. Or, would telling her be a point of no return where he would lose Miguel?

Poco a poco, on the climb, with the pushback of earth under his feet, Enrique sweats away layers of distress. He wonders if he should introduce Frankie to his family as his novia and continue to play out that story. Would Gregorio be upset enough to leave him? Should he at least tell Teresa? Enrique recycles these questions all the way to the top, not noticing the soft spun clouds or trilling birdsong.

Finally, at the top of the hill, he takes in deep breaths of cleansing mountain air and stretches his arms skyward. A wail erupts from his chest and hangs in the air. Enrique collapses on a rock among the scrub brush and weeps.

Gregorio doesn't know what it's like to live between two worlds: Oaxaca, the hip artsy city and Santa Ana, this rural, rustic pueblo with its righteous Evangelical judgments. Fuck the Bible. Why is everyone so hung up about who has sex with whom? Probably all those biblical dudes stuck out on the hillsides for months were doing it with sheep. And the Bible wasn't written by the actual hand of God. And if God made some people gay, how could he not love them? As if singing out their agreement, the bells of Santa Ana's church begin to chime.

After a few minutes of solitude, Enrique begins his walk back. He thinks about Teresa and her good nature and kindness, the reasons he was in love with her at one time and why she makes such a good mother to their son. He sees now he was starved for affection and affirmation and Teresa was there willing and pretty and so sweet to him. Three years younger, she wasn't a witness to his taunting. At that time, he felt he needed to try being with a woman, so he did. They were good together for a while, until they weren't, and he couldn't tell her why. He could barely acknowledge it himself.

Enrique understands Teresa will always live in Santa Ana. She loves the communal way of life and is proud to be such an accomplished weaver. And he also knows, with a sinking sensation, she's been in love with him all this time. He realizes this conversation could set her free but imprison him in grief. But wouldn't it feel amazing to have at least one person from his village, other than his sister, understand who he is? Could he do this for his relationship with Gregorio? Enrique watches a golden eagle circle the valley, steady and unencumbered and wishes he had wings.

An image pops up in his mind of Teresa kneeling before El Virgen de Soledad. Enrique had quietly entered the church. This was soon after her parents died in a bus accident, a year before Miguel was born. Her parents were visiting relatives in San Cristóbal de las Casas in Chiapas. The ride up is precipitous, and at the end of the rainy season, there was a horrific mudslide.

Teresa's head was bowed and the candles below the statues flickered, illuminating the edges of her shawl. He could hear her weeping but left her alone. He had been with Teresa every day since the accident, but this church was her private space where she drew strength like water from a sacred well. How deep would it go for him?

Halfway down, Enrique greets some villagers he knows, their burros packed with chopped wood, and he smells the soft pine-scented wind. In the distance, he sees farmers guiding water buffalo to till the earth. He longs for the time in Santa Ana when the fields and farms were enough for him, when he happily ran through the pueblo to greet his father. Together, they herded sheep and led the donkeys home, and he was good at what was expected of him.

Chapter Eighteen

SPARROWS

Frankie, heading to the courtyard of Café Flores, walks down streets graced with jacaranda trees, their purple feathery leaves painting the breeze. Inspired by her slower pace of life in Oaxaca and its gracious old-world style, she takes out a pen and paper. As she sips an Aztec hot chocolate, frothed with a molinillo, sparrows peck underfoot at crumbs on the cobblestones.

Dear Paula,

I miss you dear amiga. I miss our dinners at Toni's and just being able to be myself, no filters and all. Except in other ways, it's exciting to be a total unknown---anything's possible. I'm wondering how the new editing job is going? How's your mom and Stash? Are you still seeing him? I hope so because I need some vicarious excitement in that department. God, I haven't had sex since David! Argh!! I would jump on this guy's bones I've gotten to know, but he seems pretty married. I've actually been helping him find his birth family by interpreting Spanish. He found out at age thirty-seven he was adopted! Now that's some surprise! I met him at Los Niños de Amor, the place where I volunteer with the kids. He was adopted from there. It's been a real adventure. We had a second lovely dinner a few nights ago. More later...

I've been torturing myself lately wondering if it was the right decision to come down here. Maybe I should have just sucked it up and stayed in NY to figure it out, but I didn't think I could because David's everywhere. I'm also feeling more and more guilty about lying to my mom. As I told you, she thinks I'm down here collaborating with a Oaxacan dance company. Every time we talk or text, I have to remember what I said the time before and now I'm trapped in the lie.

I found a great trainer here and work out six mornings a week. I know I can't miss a beat if I want to perform in the spring. (Get the pun!) I googled NYC Moves only once because it's too painful. I've been texting with Yolanda and Philippe and Tina, but not often. I don't even know the fall season's program for the first time in eighteen years!! When I saw Raoul on the website, I ended up in a puddle.

As you can see, I am boomeranging from one subject to the other. I feel the pressure of time, every day, to make a decision about performing or having a family. Should I rethink my hard and fast rule about either one or the other? It wouldn't be easy staying with the company since Raoul is hardly pro-kids. Why did I fuck things up with David? Do you want to be my parenting partner? Should I adopt? Get inseminated? Hey, want to marry me? Ha! I could teach and choreograph like lots of dancers, but it's the performing where I'm most alive. Please help me, my all-wise friend and angel. I so value your perspective.

The kids at the center/orphanage are amazing! Lively, smart, and beautiful. I love their energy and this one little girl and boy especially tug at my heartstrings. I'm doing some admin work, teaching a dance class, creating choreography for a fundraiser, and hanging out with the kids, but it's not like being a real mom, is it? So??? Also, I'm someone's fake novia, (girlfriend)... a story for another letter. I became friends with him and his sister. Their uncle is the director of the kids' center.

There's too much to say about Oaxaca and all the pueblos around here, so you'll have to come visit. Really!!! I know I'm babbling on and on, so thanks for listening, but I really do want to hear about YOU TOO! All of it my friend...work, Stash, sex (with details), the meditation center, everything!

Love, your dancing fool, childless wonder, BFF Frankie

Chapter Nineteen

ROOTS AND TANGLES

Mac and Frankie drive in and out of fog banks as they climb from the Oaxacan Valley to Santa Caterina Lachatao high in the Sierra Juarez. The cool air is scented with evergreens and vistas expand around every corner. Frankie notices Mac is gripping the steering wheel with increasing tension as they ascend the curvy mountain road. She tucks her hands under her thighs to hide her own nervous excitement, not just about the drive, but about this whole family-finding adventure. She wants to appear calm for Mac's sake.

"I'm glad I'm the one driving or I know I'd be car-sick."

"Good to know."

"Yes, and the more I focus on driving, the less nervous I feel. I'm glad I used the bungee cord on the box Marta gave us. It's in the trunk safe from bumps."

"No worries. I'm sure the Cocijo family mementos will be fine." Mac drives on for a mile or so. "Is that a song Mac, or just random humming?"

"Oh dear, again? Totally random. I'm trying to keep my anticipation in check after that first trip."

"I understand, and up here there are many possibilities, right? I'm just saying. Marta wasn't clear she ever met your mom, and I hope your grandmother's still alive."

Mac would like eye contact but doesn't dare glance at Frankie: too few siderails and too many ravines. "It's nice you're trying to protect me, but I know someone up here will be connected to me. I can feel it."

"After the dream-visions you told me about, I believe you. Healers and spirit animals are much more intriguing than weird. They actually give me a kind of faith." She glances at Mac smiling. "Not at all fetish-like."

"Are you disappointed? Did I just say that? I must be nervous. I wish you would my wife. Oh my God, I mean I wish you would tell that to my wife." Mac groans. "Just ignore me, please. Look, Deanna doesn't find my experiences at all intriguing. She thinks I've gone around the bend and need psychotherapy. You probably do too at this point."

"I never said that. But why isn't she here? I know she's a scientist and all, but this is an important moment, right?" Mac gets quiet and Frankie hopes that wasn't too unfiltered. When he speaks, his tone is flat.

"She can't just leave her experiments midway."

"Oh, I see. I guess that's true."

"Clearly, this is more complicated than I anticipated, and it's going to take more than a few days. If Deanna were here, I'd feel pressure to hurry and guilty about what she's missing at work."

Frankie shrugs. "Maybe that's the sign of a mature relationship. You allow each other some room."

"I guess." Frankie wonders if she and David had what it takes to see a relationship through. Maybe if she had trusted him more, or more importantly, trusted herself, it could have worked. David suffered for that, and she vows never to do that to another human. And, she thinks, I may have given up my one chance at carrying a biological child.

"I kind of envy Deanna with her clarity about children. It makes life less complicated."

"Unless you're married." Mac notes with an edge.

"Of course, I'm sorry. I was thinking about my own life." Jesus, Frankie muses, I'm not scoring any points with this guy, married or not.

Frankie leans her head back, closes her eyes and finds herself reminiscing about her old life.

***

Waiting for their Friday night Thai take-out delivery, she and David relaxed on the couch in Frankie's apartment in the East Village. After a few beers, David started kissing her neck the way she loves and made his desire clear with his hands up her shirt, but Frankie, usually responsive, was still aching and spotting from the previous day's abortion.

She pulled back and said she was afraid the delivery guy might come, faked a smile then downed the rest of her beer on an empty stomach, but the beer wasn't doing it. She hadn't thought this part through and was getting frantic when the doorbell startled her.

David answered and put their take-out bags on the table. With a knowing smile, he took the beer from her hand, straddled her and continued his caressing.

Frankie gently pressed him away. David looked so concerned it flipped her stomach even more. She pulled her knees to her chest. "David, I need to tell you something. I should have told you before." Frankie couldn't look at him. "I had an appointment yesterday."

"What kind of appointment?"

"At a clinic."

"Are you okay? What's wrong Frankie?"

Her stomach twisted another knot. "Can't you guess?"

David looked completely unmoored which was unusual. "What's going on Frankie?" His voice was tight and scared.

Struck with the enormity of what she'd done, lying suddenly felt impossible. She spoke quickly. "I went for an abortion."

"What? We were pregnant?" Frankie winced. "And you didn't tell me?" David started pacing the room and rubbing his five o'clock shadow. "How could you *not* tell me, Frankie?"

Frankie spluttered, "I was confused. You might have talked me out of it. You're so persuasive David. You're a lawyer. What if you convinced me to have the baby and I left performing and resented you forever?"

David looked at Frankie as if she were a stranger. "Do you hear yourself? Resented *me*? The father? That was my child too." David's voice was breaking. "I can't believe you did this to us."

Frankie, head on knees, heard David go into their bedroom. Each drawer opening and closing was like a nail. When he stopped, she was so still, she could hear the blood rushing in her head. Frankie looked up and David stood before her with a backpack on his shoulder.

Frankie jumped up. "I'm sorry. Let's talk. Please! Don't just go."

David held tight to the shoulder strap as his lips quivered. "I can't stay here right now. If you could do this, Frankie, I'm not sure who you really are."

As David's footsteps echoed down the stairwell, Frankie's regret began in waves, cresting and plunging. All his things were packed up and gone a week later. Frankie called him on his cell apologizing over and over for a funereal month, but David was unresponsive, then he changed his number.

***

"Ah, Frankie? I think I lost you there. Where did you go?"

It takes Frankie a moment to recover. "I'm sorry Mac, I must have dozed off. I'm not used to getting up at 5 a.m." During one of their strolls around Oaxaca, Frankie told Mac a bit about David, but she certainly didn't mention the abortion, not to a man who blesses himself with holy water and prays in a Catholic church. She would have to know him a whole lot better to share that messed up part of herself.

They come around another bend revealing mountaintops of oak and pine. A flotilla of clouds cruising the sky lifts Frankie's spirits.

She spots a sign. "Mac, Benito Juarez is in three kilometers."

"Great. I'm starving and it's time to ask around about my family. Since my grandmother's a curandera, people must know her. You ready for breakfast?"

"Are you kidding?" She speaks slowly. "Remember: huevos, tortillas, y frijoles."

"Si amiga, entiendo. Eggs, tortillas and beans y café con leche por favor."

"Fabuloso! You've been studying! Hey, I'm hoping your relatives speak Spanish because I don't know one word of Zapotec."

"I hope so too." Mac looks at Frankie. "If not, you're out of a job and I'm out of luck," he quips, probably trying to cover his nervousness. "We'll have to use sign language."

They order breakfast in the only comedor in town. Across from the restaurant are the *Cabanas Benito Juarez*, wooden cabins of the communal eco-tourism business of Pueblos Mancomunados, and in front of them is a statue of the pueblo's namesake. "Do you know Benito Juarez was a brilliant Zapotec Indian who rose to become an esteemed El Presidente? He's known as 'The Father of Mexican Democracy'."

Frankie takes a sip of coffee. "It's never boring travelling with a professor, but yes, I did know that. Been doing my reading."

Mac puts down his fork. "I am impressed. Hey, maybe it's the air. I don't know, but these are the best black beans I've ever eaten."

Frankie, still chewing, tries to speak. "Yes, really good. Also, am I impressing you with how much I can pack away?"

"Definitely, and when you're done, no rush of course, could you ask the cook if he knows the Garcia Cocijo family from Lachatao? It's not like I'm looking for my biological family or anything." Mac smiles broadly.

"Okay, I get it. But, why don't I finish eating and you can practice your Spanish?"

"No, Frankie. This is too important."

Frankie finishes up. "No black beans stuck in my teeth?" She smiles with her teeth together.

"You're fine."

"Okay, no worries. I got this."

She approaches a large window to the kitchen where she introduces herself. She learns that the cook, an older man, possibly in his late sixties, and his wife have owned this restaurant for thirty years. The man, with thick brown eyebrows, is very friendly and expressive. Their eldest daughter is middle-aged and her daughter, a teenager, are working there, cutting up onions, peppers, squash and tomatoes. A huge vat of black beans is bubbling on the wood-fed stove next to a pot full of coffee.

Frankie asks them about the Garcia Cocijos. They look at each other and start speaking in what Frankie can only assume is Zapotec. She points to Mac and explains that he may be related and would like to meet them. This sets the family buzzing. Mac joins Frankie at the window.

The mother says, "We have cousins in Lachatao and we know la familia when they come back from Oaxaca. La Abuela es una curandera, muy famosa aquí."

Mac, "Yes, I hear she is. And you speak some English. I'm grateful."

She sweeps her arms out to her family. "Ah, mucha gente speak un poco de English for el ecoturismo. Tu abuela saved my nephew, mi sobrino. He had la gripa, la influenza."

Mac nods. "Yes, I've heard she's very good. And do you know her daughter, su hija, Rosario? Ella es my mother, mi madre." The kitchen gets church-solemn.

The daughter says, "My older cousin knew Rosario. They went to the same high school in Oaxaca. It's why the family moved to there. She was an artiste and muy inteligente and got a scholarship, but she never came back here." The mother says something to the daughter in Zapotec as she looks at Mac. The daughter responds in Zapotec. The mom nods and sits down in the back of the kitchen and continues cutting up vegetables.

The father says, "Lachatao es al norte. Drive directamente. There is a long hanging bridge, un puente, como aquí. You can to see todas las montañas de la Sierra Norte. It is la vista la mas hermosa, the most beautiful, en todo el mundo, in the whole world!" He opens his arms wide and laughs at his hyperbole. His wife makes chiding sounds in the universal language of older couples.

Mac and Frankie thank them and leave a big tip. On the way to the car, Frankie takes in the woodsmoke smell that for the rest of her life will evoke these mountaintop villages.

As soon as they get in the car, Mac says. "A suspended bridge, the perfect metaphor. I hope it doesn't rip apart and send me hurtling into space."

"Whoa! Where did that come from? A bit dramatic, don't you think?"

"Not really, so it's either that or humming."

"I think I prefer the humming."

***

As they drive north, dirt roads and footpaths rise up all around them into sheep farms and oxen-plowed cornfields. The expansive mountain vista is a contrast to Mac's throat tight with anxiety. He tries deep breathing into his belly as dust devils swirl by the side of the road.

Frankie touches his arm lightly. "It sounds like there's a story there about your mother."

"For sure. It's like a punch to the gut to find out she definitely isn't here. God, they all looked so ominous. Could we have read about her in the paper?"

"No assumptions. Really. I think they were just surprised, caught off guard."

"That's what bothers me. Why would they have to be on guard?"

"I shouldn't have used that word. Do you want to wait a bit? Take a walk?" Frankie pauses. "You know you don't have to do this."

Mac smiles. "Are you a dancer or therapist?"

Frankie shrugs, "I just know that feeling too much pressure doesn't help. I'm a performer. I know about pressure."

"I bet, but there's no question I've got to do this. We can't have driven all the way up here for nothing." He pauses. "You may have to listen to me hum for a while."

Frankie smiles. "No problem. I kind of like it." Without thinking, Mac reaches out for Frankie's hand. He squeezes it quickly and lets go, but the feeling of her warm skin lingers.

Mac pulls into Santa Catarina Lachatao's town plaza past the sand-colored stone church and parks in front of a comedor, much like the one in Benito Juárez. Lachatao is even more ethereal and enchanting than its neighboring pueblo. They get out of the car and stretch. The shadow of a cloud moves north illuminating a copse of pine trees in the descending diorama.

Frankie embraces the scene with arms wide open. "Forests! Mountains! Fresh air!"

"Yes amazing!" Mac turns taking it all in. "You know, we're at about 7000 feet. We probably don't want to do any sprinting, although you've had more time to acclimate, not to mention your shape. I mean that you're in good shape."

Frankie laughs off the compliment. "Well, Oaxaca's already at 5,000 feet and my workouts are intense. Hey, we don't have to rush. You'll need time to adjust." Mac looks at Frankie appreciatively as she steps ahead. She is lovely he thinks, but it's likely she could beat me at arm wrestling, not a confidence inspiring image. They go into the restaurant to ask directions to the home of the Garcia Cocijo family. This pueblo, also accustomed to tourists and la curandera's patients, happily sends them on their way.

Ten minutes later, as directed, when the paved highway, Route 175 ends, they leave the car by the roadside and walk up a dirt path at the northeastern edge of the pueblo. Both are feeling the effects of the rarified air, but Mac has to bend down and catch his breath every so often. He's carrying the family box in a backpack and his shoulders ache.

"Let's take a break." He practically throws down his pack. "I feel slightly nauseous."

"Okay, let's sit and drink some water. You may be getting dehydrated. I can carry the box for a while." Mac is grateful and annoyed. He nods and thinks, so much for my manhood.

Frankie sees the look on his face. "You can relax, Mac. It's all good." Mac thinks, yeah, for you it is. I'm definitely hitting the gym back in Amherst.

After a few minutes, they begin walking and come to a sharp bend in the path that goes to the right. They see a house made of stone and wood built back along the edge of the forest. Sheep graze in the front pasture. The side yard is enclosed with a chicken wire fence protecting the hens and roosters.

A middle-aged woman places pieces of wet laundry out to dry on large rocks and grass behind the sheep pasture. The woven tops and skirts form a kaleidoscope of primary colors. Two young women sit on chairs shucking corn and sorting something, maybe beans. Mac, breathless from the walk and acute anticipation, thinks he might throw up. Being in the modern-day city of Oaxaca is one thing, but this is an entirely different world up here. He suddenly wishes Deanna and his parents were beside him, or that he could go back down the mountain and not have to face this ordeal. Frankie looks at him closely.

"Are you okay?"

"I don't know. Those people who are most likely my relatives are looking at us like we made the wrong turn somewhere back in Benito Juárez."

The women continue staring, so Frankie waves and yells, "Hola!" They return the greeting.

The woman setting out the laundry yells, "Quieren la curandera?"

Frankie says, "They're asking if we want your grand-mother, the curandera."

Before she can answer the woman, Mac grabs her wrist. "Don't move. Look!"

Frankie looks down. "What?"

Mac is panicked, "Is that a scorpion?"

"No! Scorpions have pincers and a long tail."

"Oh, thank God. I feel a little queasy, possibly faint."

"Maybe you should sit down for a minute?"

Mac groans. "Okay, just for a minute." He sits in the road with his head between his knees keenly aware of the women watching them. He looks up at Frankie. "Do I really want to do this? Interrupt their lives? What if Rosario never told them she had me? If she did, they could have looked for me."

"Mac, take a few breaths. Look, it would have been up to Rosario to look for you, but these people are still your relatives." Frankie gives Mac a minute then extends her hand. Mac takes it, stands up and they turn towards the sound of a door opening.

An older woman leaning on a walking stick comes down the front steps and walks down the dirt driveway towards them. She's full-bodied and strong with grey-white hair in a long braid down her back woven through with bright red ribbon. She wears a dark blue cotton skirt with a white embroidered top, a flowered apron and feather and stone necklace. As she gets closer, Mac notices her eyes are a rich brown like the earth. He hopes they haven't upset her; she looks like she means business and wouldn't hesitate to use her walking stick to keep them in line. She yells in Zapotec to the women. The two young women in chairs stand up. The other drops the wet blouse in her hand.

The old woman studies Mac with penetrating eyes. This must be the famous curandera, but my grandmother, my Abuela? "Intense" is the word that comes to mind. I don't see her baking me cookies, but at least the other women are smiling, thank God. They come down the hill to join them, and as the old woman steps closer, Mac can see there's warmth in her eyes. She speaks to him in Zapotec, and the middle-aged woman, Mac assumes is his aunt, interprets in Spanish. Frankie relays the message in English.

She says to welcome you home, grandson. Mac can't take his eyes off her and has an odd urge to grab her around the waist and kneel at her feet.

Abuela switches to Spanish and Frankie interprets. "Finally, you are here in Lachatao, mi nieto, my grandson. The spirit guides said you'd be here soon. They said look for a man who likes to eat and looks like his mother." Abuela gently touches the side of his face. Frankie continues. "I usually don't say the name of your mother, Rosario, but you have her mouth and eyes. My heart is so full in this moment."

Abuela places her hands on her heart then grabs both of Mac's hands. Hers, the color of tree bark, are landscaped with branched veins and callouses. Her grip is definitive and warm. Mac's heart opens up, bringing tears, and he can only nod.

His aunt introduces herself as Consuela, and with a mixture of English and Spanish explains that Abuela speaks Spanish and some English, but wanted to greet him in Zapotec to honor his heritage. Consuela introduces his cousins, Nayeli and Inda Jani.

Looking at each, Mac says, "Hola mi Abuela, Tía Consuela, y mis sobrinas. Mucho gusto." He nods his head. "And this is Frankie, my interpreter and my friend."

Consuelo asks, "No es tu esposa, your wife?" Mac and Frankie shake their heads no, and Mac sees their disappointment.

Abuela takes his arm. "I will teach to you healing and herbs and working with guides from el mundo espiritual. You know, "cocijo", tu nombre, your name, means lightning, and Cocijo is the God of Lightning. Our name has much power." She grins. "I will teach you much. Zapotec too."

Mac laughs. "I'm still learning Spanish. Estoy aprendiendo Español."

Abuela smiles broadly, gold caps on her teeth gleaming. She holds his arm tighter. "Venga. Vamos a la casa." Mac follows.

Only a few minutes ago, this venture felt risky, possibly foolhardy, but holding Abuela's hands and hearing the welcoming voices of his aunt and cousins has changed all that. As they head to the house, Mac waits for Frankie to be by his side. She smiles and gives him a surreptitious thumbs up and hands him the backpack, the box safe inside. He hasn't looked at the contents yet, preferring to share it in person with his new family.

Chapter Twenty

OTHER WAYS OF KNOWING

Settled on the patio of his B&B, a Dos Equis in hand, Mac calls Deanna as soon as he and Frankie get back from Lachatao later that evening. They had politely declined invitations to sleep over after a full day of visiting. Deanna tells him she's in the study, and he pictures the birch trees in white paper-mâché trunks leaning over the stream, and it tugs him homeward.

Mac describes the drive to Lachatao, the hike up into the forest, and meeting his biological family. He refers to Frankie as his American interpreter leaving her gender-ambiguous name just that. "It's so beautiful there Deanna, and they were all so good to me, but my biological mother, Rosario, hasn't lived there since she was sixteen. Apparently, she's an artist and lives in Mexico City, but no one wants to talk about her. When I finally asked directly, Abuela said, 'We'll talk about her next time,' and no one chose to argue."

"Who said that?"

"Abuela, that means grandmother."

"Okay, well I'm sorry your mother isn't there. That's so disappointing."

"It is, and frustrating. I really want to understand why she gave me up, but apparently, whatever it was makes everyone uncomfortable, so I'll have to be patient."

"I'm sure that's really hard, sweetie."

"It is, but I did learn a lot about my aunt and cousins and extended family, past and present. The best part, though, was connecting with Abuela. We spent hours talking about her work as a healer, a curandera." Mac realizes he was so entranced by Abuela's charisma and commanding energy that he committed himself to helping her, and only now is he thinking about Deanna's reaction. It felt so right at the time, but a sheepishness spreads over him like a rash. "Ah, Abuela has asked me if I could help her in preserving and sharing her healing knowledge."

"What does that mean, exactly?"

"She says Rosario left a gap in the lineage and the spirit guides have led me there to help her write a book about herbs and remedies and traditional ways of healing."

"What? You just met them and now you're part of a lineage? This is feeling odd Mac, like it's coming out of left field."

"Not really, Deanna, not to me, but I can see how it would to you. It's connected to the vision-dreams. I used to have dreams like that as a kid too, but I didn't remember until they started up again."

"You never told me that. And what do you know about healing? You won't even take your own temperature."

"I'm not saying I'll become a healer, but it would be great to help her preserve her knowledge. She's a well-respected herbalist and shaman. I'll write down what she says and sketch the plants, and her granddaughters will do the translations into Zapotec and Spanish."

"Let's back up. You have a sudden interest in sketching herbs?"

"It's part of my work, part of Pre-Columbian culture."

"That's a stretch, Mac."

"Deanna, please. I want to learn whatever my grandmother has to teach. I also want to look for my biological mother. I didn't know it would be this complicated. Please, come visit, just for a short time. I really want to see you."

"Oh God, Mac. You know I hate flying and the grant deadline is coming up. I want to meet your biological family, of course, but maybe after you get to know them a bit."

"But there's always a deadline. Everyone gets to take some time off, even you."

"Well, realistically, how long do you think you'll be there?"

"A few weeks at least. Maybe a month since Rosario lives in Mexico City which is a plane flight away."

Deanna sucks in her breath. "Oh Mac. Look, I'm happy you've connected. I really am, but it's been less than a week and I already miss you. So does Pumpkin."

"I miss you too, but I need to make the most of this, especially while I'm on sabbatical, and you've got to meet my grandmother. She's a force like you and has a lot to teach me."

Deanna delivers a long sigh. "I still don't understand this sudden interest in herbs."

"I'm more the messenger, someone to bring her knowledge to the States. She's connected to a place called Sage Mountain in Vermont." Mac paces the patio. "And, I have to be honest Deanna, I'd like to learn more about shamanism and Abuela can teach me." There's a long pause and a sound, but Mac can't tell if it's a cough or Deanna's crying. He feels awful.

"I'm sorry, Deanna. I know this isn't what you were expecting to hear."

"So, your grandmother is somehow connected to those dreams, I'm sorry, vision-dreams you have?"

"Yes, those are the spirit guides she works with in her healing." There's silence on the other end like a vein's been severed.

"I don't know what to say, Mac."

"Oh God, I wish I were there in person to help you understand."

"Me too. It feels more and more like we're operating out of parallel universes. What about preparing for next semester?"

"I can teach most of that stuff in my sleep, except the new course, and learning about shamanism will help me complete the syllabus. And here, there's a chance for me to learn so much more than what I'll need for my coursework."

"But Mac, I thought you loved teaching. You mean you'd consider giving it up?"

"I didn't say that. You're getting ahead of yourself."

"Speaking of teaching, one of your students, Adriana, has left three or four messages on our home phone. Can you get in touch with her please?"

Mac bites his lip. "Sorry, will do. Deanna, I wish you were more excited for me. I'm exploring. I'm learning about my people."

Deanna's voice drops low. "Your people?"

"Well, some of them, yes. But of course, you are my main people, Deanna. You know that. You and my parents and my extended family and my students."

"Well, that's good to hear. And without being sarcastic, I mean you know there's science now, right? So why are you going back in time to work with a traditional healer?"

"This isn't going backwards. People have used herbs to heal for millennia. A lot of pharmaceutical companies try to reproduce their properties. You know that, and there are thousands of herbal products on the market. Shamans and healers have existed in every culture long before modern science. Healing isn't just science; it's also an art with a spiritual side."

"Wow! Okay. Good to know. What an afternoon you've had! You sound like a convert. Possibly a pagan. And here I thought we were a Catholic family."

"But when was the last time I went to Mass? I've been exploring other religions for a while. And many Catholic churches, just so you know, were built on Indigenous temples because the Spanish recognized their sacred power."

"Okay Mac, you've made your point, but it all feels pretty out there to me. Have you forgotten about how rigorous science is?"

"You know I respect science. You observe tiny worlds under a microscope and manipulate them in a lab and come up with amazing discoveries that change the world, but there are other ways of knowing."

"But other people can verify what I see."

"True, but couldn't you try to be more open? Are we all supposed to find one thing to believe in or work at and that's it? That may work for you, but it doesn't for everyone."

"Whoa. Calm down. When did I say that? I'm just trying to understand what's happening to my husband. We've built a life here and...."

Mac interrupts, "How do you think this is for me?"

"I don't know. I mean you sound excited."

"I am, sometimes, except it's turned my world upside down. Finding out I'm adopted at thirty-seven. Having these vision-dreams. I need some support here."

Deanna is quiet for a few moments. "Mac, I will try to be more supportive. But you need to understand, it's turned my world upside down too. Bottom line, I'm feeling lonely here in Montague. It's starting to get chilly in the evening and darker earlier. I miss you warming my feet up at night."

"I miss you too." Mac tears up.

"I guess I'll have to get used to the idea that you very possibly could be gone for a month or more."

"So come visit."

Deanna speaks so softly Mac can barely hear her. "Let me think about it." Deanna takes a long pause. "I'll let you know, but right now I have to head back to the lab for a few hours. I came home to feed the cat and water the plants, but it's too quiet. I even miss your humming."

"Try to be patient, my love."

"I promise I'll try. Have a good night, Mac. I love you."

"Love you more."

Chapter Twenty-One

DOPPELGANGER?

It's been two days since Mac's first trip to Lachatao, and tomorrow he'll make a second trip with Frankie to have his first real lesson. Tonight, he plans to meet up with her at El Saguaro for a bite to eat, and when she mentioned Enrique won't be working, Mac was relieved. He takes a shower and shaves. As he's getting dressed, the light between the wooden blinds casts soft geometric patterns across his body and the bedspread. He hears a bird singing by the patio, dogs barking down the street, and a truck engine revving up. Soon it's quiet again, and for a few moments he is content, bathed in a pleasant calm, but then Deanna comes to mind, alone in their study, staring out at the birch trees.

All knotted up after the conversations they've been having, Mac decides to take the long way around to the restaurant to clear his head. He understands why Deanna wants him home, but she doesn't seem to want to accept or understand why he needs to stay. He wonders if he's being selfish. Heading down Guelaguetza Avenida, his muscles begin to loosen with each stride. Mac starts to hum a favorite jazz piece while imagining he's playing it on his keyboard.

Every time Mac goes for a walk, he uses a different route hoping to uncover and experience all of Oaxaca before he leaves, and this route has brought him to a street that runs in back of El Saguaro. As he approaches, he notices a lone red motorcycle by the curb. Mac thinks he's alone until he notices two people kissing under the awning of the back door. One strong hand is on the back of the other's head holding it tight. The person with his back to the parking area looks a lot like Enrique, but that can't be. Mac, not wanting to disturb them, backs up under the shadows. Then the couple move apart, and Mac clearly sees Gregorio, dish towel on his shoulder, turn and walk back into the restaurant. The other man emerges into the sunlight. Oh God, it is *indeed* Enrique! He jumps on the red motorcycle and speeds off over a tope, the ubiquitous Mexican speed bump. Enrique glides airborne for a moment before touching down, revs it once and turns the corner.

What the hell? This is crazy! Is Enrique stringing Frankie along for some kind of green card deal? Is her heart going to be broken? Is he bisexual? Now Mac doesn't know what to say at dinner. Should I tell her? That's what a friend would do. He had been looking forward to this evening, but this is not an auspicious start. If he tells her, things could get awkward and serious and he longs for a lighter fare, a break from the intensity with Deanna. He'll just have to play it by ear.

He thinks about topics that might be engaging or even funny, but then gets distracted imagining what Frankie will be wearing. He admires her style, physicality and warmth. He has to admit there's an attraction on his part but senses nothing flirty from her, certainly nothing overtly suggestive. For the decade he's been married, Mac's been faithful to Deanna. No one's turned his head, not even the lovely underclad undergrads. Plus, Frankie knows he's married, and she does have a novio. But does she? That was quite a kiss! He hopes for Frankie's sake that Enrique has a cousin, or a Oaxacan doppelganger.

Chapter Twenty-Two

FIRESIDE IN LACHATAO

The next morning, with roosters crooning across the valley, Mac is up, tossing his overstuffed bag in the back seat. He's on his way to pick up Frankie, and they'll spend the night in Lachatao with his newly acquainted family. Nearing Jalatlaco, he hopes Frankie will be ready. She's become a trusted interpreter and is becoming more and more a confidante and friend. And there she is, out front waiting. He sighs and realizes he's been tense all morning.

Less than two hours of driving, constant conversation and three cups of coffee later, Mac and Frankie arrive in Lachatao. Abuela is ready and waiting on the porch, cane in hand with Nayeli by her side. They hike up behind the house into a pine forest draped in Spanish moss and mist. Mac can't believe he's really here with his biological grandmother and cousin. Abuela carries a woven basket to collect herbs.

Mac catches up to her. "Here, let me carry the basket for you."

"No es necesario, mi nieto." She uses her cane like a third arm, sweeping away grass. Abuela points to a plant she identifies as una planta de bee pollen and says it's used to treat arthritis. She bends to pick one up and holds it out to Mac. He sketches and takes notes as she describes making a poultice. He appreciates the help from Frankie and Nayeli who jump in to interpret whenever there's confusion.

They travel further into the forest and Abuela picks simonillo flowers used to make tea for stomach problems, explaining that it doesn't taste good but works. Mac draws and writes like mad.

"Abuela, I'm happy to be helping, but you know I have no background in healing."

Abuela locks eyes with him. "I know nieto, but there is some in your blood, and we need you to learn about herbs and healing to bring to your country. This is mi obligación. There are healers still receptive to old ways. I will give you names in Vermont near to where you live. We need nuestras plantas to go out into the world, so we don't lose them forever because of the horrible things we do to Mother the Earth." Abuela touches his cheek with one of her hands. "Understand?"

"I'll do my best Abuela." Her face lights up and she nods and smiles as if expecting no other answer.

"Soon I will do a limpia, an emotional and spiritual cleansing with you and you will understand more. She points to a clearing. "Look, see that beautiful planta, that's heno for coughs." She gathers heno and invites Mac to help. Her basket is full so she uses the big front pockets of her apron. "The government does not protect nature so we must to be las guardíanas." Abuela opens her arms to include the forest and mountains. "All over the world we need guardíanas de la naturaleza or life will disappear."

Nayeli smiles at Mac as if to say, welcome to Abuela and her world. "Abuela, I will try, but like I said, I have no background, no prior knowledge of this."

"Si, pero you are muy inteligente, no? Of course, you are my grandson." She giggles. "Who else do I teach? Nayeli and Inda Janu use herbs solamente for cooking like their mamá. When Rosario left, there was a hole."

"I understand, Abuela, but remember, I have a wife at home, my students, even a cat, so I can help, but my time is limited."

"Díos helps all, my grandson." Mac can see Abuela's not listening. "Your mamá is not here, so now you are here, but we have not to talk about her." Mac sees Frankie give him a sympathetic look. She knows how much he's aching to learn about his mother.

Mac turns away from Abuela and breathes in the pine and moss smells. He doesn't want to squander these precious moments with impatience. He turns back. "It's beautiful here, Abuela. So quiet."

"Si, y es tu casa aquí. It's your home here." Mac, humbled, makes a quick bow.

Mac has assiduously recorded everything in his notebook for the past three hours. Thank God he can sketch well. But still acclimating to the altitude, he tires easily and is ready for a break. His stomach agrees, grumbling away what's left of his coffee and breakfast. Frankie and Nayeli look like they could use a break too, but Abuela appears as vibrant as her colorful stream-washed clothes. She looks at Mac and Frankie, and without a word, turns and heads downhill.

Mac hurries to keep up, breathing like a chain smoker and thinks, now is as good a time as any. "Abuela, when can we talk about Rosario?"

She stops and they fall into line like dominoes. "When she left, I said I would never speak her name again, pero for you, my nieto, I do this. In the box from Oaxaca are las fotos with old notebooks from the school. She always loved to draw. All the time. Maybe it's why you can do sketches so good. I left those things in Oaxaca to be finished with Rosario, but the past is tocándome, touching me, on the shoulder." She lightly taps Mac's shoulder. "Tonight, after dinner, we talk."

***

After the morning lesson and lunch, Mac climbs the hill behind the cornfield. At lunch, Frankie had asked his cousins to teach her some Zapotec. He admires her friendliness and ability to find common ground. Their laughter follows him from the side yard and makes him smile. He comes upon a hammock at the edge of the forest, a green and yellow weave suspended between two pines. Craving a solitary space to absorb all that's been going on, Mac cocoons himself inside it. Here at the heart of the place he's meant to be, he has no need for vision-dreams. Rocking in and out of streaming sunlight, his body feels like it's floating in a river of liquid gold, and soon a sweet deep rest comes over him.

***

After giving Frankie a lesson in Zapotec, the cousins leave to help a neighbor harvest beans, and Frankie lies back on the grass and relaxes. She hopes Mac will continue to bring her here even though he's learning more Spanish and Nayeli knows a lot of English. She loves being with him, and watching his story unfold is compelling and poignant. As well, being in Lachatao's forest with Abuela is a unique adventure.

As if thinking about her made it so, Abuela appears. "Frankie, would you like una limpia? It is good for you. Next time Mac comes, I do one for him. La limpia is a cleansing of your body y espíritu. I pray to God, to Jesús Cristo, y La Virgen de Guadalupe and my guides to help." Frankie hesitates but has no idea how to refuse someone like Abuela, and she wants to be a good guest. She remembers her promise to stretch herself and one of *The Four Agreements: Do Your Best.* She doesn't know exactly how she feels about this kind of healing using spirit guides but is open to it largely because of Mac.

"Okay, Abuela."

"Vamos." Abuela leads the way to her healing space in a small wooden building next to the cornfield. They stand in front of her altar. A crucifix hangs above the framed pictures of El Virgen de Guadalupe, Jesús Cristo, and Santo Francisco de Assisi. White carnations and red roses adorn the altar, and a clay brazier of copal sits next to several white candles. Abuela explains that the basin of water on the floor is there to absorb any negative energy released during the cleansing. She lights the candles and copal. Frankie tries to ignore the inner voice saying, WTF, this is so weird.

"Come to sit." Frankie sits in a chair in front of the altar, and Abuela smudges (cleanses) her with the smoke from the copal, circling her several times with the brazier until the entire room is filled. "Many curanderos use an egg to rub on the body to diagnose, but I call on to God and saints and guide-helpers." She takes a hefty bouquet of rosemary, basil, and piru leaves from an urn and brushes Frankie's body from head to toe, praying and lightly whacking Frankie to unsettle and release unwanted energy to help rebalance her. Frankie almost laughs out loud as she imagines Raoul and the dancers witnessing this, and Abuela, possibly reading her mind, surprise spritzes her with mezcal to further cleanse.

"Come to lie here for a massage." Abuela points to a wooden platform bed with thick woven blankets and Frankie obeys. For an older woman, her hands are incredibly strong as she works on Frankie using her bodyweight to press and release any muscle tension and increase blood flow. Frankie gives herself over. She stopped judging or thinking the moment Abuela's hands touched her body. It's glorious to feel pain shapeshift into pleasure.

Frankie hears a distant voice. "You can to sit up when you are ready." She must have fallen asleep, and as objects and sounds come into focus, she reluctantly sits up. Her body feels relaxed like she's just bathed in a warm salty ocean.

Abuela holds her gaze and both of her hands as she speaks. Frankie feels her warmth surging into her. "What I see is a body who need to move, always to move. You strong but some time is too much. Your neck and shoulder too tight. And I see conflictos with tu mamá and confusión, como una tormenta, like a storm around you. With big decisions comes the peace. Be patient. I will give you herbs for your muscles to use en la noche, at night. I put in a soft cloth for you, and lavender tea will relax you to sleep."

Abuela looks at her in such a loving way, Frankie feels like crying. She then leads her by the hand outside and points towards the driveway. "Go to walk, to sit by the stream. The water will absorb las cosas, the things, you need no more. Keep your heart open. No too much thinking."

Sitting by the stream, Frankie lets the tears flow. There's no sudden epiphany, but a steady letting go, like river ice breaking up in the spring and melting back into itself. Afterwards, she feels calmer, like the massage worked on the inside too. When Frankie feels done, she heads back towards the house and sees Mac coming down the hill. She walks his way, resisting the impulse to run and throw her arms around him.

"Abuela just gave me una limpia, and I'm *so* relaxed. Your grandmother is an amazing curandera, that's for sure." Mac gives her his razzle-dazzle smile.

***

Dinner is fresh trout from the stream, rice, and roasted peppers and corn, cooked over the wood-fired stove. The aromas are intoxicating. Everyone sits around a large homemade wooden table, including Consuelo's husband, Francisco. He's just arrived home from San Miguel Amatlán where he was cleaning eco-tourism bungalows, one of the duties the people of Los Pueblos Mancomunados share. Francisco is famished and tired. Aunt Consuela is a talented cook, and the two tour companies from Oaxaca have hired her to teach cooking classes whenever the groups come to Lachatao.

Mac says, "Thank you. This food is delicious!"

Frankie, swallowing a mouthful, adds, "I've never had corn roasted like this."

Abuela scoops more rice onto Mac's plate. "I teach Consuela all about the herbs, pero su tía no es una curandera, but she heals with her food. No?"

Mac holds up an ear of corn. "I feel better already. Speaking of healing, I know someone who's studying to be a nurse and a midwife. She's from Santa Ana del Valle. Frankie knows her too. Maybe she could learn some things from you?"

"Si, cómo no. We all go together to the forest."

"Frankie, don't you think Raquel would love to meet Abuela? I bumped into her near the zócalo and told her how much I'm learning. I'd love to pay her back for helping us find my birth records."

Frankie looks at him blankly for a moment as if she doesn't know Raquel and says, "Of course," then focuses on her trout.

"Maybe we could all come up next week?" Mac looks at her expectantly.

"Sorry, next week I'm really busy at Los Niños." Mac's disappointed and wonders at Frankie's aloofness, a side he's never seen.

Inda Jani gets up to heat water to make coffee. She first serves nicuatole, a dessert with a corn base and flan-like texture. Consuela sweetened it with maguey syrup from the local cactus and topped it with pineapple and coconut. For a few minutes, the only sounds are the click of spoons and murmurs of satisfaction.

Nayeli starts a fire in the huge stone fireplace which covers the whole north wall. The nights get chilly at this altitude, down into the low forties Fahrenheit. Mac is happy he threw his maroon and white UMass sweatshirt into his bag. Consuela hands Frankie a rebozo, a shawl, and they settle around the fireplace. Abuela, Consuela and Francisco sit on the couch facing the fire. Nayeli, Inda Jani, Mac and Frankie spread out on the floor on pillows on top of woven rugs. They sip their coffee and gaze into the fire.

Abuela says, "Por favor, Consuela, you can to start the story about Rosario for Mac y Frankie."

"Si, mamá. Mac, I was thirteen when your mother left and I remember her with much affection. We were four years apart but she shared her clothes and stories with me.

She never made me feel bad because I was younger or not as smart. Rosario was muy inteligente and creative. Such an imagination! She was always drawing and painting. I think she slept with her paintbrushes." Everyone smiles, but Mac notices Consuela is using the past tense as if she were deceased. "We moved to Oaxaca because she got a scholarship to study at an excellent high school there, and Abuela didn't want her alone that far from home."

Abuela interrupts, "Pero, she no grateful."

"Abuela, she was young and fell crazy in love."

Abuela continues. "Your mother got involved with a man from Mexico City. He went to their school to lecture about art history, like you maybe. She see him in secreto. She did not talk much about him. It was dos casas, two houses, of course for him. His real wife, y sólo Dios sabe, only God knows, how many children he had, lived in D.F., el Districto Federale. That's how we call Mexico City. Rosa was not careful. I taught her about herbs and still she be with baby." Mac sees that Nayeli and Inda Jani are rapt, finally hearing the forbidden truth about their estranged aunt. He's certain they were smart enough growing up to never ask questions.

Their mother tag-teams with Abuela. "We wanted to support her to get through school even with a baby, so we made clothes for you and set up your crib in her room. We already loved you."

Abuela cuts in, "But she is no good. She went to hospital to have her baby. I am midwife with all the herbs waiting for when she be in the labor for the new life." Abuela shakes her head with decades-old resentment. She betrayed me y todo, all, that is sagrado to me." Abuela stops abruptly and stares into the fire.

Consuelo continues, "We only knew she gave birth because she didn't come home one night and the next day a nurse from the hospital called. She said she had a note from your mother. In the note we learned Rosario moved to D.F., that her professor is helping her, and she put you in a place to be adopted so you will have a better life. But she didn't tell us the name of the place."

Abuela takes up the thread. "Why she did not like our life, I don't understand. Is so beautiful here. We eat food from the garden. We have una buena comunidad. I think el problema es el profesor said he can't take her with a baby. He said him or the baby. No the both." Jolted by this thought, Mac feels slightly out of his body. This story is intimately about him, yet totally alien like he's watching a bad movie.

Abuela trades anger for tears. "She broken our hearts. Not because she just leave us, but she keep you away too, mi nieto. She too selfish and stubborn." The pine logs crackle and shift; blue and orange flames dance. "Over time my spirit guides tell me she is alive. You too. I pray they find you and finalmente, you come home."

Everyone is subdued. Mac thinks each must be imagining the past from their unique frame of reference. Mac rocks a little back and forth, his arms wrapped around his legs. Frankie moves closer. He wishes for the comfort of an arm around his shoulder, but she doesn't offer one.

Consuela speaks softly. "It was a horrible time. Our house became too sad. Mamá y papá lost a daughter and grandson; I lost a sister and nephew. So, after a few months, we moved back here. Started life again." Francisco has nodded off and snores with impunity. Everyone laughs, grateful for a reason to.

"I could breathe again." Abuela demonstrates a deep breath. "The air in Oaxaca, not so good. Then here Consuelo she meet Francisco." A snore punctuates her sentence. She tilts her head towards him. "He mas lively then." Everyone laughs. "Pero, tu abuelo, your grandfather, in one year, he die. He is a good man. I'm sure he be proud of you, Professor."

Mac is touched and makes a little bow to Abuela. "Thank you."

He stares into the fire. Unfortunately, none of this story has made him feel better about Rosario or closer to this present family; instead, he's irritated at Abuela. She can't seem to say anything positive about a daughter who was clearly intelligent and artistically gifted, not to mention, his mother. He looks around at his relatives. "Has anyone ever tried to find Rosario?"

Consuela looks to her mother, "Abuela?"

"I will no more speak about Rosario. She made a big hole in my heart no herbs can heal." Mac doesn't know what to say. He's torn between a sense of gratitude to this family and a reflex to defend his biological mother.

Consuela speaks up on her sister's behalf. "But, it's important to remember she was very young, only seventeen.

She probably regrets what she did and is too ashamed to come back."

That thought lingers in the air. No one speaks for another minute or so, then Abuela is the first to get up. She says good night to Frankie and Mac, and the rest follow and they begin their preparations to go to bed.

Mac sleeps on a sheepskin pad near the fire and stays warm under bright woolen blankets. Frankie, with eyes already closed, lays on the couch five feet from him. The smell of woodsmoke mixes with the lavender, chamomile, and mint herbs hung from the rafters to dry.

A disquieting miasma settles over Mac, and he tosses and turns. He becomes increasingly aware of Frankie's proximity, and in his vulnerability, her physicality and strength draw him. As he watches her sleep, he's seized with a desire to hold her body close. He imagines his hand on her breast, but guilt strikes him blind.

Mac rolls over to face the fireplace. God, if Deanna were here, he thinks, I wouldn't be having these fantasies. I could wrap my arms around her softness and be comforted. Even furry Pumpkin would be of solace. He watches the glowing embers that mesmerize him until he falls asleep.

Chapter Twenty-Three

LA OLLA (CAULDRON)

Frankie waits at a window table at La Olla. It's a lovely restaurant a block from the famous Oaxacan cathedral, Santo Domingo, where artisans sell their wares along its side. From where she sits, it looks like an impressionistic painting.

Frankie wonders about Mac's trip with Raquel to Lachatao. She felt so dismissed when he mentioned taking her. Maybe he'd prefer Raquel as an interpreter since she knows Zapotec? Argh! What gives beauty such annoying, undeserved power? The idea of Mac and Raquel being together in his cozy car for so long lodges like a splinter in her chest. But then she reminds herself that Mac is quite married, so end of story, thank you.

She thinks of their last time together in Lachatao, sitting by the fireside hearing Rosario's story, and Frankie is washed in a tenderness towards him. She knows how deeply disturbing it was. No one wants to hear their mother has chosen someone else over them. She longed to put a comforting arm around his shoulder and now regrets she didn't.

Frankie moves the candle on the table closer hoping to share some of its glow, then sees Mac at the door and waves.

He sits down and she sees him take her in, a tiny thrill in itself. “That’s a pretty green. It looks great with your hair.”

“Thanks.” His words gently remove the splinter, and she notices his dark eyes are smiling. As he brushes his hair back, Frankie admires his strong beautiful hands and gets a little shiver. God, I need to be careful, she thinks, but at least there’s no expiration date to all this looking.

They order dinner and Mac talks about his visit to Lachatao and how Raquel and he learned so much about herbs related to pregnancy and delivery. He said he filled up half a notebook and didn’t get queasy once. Frankie unconsciously twists a napkin in her lap, only stopping when Mac says, “You know, Raquel feels like the sister I never had.”

“Uh huh.” She could make a joke about incest, but is afraid her relief would show, and Frankie knows being relieved is messed up.

“Yes, I mean it’s even possible Raquel and I are related if you go back far enough.” Mac smiles and shrugs.

“I didn’t think of that.” Frankie smiles back.

After dinner, they order coffees and a flan to share. When it arrives, Frankie eyes it. “Yummy.”

“Go ahead Frankie. I’m sure you’ll exercise it off at the gym.”

She takes a bite. “Okay, but then you get the very last bite. That’s how it works.”

“Deal.” Mac leans back and crosses his ankles. “Remember last week we were talking about the whole nature/nurture thing…you know, which is strongest and all that? So, do you think you were born to dance or did you learn to love it?" Talking about nurturing makes Frankie think of Rosario and she wonders why she made the decision not be Mac's mother.

Instead of answering, she asks, "Mac, do you think you'll try to find your biological mom after all the things Abuela said?" Mac pauses and Frankie wonders if she was too blunt, but he doesn't seem fazed.

"Definitely. In a weird way, it makes me want to find her more and hear her story. What about you? Does all of this make you think more about looking up your dad?"

"Not yet. I've got too much on my mind. And to answer your previous question, nature wins out. I would have been drawn to dance no matter what. Absolutely."

"And are you any closer to figuring things out? You know, about dance or having a family?"

"Not so much. I'm using the 'poco a poco' approach hoping that will work. And, living here has opened me up to looking at the idea of family in a different way."

"That's one of the great things about being in another culture. So, how are things going with Enrique?" Frankie sits back wondering why Mac is asking. "Would you say your relationship with him is serious?" Frankie's heart races. Why would Mac care if it were serious? When she doesn't respond, Mac says, "I hope that's not too personal."

"No, I'm just thinking about how to answer." Frankie knows she needs to keep up the novia pretense but wants to downplay its importance. “I wouldn’t say it’s too serious, somewhere between a fling and a real connection, but I don’t really know where it’s going.”

“Frankie, I really like you.” The butterflies in her stomach do swan dives. The word “swoon” comes to mind.

“I like you too, Mac. A lot.”

Mac’s mouth smiles, but his eyes show a slight confusion. “Well, you’re a wonderful person, and I feel a little protective of you. I don’t want you to get hurt.”

Damn, Frankie thinks, wrong direction. “What are you saying?”

Mac circles his thumbs together. “I don’t know much about your relationship with Enrique, but I think, in case you didn’t know, I should tell you. It seems he has tendencies towards men, or maybe it’s just one man.” Frankie’s disappointment morphs into relief and amusement. She smiles which confuses Mac.

“I saw him kissing Gregorio the other day and it wasn’t just a peck on the cheek. I’ve been meaning to tell you, but I’ve been uncomfortable and avoiding it.”

Frankie starts laughing. All the heightened emotions she’s been juggling about Mac, performing, motherhood, and Enrique join forces. She doesn’t want to stop herself. It feels too delicious.

Mac looks annoyed, but Frankie’s laughter is contagious. “What’s so funny?” A few customers look their way. “So, you knew?” He talks while laughing, “But really, what’s so funny?”

"He is totally gay. One hundred per cent! I've been meaning to talk to you too, but I had to be protective of Enrique. I'm a cover for his relationship with Gregorio because he's not out yet. I felt badly not telling you, but I couldn't out him. I made a promise."

"Well, I am relieved."

Frankie stops laughing. "Why?"

Mac looks a little puzzled. "Well, this means you won't get hurt."

Frankie looks into Mac's eyes and thinks, is that all? She says, "Thank you. That's very sweet." The waitress returns and they decide to top off the evening with Drambuie.

Frankie thought she'd feel freer with Mac once the novia gig was up, but free for what? A fake relationship with Enrique compared with the weight of Mac's very real marriage hits her. How did she get in so deep? She came to Mexico looking for answers and ended up a fake novia and a novia wannabe. As she polishes off her Drambuie, relishing its numbing effect, she asks herself, am I a walking telenovela, or what?

"I see you eyeing that last bite, Frankie. Go ahead. My next workout is always mañana."

The flirtatious Drambuie speaks up, "Only if you promise to come hiking with me in San Felipe this weekend." Now she's playing with matches again.

"Deal. Wait a minute, isn't that a lose-lose? No flan, just exercise?"

Frankie giggles. "Kind of. But you'll love it. San Felipe's in the foothills of the Sierra Madres and there's a park there with views of the valley. It's rural with small farms with chickens and cows. I even saw a bull up there the other day."

Mac's eyes widen. "A bull? Like out in the open?"

"Exactly," Frankie says as she savors the last bite of flan. "Horns and all, no bullshit." They laugh.

"I may have met my match in punsters."

"I think you bring them out in me. Really. I never used to make puns." Frankie feels happy, and Mac seems to enjoy watching her eat the last bite of sweetness. In the next second though, Mac's smile flattens and he looks pained. Frankie hopes it's not food poisoning, or could the idea of hiking be that daunting?

"Are you okay?"

Mac says, "Oh, my God. It's Deanna."

Frankie's heart does a swoosh slam-dunk as she looks towards the doorway. Oh Jesus, here's the wife, the one who hates flying, who's come thousands of miles to surprise her husband.

Mac's face, an unravelling map of shock and surprise, lands on happy, genuinely happy. Frankie thinks, why is this a revelation? Fuck me. I have been swimming in the river of denial and now I'm going to drown. Right here, right now after eating this stupid highly-caloric flan. For a few minutes before Deanna's grand entrance, something true had passed between them. She felt it the moment Mac understood Enrique wasn't her real boyfriend. Didn't she?

Deanna doesn't look very happy either, but Frankie's too self-absorbed to care. Mac rises from his chair and they meet halfway across the restaurant and embrace, hanging on until a waiter needs to get by. Frankie looks down at the cloth napkin in her lap. If she could fold up into an origami bird and fly away, she would. Gladly. When she looks up, Mac is introducing her to Deanna. Deanna has her hand out. Frankie shakes it.

"Nice to meet you, Deanna." Frankie stands up. "I'll leave you two to catch up. I'm sure there's a lot to talk about and I was just heading out anyways." Frankie grabs her bag from the back of the chair. She gives them a nod and weak smile, and glides through the tables like a feral cat, disappearing out the doorway.

***

Deanna sits in Frankie's seat and Mac sees her noticing the flan dish he and Frankie shared, forks pointed towards each chair. She's also probably noticed his credit card still on the table.

Mac feels pressure to explain Frankie to Deanna even though he knows he hasn't crossed any lines. "Frankie's my interpreter and her boyfriend, Enrique, is the nephew of the Director of the orphanage and children's center where I was born. She volunteers there." The sentence squirms like a flapping fish, and Mac wishes he could throw it back.

He moves his chair closer to Deanna. "Why didn't you tell me you were coming? I could have picked you up at the airport."

"I wanted to surprise you, so I went to your B&B, and they let me know where you were. But, I guess I'm the one who's surprised. You usually don't make friends this quickly." She crosses her arms and sits back in her chair.

"Do you mean Frankie? She's become a friend. She has a boyfriend. She's been really helpful interpreting."

"I bet! And sharing desserts? It took me years before you let me touch your food. And I watched you two laughing." Deanna waves her hand over the table. "And it looks like you've had enough drinks for an entire wedding party."

"You're getting the wrong idea, Deanna. Really, Frankie's a friend. And it didn't take years for me to share." He unconsciously pushes the dessert plate to the side. "Let's get out of here. We'll walk through the zócalo, and go back to the B&B and relax. What do you say?" Deanna's face softens.

"Okay Mac. Let's go." He's relieved to hear a warmer tone and eager to leave La Olla which now feels like a crime scene. He replays Frankie's escape out the doorway and his guilt is tainted further by a definitive pang of regret.

***

Fleeing the debacle at La Olla, Frankie is barely able to make it into her apartment before decomposing. She renames La Olla, or big pot, "The Cauldron of Horror," a stew of embarrassment, shame, jealousy and stupidity.

Why don't I just keep in my own lane? She thinks. ARGH! Frankie sits on the bed to have a good cry. This whole situation is making her miss Raoul and her dance company, and even David. She thinks, I could have had a two-year old by now, but here I am, alone in Oaxaca. I don't even feel okay calling my mom since I'm living a big fat lie. And Paula, who will be visiting in only a few days, won't like any of this. Yikes! Maybe it's a good thing Deanna's here. Who knows how far it would have gone tonight and then what a mess!

"Pull it together," she says aloud. "Think about what's working." Frankie pours herself a glass of water and thinks of Esme, Leonel and Julio and the dance recital that's in the works. She thinks about helping Enrique as his "novia" and working out to keep up her dance stamina. This reminds Frankie she has a session tomorrow morning at 6, so she starts drinking glass after glass of water to dilute the alcohol.

She raises her hands to her heart, acknowledging she was falling for Mac, and starts to cry again. She goes into the bathroom and splashes cold water on her face and dries it roughly to make the skin tingle. Then she stops to breathe deeply. I'll try to do what Paula taught me. Be in the moment. No matter how shitty! No running away. Just breathe. At least I didn't kill anyone and I'm not dead. I can still dance. She brushes her teeth and puts on her pink NYC Moves t-shirt as pajamas, burrows under the covers, and waits for the merciful curtain of sleep to descend.

Chapter Twenty-Four

HEART TO HEART AT THE B&B

After a short stroll from La Olla to the zócalo, Mac and Deanna settle on the patio at the B&B. Mac grabs two Dos Equis from the frig. He would prefer to table any discussion until the morning, but Deanna is unusually insistent.

"Mac, I came to support you and I want to meet your biological family. I really do, but I also came because we need to talk face to face."

Mac groans, "But what about our rule? No discussing anything serious past 8 p.m. You know that's potentially disastrous."

"I got on a plane and flew all the way down here to see you. I can break a few rules. You certainly may have. Plus, I'll never sleep unless we talk, at least a little."

"If you really need to." Her eyes fill. "Okay, I'm listening." Mac moves his chair closer so their knees are touching.

"Thank you. Look, I want to understand what you're going through, but first you were coming for a week, then two and now possibly a few months. What about your sabbatical work? Your research? And this herb gathering with your Abuela. I don't understand how it suddenly seems more important than the rest of your life. And you said she's connected to your dream-visions and shamanism. I can't keep up Mac, and now I have Frankie to add to the mix."

"This isn't about Frankie, Deanna. It's part of my pre-Columbian world and my roots. I can't help it that my parents waited half my life to let me know where I come from. I want to learn from Abuela. And yes, she is a curandera with strong spiritual connections that are linked to me, but why is that bad? You'll understand so much more when you meet her. Let's drive to Lachatao tomorrow."

"Okay. I want to meet your family, but why months Mac? Fall is our favorite season together and I'm getting sick of going to potlucks alone." Deanna looks like she's going to cry.

"I'm sorry about the time it's taking."

"You're truly that interested in herbs and healing now?"

"It's partly that, but more so I want to help Abuela pass on her knowledge. The more that people grow the herbs and use them, the less likely they'll disappear from the earth."

"Why you?"

"I don't know. Destiny, I guess. Abuela learned from her mother, who learned from her mother, and she was supposed to pass her knowledge on to Rosario, but that never happened. I've already learned about limpias, or spiritual cleansings, from Abuela, and I've had a temazcal which is like a steam bath with herbs. She learns from her spirit guides the best herbs and remedies for her patients, then she prescribes them in teas and tinctures and medicinal baths." Mac can read the disdain in Deanna's face before she speaks.

"Jeez, I wish spirit guides could tell me how to do my research."

"See. This is why we decided not to discuss things at night when we're both tired. And you can make fun of Abuela, but she's good at what she does."

"Okay, Mac. I'm sure you're right, and I'm sorry for being sarcastic. Let's finish talking tomorrow."

The chilly air sends them inside where they sit on the couch.

Deanna puts her hand on Mac's thigh. "Even though this is hard for us, it's good to see you and feel you instead of texts and voice messages."

"I know. I've really missed you, too." He sees Deanna's attempt at a smile and understands how exhausted and apprehensive she is. He pulls her to him and holds her close. He knows he's asking Deanna to make a giant leap of faith when hard science is her life. She spent a decade earning a Ph.D. in epidemiology and loves her work with a passion. Through many dinner conversations, he's learned about her research and is proud she excels at it. Mac hopes that tomorrow she'll try to be open about Abuela's work rather than judgmental.

They climb into bed together for the first time in almost a month. But instead of a rush of libido, Mac feels awkward and senses Deanna does too. He rolls towards her and whispers, "Can we just cuddle? I've missed holding you, but I'm too tired for anything else."

Deanna, exhausted, agrees, and Mac, knowing it's unreasonably so, feels a little hurt she so quickly agreed. Shouldn't they want to ravish each other? Mac reaches his arm around her, pulls her tight and they spoon, knees tucked and fitting like puzzle pieces. The evening air caresses their shoulders as he strokes her arm and breathes in the scent of her hair. They lay awake for a while listening to the dogs of Oaxaca do their call and response. A few fireworks explode, a baby cries down the hall, and then more barking. Strange sounds, strange bed, but even stranger, the feelings in their marriage. Mac continues to hold Deanna until she's snoring lightly, then rolls onto his back. As he finally drifts off to sleep, he sees Frankie moving like a dancer through the tables at La Olla.

Chapter Twenty-Five

UN POCO LOCO

At 2 a.m., after a long Saturday night as a DJ, Enrique starts up his motorcycle. He loves his work; it's like mainlining speed, all the percussive rhythms and dance moves and ecstatic energy from the crowd, but the come-down is a noiseless descent into a funnel of exhaustion. Gregorio didn't seem himself tonight, Enrique thinks. He can be particular about the way things are done at the bar, but he's not usually moody. He was clearly not interested in our spending the night together which is a first. Maybe he's still annoyed about Frankie? They haven't discussed the situation since Enrique stormed out a few weeks ago. He tells himself that Gregorio is overtired and decides to check in on him tomorrow.

Sailing through the now silent streets of Oaxaca, Enrique swerves to miss a stray dog. He's grateful for the wind pummeling him awake. By the last leg of the uphill trek into Santa Ana, Enrique feels like he's riding through a dream. His house, north of the pueblo's plaza, is a typical adobe home with a courtyard in the center with hammocks and a pila, a stone sink. They've had running water for the past ten years, but no electricity yet on his street so they use propane lanterns. His dad, as usual, has left one on for him by the front door.

In bed by nine, his dad is usually asleep when Enrique gets home and is up and out of the house by five. His eighty-year-old Abuela, Florencia, wanders around all hours of the night with insomnia and naps during the day. Enrique loves her dearly and she always lights up when she sees her nieto. He only sees his dad every few days and that's enough. He remembers tomorrow morning his father's going to help a neighbor harvest squash and corn to sell at the outdoor market in Benito Juárez.

Enrique sleeps deeply and is awakened gently by an Aztec thrush in the pines outside his window. After a shower and some strong coffee Florencia left on the stove, Enrique fries up eggs to have with tortillas and makes a bowl of steaming hot chocolate with enough cinnamon to scent the kitchen. He's in a contemplative mood as he sits at the table in the sunny courtyard. The warmth from the cement floor seeps into the soles of his bare feet as the sun dries his hair. He eats and sips his hot chocolate and smiles when he hears Abuela snoring like a bear cub.

Enrique hikes down to Teresa's house to spend time with Miguel. When her parents died, she inherited the house because her two older siblings had their own families and houses in Santa Ana and Teotitlán del Valle. She's grateful to have this place to call home.

Three mornings a week, this is their routine. He passes the village center, and coming around the last bend in the road, is surprised to see a young man chopping firewood and stacking it next to Teresa's back door. As he gets closer, he recognizes the man is Esteban, a cousin of his best friend from school, Chaco, the only friend who stood up for him no matter who was doing the taunting. He wonders if Chaco ever mentioned his sexuality to Esteban and if Esteban has said anything to Teresa. He hopes not because she's never doubted it as far as he knows. Miguelito is outside trying to drag a log as big as he is to help Esteban. Enrique's heart blossoms in a way he'd never felt before becoming a father; it's made him a bigger person. If it weren't for needing to support Miguel, he wouldn't have to work at the gas station. DJ'ing would give him enough money to survive, but he fully embraces the responsibilities of fatherhood.

"Buenas días, mijo!" Enrique yells.

Miguel immediately drops the piece of wood. "Papá – ya voy," and he runs out of the yard and flies into Enrique's arms. As he's swooped up, he shrieks and lands on his father's shoulders. The young man puts down the axe and disappears into the house. Seconds later, Teresa emerges from the front door, wiping her hands on her apron and walks up to meet father and son.

Enrique gives her a kiss on the cheek and she giggles which is unusual. "Is that Esteban, Chaco's cousin? If so, he's grown about a foot since I last saw him."

Teresa looks embarrassed. "Si, Enrique. I didn't know you knew him. Miguel, go run to the house and get mamá's rebozo, my shawl. It's on the back of the kitchen chair." They watch him race to the house.

Enrique takes a deep breath. "I've been wanting to tell you something."

Teresa looks down at the dirt road and back at Enrique. "Yes, Enrique, I understand you will never ask me to marry."

"What? Who told you that? Was it Raquel?"

"No, not Raquel. You know there's always gossip. I heard about your novia, la Americana, the one I met here last month. You should have told me Enrique."

Enrique glances up at the sky. "I'm sorry, but it's not what you think."

Teresa shrugs in disbelief. "I need to tell *you* something." Miguel runs towards them with her rebozo. Teresa speaks quickly. "Esteban asked me to be his novia. He spends time here having meals with us and helping me out, and I finally said 'yes' to him. He's a good man. He loves Miguel, and he loves me." Miguel, dragging the rebozo on the ground, reaches his mom and grabs her leg.

Enrique smiles. "I'm happy for you." He helps Teresa adjust the rebozo around her shoulders. "And I'm sorry you waited so long for me."

"I understand Enrique."

He nods. "I'll need to talk with Esteban. If he's going to be with my son, I want him to understand Miguel will always be mijo, *my* son, and I will always be there for him."

"Yes, of course." The three head back to the house, Miguel between them holding their hands and swinging like a monkey.

Enrique asks, "Could we meet later today to talk? Just us? I want to tell you something, too."

Teresa looks surprised. "Of course."

"You know Teresa. You'll always be the most special woman in my life." Teresa makes an inscrutable face as she steps back to look at Enrique.

"You are loco."

Enrique swoops down, grabs Miguel and spins him around. "You don't think your papá is loco, do you?"

"Un poco." Miguel says laughing.

Chapter Twenty-Six

MIDNIGHT REVELATIONS

Leaving the heaviness of last night at the B&B, on their drive to Lachatao, Mac and Deanna fall into their ten-year-old rhythm of chatting, then letting stretches of quiet time elapse.

"This is really beautiful. Remote, but beautiful. I love all the greenery." She inhales deeply out the window. "I've never breathed such clear air."

"Wait until we walk in the forest. The pine scent is amazing. The whole woods smells like our living room right after we've put up the Christmas tree."

"The one last year was the best. So full."

Mac nods. "And the twinkle lights on the rhododendrons looked great."

Deana smiles. "They really did."

"We only have about ten more minutes to go."

Deanna looks over at him. "You look like you've lost weight. You look more fit. I think all this walking is good for you."

"Well, thank you for noticing. And the food in Lachatao is really healthy, all homegrown."

"So, tell me everyone's name again."

Mac prepares Deanna and reminds her that Abuela speaks a mix of Spanish, English and Zapotec, so his cousin Nayeli can interpret if Deanna needs any help. "I can help too. My Spanish is improving and I'm picking up a few words in Zapotec."

Deanna reaches over and covers his hand with hers. "Don't get too multilingual on me. I won't be able to keep up."

***

An hour later, Deanna has met the whole family and together they sit down to eat papáya with lime juice and delicious homemade bread. She joins the trek for herbs in the woods with Abuela, Nayeli and Mac. Mac focuses on capturing Abuela's every word. Even though it's related to healing, Deanna isn't very curious about herbs and finds herself drifting, feeling the odd one out and wondering what's going on at the lab in Greenfield. There's one place in town that has the internet, but it closes at 4, so she'll have to wait until morning to communicate with her team. The grant, funding fifty-percent of their research for the following year, is due early next week, and Deanna feels the weight of it. Although everyone seems very happy to have met "Mac's esposa" this morning, Abuela is focused solely on Mac, almost obsessed with him. Deanna hangs back, feeling irritated and hurt. Abuela's initial welcome was warm, but there's something slightly less than enthusiastic in her bearing towards her.

Deanna's grateful when dinnertime arrives and she and Mac can sit down to eat with the whole family. It's a hearty chicken, rice and vegetable stew served with tortillas.

After dinner, they move into the living room around a cozy, comforting fire, but Deanna feels more like she's at camp and doesn't understand the draw for Mac. In Montague, he won't even go barefoot in the summer and heats up a microwaveable bed warmer in the winter. But here, he seems surprisingly at home, the prodigal son returned at last with four female relatives to dote on him. No wonder he isn't in a rush to return home. Not to mention Frankie, the svelte New York City dancer, Mac's personal interpreter, and who knows what else. But no, she won't ask him for details, not here. In a word, Deanna is miserable, but tries to be the good wife with appropriately timed smiles and nods.

The family retires early, and she and Mac sleep on the floor by the fire. It's comfortable with padding and blankets, but Deanna can't sleep. Travelling disturbs her routine, and her nerves are vibrating like an out-of-tune guitar. She gets up slowly and carefully so as not to disturb Mac, wraps a blanket around herself and wanders outside to stand under the stars. The cool night air is like a loving hand on her cheek, and she draws it deep into her lungs, her head gradually clearing. The sky is magical at this altitude. With so little pollution, the constellations are etchings of light and the solitude a balm. She hears an owl hooting.

Suddenly, there's a hand on her arm, and Deanna screams and jumps back.

"We are sorry to frighten." Quiet as wood nymphs, Abuela and Nayeli have materialized. Deanna's heart is racing like crazy.

Abuela doesn't release her hand. She repeats, "So sorry to frighten." As Deanna's heart slows down, she notes that Abuela has spoken gently, almost maternally.

"We see you are unhappy my daughter. But I to help you. My herbs are very powerful. Yes, you can have a child. I will clear the energy inside. Have faith."

Deanna feels like she's been transported to another planet. She looks at Nayeli. "Please tell Abuela I have no idea what she's talking about."

Abuela shakes her head. "But Mac, he told me he wants los niños, the children. He said maybe is a problema with you, so I want so much to help."

Deanna pulls the blanket tighter. "But I don't want children. I could probably get pregnant if I wanted to, but I don't." Nayeli translates this into Spanish and then Zapotec in case Abuela is confused. Her face falls. There's no confusion there. Deanna starts trembling and feeling very far from home.

"But why marry Mac if you don't want una familia?"

She can't face Abuela's insisting presence so turns to Nayeli. "Please, tell Abuela I'm a scientist and I help children through medicine. I don't need to bring more into the world. But thank her. Tell her I'm sure her herbs are wonderful."

Deanna waits until the words are translated. On some level, she actually feels badly for Abuela. "Nayeli, please tell her I'm very sorry." The three remain motionless until Deanna turns and disappears into the house.

Once inside, she quietly packs her things, wraps herself in the blanket and sits on the couch. She watches embers turn to ash as she waits for Mac to wake. A rooster crows, out of sync with the dawn, useless, like Deanna feels. Finally, the darkness and heavy blanket coax her eyelids closed.

A few hours later, still in a sitting position with one arm around her backpack, she wakes to women softly talking as they bank a fire in the woodstove and crack eggs. These simple acts bring tears to Deanna's eyes and she longs for home. Mac rolls over towards her, blankets pulled tight and opens his eyes. He's barely able to focus when Deanna speaks from across the room.

"We need to leave."

"What? Now? Why?"

"I can't talk here."

He repeats his questions several times. Deanna won't look at him and responds with icicles of silence. He tells Abuela and Consuela that there's a problem at Deanna's work and she needs to return to the lab right away, but everyone knows it's a lie. Mac packs up and drives away from the house clueless without even a cup of coffee.

Finally, at the outskirts of Lachatao, Deanna's tension starts to ebb and she finds her voice. "At midnight, I learned from your Abuela that you want children, and you told her I have a problem. She thinks I'm not fertile. What the hell, Mac!"

"Oh, Christ. Is that what this is about? I *did* tell Abuela that, and only her, but she took it out of context. I never said I was clear."

"You can't want kids in a context, and you know *I'm* not having kids, so?"

Mac is silent as Deanna stares out the window.

"Last time I checked, we were okay without them. What else don't I know? Maybe you even have a dancer girlfriend."

Mac focuses on the road ahead. "This isn't about Frankie!" He tears up. "Damn it, Deanna, I'm confused." Mac pulls the car over to the side of the road. He shuts off the engine and turns to Deanna who has her hand on the door handle as if she's going to make a run for it.

"But why now, Mac? Ten years we've been together, and I didn't know this. What else don't I know?"

"I was never one-hundred-percent sure about not having a family like you are, but spending time at the kids' center and meeting my biological family, it's making me think about being a father. Is that so strange?"

"Okay, fair enough, but those are conversations you have first with me, your wife. Certainly, before someone you met three weeks ago, even if she is your grandmother. Who, by the way, doesn't seem to like me very much."

"She's not so warm and fuzzy, no. But Deanna, I didn't bring up the idea of children with you because I'm not clear, so why make it an issue?"

"Well, *she* sounded pretty clear." They stare straight ahead at the road.

Mac speaks quietly. “Going to NNAA where I was an infant and seeing all those kids. It’s like there’s this huge family of adopted kids from everywhere in the world I’m a part of. And I’ve been having so much fun with them. I was one of them, and now I’m old enough to be someone’s father.”

Deanna drags the stone in her gut aside. “Wow, this is big Mac.” She shakes her head and has never felt so unmoored. Mac’s always been her anchor, but he seems to have pulled up overnight and set sail elsewhere.

“Does it have to be a closed book?”

Deanna ignores the question. “Don’t you miss your teaching? And music? Montague? Your annoying student who keeps calling?”

Mac nods. “Yes! All of it. I miss playing with the band like crazy and my students like Adriana and teaching. Of course, I miss Montague. It’s home.” Mac puts his hand on his chest and pats his heart. Deanna sees him tear up again. She wants to reach out to comfort him, but then again, damn him, she doesn’t. He starts up the car.

Deanna looks at her cell phone. “Dear God, 8 a.m. has never felt so late.” Or awful, she thinks.

Chapter Twenty-Seven

THE BIBLE SAYS

Enrique heads to Santa Ana on his motorcycle after his Friday night DJ job at El Saguaro. It's almost 2 a.m. Thank God, Gregorio seems to be in a better space lately, and they spent the previous night at his apartment. Tomorrow morning, Gregorio will head to Guanajuato to spend time with his family for a few weeks, especially to be with his dad who's dealing with some health issues. As well, El Saguaro's closed for two weeks while the owner's off to Los Angeles to visit family.

This frees up Enrique who hasn't been home in a few days. As he drives up to the house, he sees there's no propane lantern left out. That's weird, he thinks. He parks the bike by the side of the house and quietly enters the kitchen careful not to wake anyone. He sees ominous shadows on the wall before registering their source: his father and his open Bible at the candlelit kitchen table. "Papá, what are you doing up?" He notices Abuela hovering in the courtyard like a guard dog.

"Two nights up I'm waiting. Teresa's cousin, Eduardo, he came to tell me mi hijo is a homosexual. He said it's why you never married to Teresa."

Enrique wants to flee back into the darkness. He considers getting back on his bike and going to Gregorio's but can't get his feet to move.

"If you can father a child, then it's the devil talking sickness when you want men. But we pray together Enrique. You can to change with God's strength. Right now, we go to the church. We pray." His father stands up. "God can forgive."

Enrique feels sick to his stomach. "Papá, listen to me. I was born like this. I'm not going to change. I can't."

His father slams his hand on the table. "I am so happy tu mamá is not here to see this shame."

Abuela emerges from the shadows. "My daughter loved Enrique cómo he is."

Papá dismisses her with a flick of his wrist. "Bah!"

Enrique is quick to go stand by his grandmother's side. "Mamá didn't care about those things. You let the Evangelicals get to you after she died. They took advantage, and you lost Catholic friends over it." Enrique was bone-tired, but now his adrenaline's pumping. He speaks evenly hoping to control it. "God is not righteous or hateful."

"Don't speak to me about God. You never go to the church."

"God isn't just in church. He's out in the world where there's room for him."

Abuela puts her arm though Enrique's. "El Díos, he loves all people."

"You don't know what you're talking about. You can't even read. You don't know what God's words say." Papá faces off with Enrique. “How can I live in this comunidad with you living un abominación?”

“It’s not even clear what the Bible says about homosexuality. And, you know the New Testament was written years after Jesús lived, right Papá? By people who never even saw him. The Bible is a book, not God.”

“The Bible is God’s word, and don’t call me Papá. Go now. Come back when you can be a man.”

His father points to the door. “Get out! Now!”

Abuela steps forward and sweeps the Bible onto the floor. “Es suficiente!” No one moves.

Wow! Enrique thinks, that took cojones! His father glares and picks up the Bible, brushes it off and retreats to his room slamming the door. Abuela sits down and Enrique stands behind her, his hands on her shoulders. She reaches up and grabs a hand.

“Your papá, he is no good since your mamá died.”

***

Ten minutes later, Enrique cuts the engine at the top of the hill and glides down to Teresa’s house. He maneuvers very slowly because Abuela, her bony arms crushing his waist, is terrified to be on a motorcycle. He gently stops the bike and helps her off the back. She stands in the dark as he goes to the side of the house and calls out to Teresa. She appears moments later at the front door in her cotton nightgown and sweater.

"What's wrong Enrique? Is it your papá? Your abuela?"

"Papá, si, but not how you think."

She notices a figure by his bike. "Who's that?"

"Es Florencia."

"Oh, dear God, Abuela."

"He kicked me out. Eduardo, your cousin, he told him about me."

Teresa looks stricken. "What? I didn't tell him Enrique, I promise, but I think I know who did. I'm so sorry. Let's get Abuela in the house." She motions for Abuela to come over.

"Come. I'll make some tea."

A few minutes later, they're sitting on the couch with blankets around them drinking tea. "I'm no longer welcome, no longer his son." Enrique coughs to stave off tears.

"Why don't I try talking to him?" Teresa asks.

"Good luck with that."

Abuela puts her hand on Enrique's arm. "Enrique cannot stay en la casa, so I will not stay."

"Abuela, you can stay here of course. You can sleep with Miguelito. He will be so excited to have his only bisabuela, great-grandmother, here."

"Yes, and I help con Miguelito. I think Papá will change his mind soon. I pray for him."

Enrique clears his throat. "I think you two should go to bed. It's three in the morning. But I'd like to take off on my bike if you're both okay with it. For a while, I've been thinking about taking a trip to Juchitán de Zaragoa on the Isthmus. El Saguaro's closed for two weeks and I have a few days off at the garage. Most of my clothes are in my backpack anyway. It's just for a few days."

Florencia nods. Teresa says, "That's fine, Enrique. Now that I understand how things are, I think it'll be good for you to get away."

Enrique looks at Abuela. "And you're okay staying here for now?"

Abuela nods but continues to hold Enrique's arm. She pleads, "Don't leave. Wait for the morning,"

Teresa joins in. "Yes, sleep on the couch."

Abuela pats the couch. "Si, niño, it's too late."

"No, really. I want to get moving. I'm super awake." Enrique clears his throat. "Give Miguelito a hug for me. Tell him I'll bring him back a surprise, and don't worry about me." He kisses them both and heads into the night that feels safer than home.

Chapter Twenty-Eight

INTIMACY – THE LITTLE THINGS

After the harshly illuminating trip to Lachatao, Deanna needs most of the day to catch up on her sleep. Post-siesta, she communicates with her team in Greenfield and is relieved to hear things are moving forward in a timely fashion for their grant deadline. She takes a shower, washes her hair and starts feeling more like herself.

Having agreed current circumstances warrant rule-breaking, Mac and Deanna decide to wait until later that evening to discuss anything serious. In the late afternoon, they explore Oaxaca together trying to establish some sense of normalcy. After sight-seeing, Mac takes Deanna to Las Tres Hermanas where he ate once and loved it. They catch up on the little things about family and friends that bundled together create intimacy. After, strolling through the zócalo hand in hand, they stop to listen to a marimba band and admire the flowers surrounding the giant trees. Mac notices the Oaxacan families out enjoying the beautiful evening. He finds the children here beautiful but keeps any thoughts of children to himself. Instead, he hums.

Deanna smiles. "I must admit, I've missed your humming and the keyboard too. The house is too quiet."

***

They're back at the B&B by 10. Mac is in a t-shirt and boxers and Deanna puts on a silky pink nightgown. She leans back against the headboard sipping red wine as Mac gets comfortable next to her. He gently circles one finger along her thigh. "Can we talk about children now?" Deanna nods and takes another sip of wine. "I'd like you to consider the possibility of adoption. You wouldn't even have to be pregnant."

Deanna places the wine glass on the night table. "But Mac, I'd still be a mother."

"What if I agreed to take on the lion's share? Be the more active parent. Pick up and drop off, lunches, midnight feedings, all that."

She stares at her hands. "But I'd still be the mother. I don't know if I'd be able to focus on my research in the same way, and with that set-up, you'd end up resenting me."

"No, I've thought this through. I'm sorry again I didn't tell you I was unsure when we got married, but you were so certain, I was afraid I'd lose you." Mac tries to catch her eye with his sincere deep brown ones, but no luck, and then in a sudden panic, turns his back to her. "Is there something crawling on my shoulder blade? It's not a spider, is it?"

Deanna laughs. "No Mac." She brushes his back. "It's just an ant."

"What do you mean *just* and *is*? You got rid of it, right?"

"Yes, Mac." Deanna laughs again. "You'll have to be braver about bugs if you have kids. They love to collect them and bring them in the house to show you." She playfully runs her fingers up his back like a spider. "Sometimes they even let them out."

"Fine, but not funny. I'll work on it." Mac turns back to face her.

Deanna puts her hand on his chest. "I do wish you'd been honest before we got married."

"I know and I regret that, but things have changed. Look, I promise I won't argue with your answer. Whatever you say, I'll agree with." Deanna looks surprised.

"So, does that mean if I say no, we're still married? I'm confused."

"I don't know. Your answer has to come from the heart, so all I can promise is I will accept whatever you say after you've come to a decision."

Deanna cocks her head. "Are your parents pressuring you to have kids? I know Sophia would love a grandchild. Your dad too, I'm sure, although he'd never say it."

"No, nothing like that. I never brought up the idea of kids because you were so against it."

"Remember, I told you I had dinner with them last week. Well, I think your mom's nervous you're so angry with them, you'll stay here forever, for spite."

Mac laughs, "She tends towards the dramatic, but she knows that would never happen."

Deanna looks surprised. "How would she? I'm not sure you'll be back either. I mean now you want to visit D.F. That means you could be gone until December. And you most likely want a child knowing I don't. No, I think your mom's fears are justified."

"That's craziness." Mac pauses. "I promise I'll be home by Thanksgiving. How's that? And if I haven't found my biological mother by then, I'll come back in December or during the January intercession."

"So, you will be back to teach next semester?"

"I think so. I'm as sure as I can be. Why wouldn't I be?"

"Oh my God, this is the man who keeps his clothes color-coded and neatly folded and pays his bills in advance, but you're not sure about the perfectly good job waiting for you?"

"Deanna, don't go off on me. We've been having a good conversation so far, and I've never once said anything about quitting my job."

"But what does it all mean? It sounds like you might decide you want to stay here harvesting herbs in the forest with Abuela like a flower child. Or, assuming you'll be home, you may or may not decide you want children."

"I'm sorry, Deanna, but I'm just not clear right now. I'm having an identity crisis, like someone's rewriting my bio, one that features shamanism and Indigenous lineages and a mysterious mother."

Mac gets up and paces, then stands at the end of the bed. "Look, I'm sorry. I know this is making me totally self-absorbed, and I can't imagine how hard it is on you. But Deanna, can you just do this? Consider the possibility of a family?"

Deanna finishes her glass of wine, gets up to pour another and walks out to the patio. Mac follows and they sit in silence for a minute.

Mac nervously taps his leg up and down and speaks very softly. "And you're busy with your work, Deanna. Very busy. Half the nights you come home, you're too tired to talk, never mind make love. Sometimes I wonder if you're more in love with your research than me."

Deanna looks startled. "Whoa, that's a new one. Boy, the things we have to work through are mounting up."

Mac clears his throat. "I've been thinking, maybe we could use some help. Some couples' counseling."

Deanna groans. "Oh, we're going to be one of those couples?"

"Just think about it. We could start when I'm home at Thanksgiving. Dave can give me a reference. I think we'll need help with this question about children."

"Didn't he end up divorced?"

Mac ignores the question. "Look, it's past one o'clock. Let's try to get some sleep."

"I would love to, but you just dropped a bomb, Mac. This isn't just about having a kid anymore."

"No, it's not, but all marriages go through rocky times. We just need to try and work through this, and with all that I'm going through, I could use the outside support."

Deanna stares at him. He's grateful that at least she's not saying something sarcastic.

Mac gets up and reaches his hand out. "Come, please." He pulls her up and leads her back to the bedroom. They go to bed and spoon again, Mac behind Deanna. He pulls her tighter and starts rubbing her back in circles the way she likes. The wine must be working its magic too because Deanna snuggles closer and then turns over towards him.

Mac takes her chin in his hand. "Hey, look at me." Deanna looks up and Mac takes her face in his hands. "We'll work through this. We will."

He so hopes that's true as he kisses her lightly. The kiss becomes deeper as they toss their contradictions and then their clothes aside. Finally, it's the familiar feel of skin on skin, and they make love adjusting pillows and positions. The tension and edges of desperation make their releases more intense as they take one other far from the room in Oaxaca.

In the morning, Mac wakes before the alarm and in the pale light watches his wife sleep. She's on her stomach, head turned away with blonde tussled hair draped over her shoulders. His fierce scientist looks vulnerable, like a sleeping angel. The tenderness he feels is so acute, it makes his chest ache and his eyes burn.

Chapter Twenty-Nine

MESSAGE IN A BOTTLE

The morning after the "cauldron of horrors" evening, Frankie stays in bed replaying every searing second of Deanna's appearance. Frankie imagines having a conversation with Deanna to convince her she harbors no thoughts of hitting on her husband, but the sprawling lie is so big it pushes her out of bed.

After breakfast, sick of obsessing, Frankie takes her frustrations out on interval training at the gym. On the way home, she buys a tlayuda for lunch, a big crunchy tortilla with toppings. Her favorites are refried black beans, Oaxacan string cheese and avocado slices. After eating, she spends the afternoon choreographing one of the numbers for the fundraiser. Being productive eases her self-loathing, so it no longer feels like it's on speaker phone in her head.

By the following day, Frankie wakes feeling much better about herself. She brews Mexican coffee, adds a pinch of cinnamon and pours it into a terra cotta mug. Breathing in its rich earthy aroma, she carries it out to the patio, but for no apparent reason, her feet become unsteady like she's on a boat. Simultaneously, she hears crashing behind her as cups and plates get tossed from shelves. Frankie lurches forward thrown by an unseen force as the patio wall comes crashing down in front of her. The last thing she hears is the frantic barking of a neighbor's dog which stops suddenly.

***

Eight hours later, Frankie swims her way up from a sludge of drugs and pain to a semi-conscious surface where sensations and words try to coalesce as thoughts. She becomes aware of hospital beds all around her and down a corridor. An undercurrent of coughs and moans is punctuated by people crying out. Her memory clicks off images like a camera: the trembling mug, a ceramic pot of yellow hibiscus fissuring, and bright red flowers whirling. She thinks about sitting up but a tsunami of fatigue presses her back and an undertow drags her below the surface.

***

Paula, on flight 207 from New York's Kennedy Airport looks forward to the 8 a.m. landing in Dallas with a two-hour layover. Most people merely tolerate layovers, but Paula enjoys the on-the-move vibe in airports, notices the various ethnicities and listens for accents. She's a pushover for the caress of Portuguese vowels or a smooth sexy Southern accent, like the one from the man behind her in the coffee line. Paula buys a bagel and latte, and when she turns to find a place to sit, notices a large group of people gathering under a TV screen. Two reporters speak in rapid-fire Spanish as an English text crawls below with agonizing accuracy.

"A 6.1 earthquake strikes the southern state of Oaxaca, Mexico. The eastern section of Oaxaca City and a twelve-mile radius have been the hardest hit. Currently, eleven people are dead with dozens of casualties. Emergency crews are digging people out from the rubble and clearing debris from the roads."

"Oh, dear God!" Paula leans on the nearest wall, slides down to the floor and searches with shaky hands for her cell phone. She dials Frankie's number but it goes directly to voicemail. At least her phone is functioning, she thinks, or does that even mean anything? She doesn't know who else to call. She never asked Frankie for her landlady's number. It wouldn't do any good to call Frankie's mother, Tricia, or Raoul. They wouldn't know any more than she does and might get hysterical. Paula scans the departure screen; her flight to Oaxaca is delayed until further notice.

She closes her eyes and calls on her years of Buddhist training. Focus on the breath, don't let thoughts create panic, find equanimity. Basically, "Don't bleed 'til you're shot," as a work colleague always says when they're under editing deadlines. Paula breathes as mindfully as possible and pictures Frankie as whole and happy away from the earthquake's most destructive area, then she sends metta, lovingkindness, to Frankie and everyone involved. Finally, she starts to cry, like many of the passengers around her and realizes she's trembling.

***

Ten hours later at 2 a.m., Frankie wakes and is able to stay conscious. She wiggles her fingers, and sees that a cast and sling is on her left arm and her right arm is bandaged. She wiggles her toes. "Thank you, God," she whispers. "I can feel my toes." Next, she tries to move her legs, but they're aching and so heavy she can't. Full blown panic courses through her body as she tries again to lift them, screaming inside, *no, not my legs*! She tries again, comes up against some intense pain and stops. But if I can feel them, they're not paralyzed, right? But could my bones be totally shattered? Frankie starts to yell for the nurse across the room, but her blue uniform blurs as Frankie, done in, falls back on the pillow and sleeps.

At 7 a.m., awakened by a nurse, Frankie sits up and tries to move her legs again. "I can't lift my legs." She searches the smiling nurse's face for clues but realizes as she reaches for the chart, that her cheerfulness has nothing to do with whether Frankie will be able to walk again or not. She's sweating from fear, the skin under her cast is beginning to itch, and her body is screaming with aches and bruises.

"Do they feel heavy?" the nurse asks.

"Yes, what's wrong?" Frankie's heart races as she waits on the precipice of the answer.

"Nothing to worry about. The night nurse put restraints on your ankles and thighs. With the hospital over capacity, we can't watch each patient. We don't know how someone's going to react to pain meds and didn't want you falling out of bed or trying to get up yet. Your legs are badly bruised, but no broken bones, not in your legs."

Frankie bursts into tears. "My legs! Thank God!" She blows her nose and looks at the nurse. "I'm a dancer." The nurse lovingly pats her shoulder.

"You're one of the lucky ones. But, your left forearm is broken, both the ulna and the radius, and your right arm is bandaged where you were cut from glass and braised by cement. Also, you sustained a concussion, another reason for the restraints." The nurse opens a drawer and takes out a mirror to show Frankie a triangle-shaped shaved spot above her right ear. "That's where they removed pieces of debris. You're going to be alright."

As the nurse removes the restraints, Frankie hears the echo of, "You're going to be alright," and starts to cry again. She realizes the earthquake is her message in a bottle which makes her cry harder.

Once the restraints are off, Frankie gently moves her knees and legs and sighs deeply. "Was Xoxocotlán affected?" Frankie's been dreaming of the children at Los Niños de Amor and sending prayers for them, the volunteers and Uncle Pepe.

"No, the earthquake was on the east side mostly." Frankie fears for Mac and even Deanna.

"What about near Santa Domingo? And Los Pueblos Mancomunados?"

"The pueblos are far enough away, but there is damage near the church, not so much to the church. This one wasn't nearly as bad as seven years ago." Frankie says a prayer for Mac, Enrique, Raquel and everyone who's hurt and suffering. She wonders where all this praying is coming from. Maybe it's a Oaxacan influence, or perhaps the stakes have never been this high, and she doesn't know where else to turn.

By late afternoon, they have her up using a walker and are administering smaller doses of pain medication. Frankie is used to physical pain, but not throughout her whole body like she's been pulverized, and her head is throbbing from the gash. Exhausted and back in bed, she dozes in and out of dreams and watches the tv above her bed, sometimes confusing tv characters with those in her dreams. She sips ginger ale to stave off painkiller dry mouth and has just taken the last sip when she looks up at the doorway and thinks, oh dear God, too many drugs. Then the hallucination moves closer.

"Mom? Paula?" Frankie looks at them, happy but confused. "Oh my God, it's so good to see both of you. What day is today?"

Tricia rushes over and grabs Frankie's hand. "How are you sweetie?" She brushes the hair off her face. "Oh, that cut looks nasty. What's wrong with your arm?" Before giving Frankie a chance to answer, she looks at her from the waist down and puts her face closer. "Your legs?"

"They're good. Badly bruised though."

"Thank God." She holds Frankie's hand to her heart and tears up.

As Tricia steps away to find a chair, Paula moves towards Frankie and kisses her lightly on the forehead. Frankie remembers Paula's aversion to hospitals. She hates all the beeping machinery and antiseptic steel. As well, she's an empath and is probably suffering just looking at Frankie.

"Thanks for coming. I know this wasn't the trip you imagined."

Paula smiles weakly. "Do you need anything? Water? Ginger ale?"

Frankie touches Paula's hand. "Just you."

Tricia comes back and scooches the chair close. "Don't worry about anything, Frankie. We're here now. Just focus on getting better. What happened?" Frankie describes her experience in the earthquake, what's broken, sprained and bruised, and her prognosis.

"I should be out once they're certain my concussion's gone. Wait a minute, how did you two come together? And how did you find me?" Frankie looks at Paula.

"I got grounded in Dallas. Then your mom and I talked and she met me there the next morning. We found the hospital closest to your address."

"Yes dear, and we booked a place on the west side of Oaxaca which was not so damaged by the earthquake. It's called La Casa de Isabel, and I've already booked you a room. Your apartment must be in ruins, so you'll come stay with us. Maybe stay until you come home, or better yet, just come home. Unless of course the show must go on somehow."

Frankie, overwhelmed with gratitude, starts to cry. Professional dance has toughened her, but not for something like this. “Thanks, you two.”

“Sweetie, what about Raoul and the other dancers? I hope to God they’re alright and the Mexican dancers. Where is everyone staying? I told you staying alone in a strange city wasn’t a good idea. No flowers yet or a card? Raoul must be hurt. Have you called him?” Frankie gives Paula a beseeching look like, *Oh shit, please make her stop, and now what do I do*?

Paula shrugs helplessly. “I’m going out for a breath of air. Want anything?”

Frankie shakes her head “no,” and touches Paula’s hand again. “Take your time. No worries.” Besides hating hospitals, she knows Paula is uncomfortable being an accomplice to Frankie’s lie to her mother about why she’s in Oaxaca. Tricia and Frankie watch Paula leave.

Frankie fakes a smile, leans her head back and keeps her eyes closed. “Mom, I think the dancers are okay. They’re staying north of the zócalo.” She hopes she can figure her way out of this mess. Fat chance. Just thinking about coming clean fills her with filial agita.

“Sweetie, looks like you could use a nap.” Tricia rubs her hand gently up and down on Frankie’s cheek. “I’m going to grab some coffee and come right back, so I’ll be here whenever you wake up. Promise.”

Tricia’s low-heeled sandals echo down the hall. Bottom line, Frankie’s relieved to have her mother there, but at this very moment, happier to be left alone. It's not her mother's fault that her daughter's a liar. Well, maybe a little bit.

***

Mac thanks God that Deanna was safe in the sky, probably somewhere over Vera Cruz before the earthquake struck. The B&B sustained cracks in a few inner walls and the main floor, but nothing came tumbling down. Mac waited to feel aftershocks, but there were none he could sense. He knows the kids are fine at NNAA because he's been tracking the earthquake on television and called Uncle Pepe, but he's sick with worry about Frankie. He couldn't get through on her cell phone and tried to get to Jalatlaco yesterday, the day after the quake, but the roads were blocked with debris and emergency vehicles.

Today he succeeds. He feels guilty for not pitching in with the recovery efforts but knows his limits with blood and trauma and is doubtful his Spanish would be sufficient. He's better off staying out of everyone's way. When he gets to Frankie's apartment, he can see the damage through the gate. The landlady's home is mostly intact, so he knocks.

He learns Frankie is in Hospital La Reforma, but the landlady doesn't know her condition. Mac tries to block devastating images from his mind as he wends his way there. When he finds Frankie's room, he sees two women close enough to obscure her, but he can hear her voice and it sounds strong. He stands in the doorway breathing relief;

he's been too tense even to hum. He assumes the younger woman is her friend Paula who Frankie said was coming but doesn't know who the other woman is.

He asks about Frankie's condition at the nurse's station, and they assure him she'll be alright and discharged once her concussion symptoms are gone. He's finally able to release the fearful images that have been making a mess of him.

"Please, tell her Mac was asking about her and that I'll be in touch soon."

Chapter Thirty

NIGHT FLIGHT

Bathed in an orange and pink sunrise, Enrique, cruising along Route 190, heads southeast towards Juchitán. The sunlight polishes his bike silver as highway lines slip past in a dizzying relentless escape. Juchitán is on the Isthmus of Tehuantepec. To the north, is the Gulf of Campeche, part of the Gulf of Mexico. To the south, is the Gulf of Tehuantepec, part of the Pacific Ocean. On each side of the highway, green-blue agave plants open their spiked leaves to the sky, and saguaro cacti stand guard over the landscape like man-sized prickly pickles.

Enrique should be exhausted, but he's as revved as his Honda Rebel 500, and more so the further he gets from his father and his damned Bible. He's wanted to visit this city since he was thirteen and first heard of muxes (moo-sheys). He's learned about them from articles and conversations with his friends in Oaxaca. Gregorio was never interested. It seemed passé to him, but then again, he didn't grow up in Santa Ana.

About an hour later, Enrique notices the land is starting to flatten and the air is getting warmer and more humid. His shoulders ache from all the hunching forward, and as much as he knows he should stop to rest, he's not going to. As Enrique gets closer to the Isthmus, massive fields of wind turbines usher him south. Sultry gusts pick up and he leans into them, his senses alive and attuned to the changing winds.

During this past summer, he befriended some Tehuanas who frequented El Saguaro. He remembers them saying that the Isthmus has been home to Zapotec men, women and a third sex, muxes, long before the conquistadores came. Muxes are men with feminine sides they are culturally free to express. They're also called the two-spirited people. Enrique wonders if he'll wish he were a muxe or be attracted to one. He's heard they don't date each other but often date men who are married and not considered gay. Do muxes date gay men, he wonders?

Enrique finds a room at the Hotel Centrale near the Palacio Municipal and mercado, the market which borders the zócalo. The room is inexpensive but clean. He takes a shower and crashes on the bed, his limbs still vibrating from the motorcycle ride. He falls asleep quickly but tosses and turns. Enrique is excited to be alone in a strange city, a first for him, but his sense of adventure is tempered by the image of Abuela flinging his father's Bible to the floor. He hates that his sweet Abuela is involved in this drama, and as much as he wasn't shocked by his father's outburst, it leaves him feeling orphaned and bereft.

Enrique rouses from his nap at five, shaves, combs his hair, adds a little product, puts on cologne and dresses in his best white cotton shirt and jeans. He heads to the marketplace which is inside the columns of the Palacio Municipal. It looks like any other outdoor marketplace in Mexico, except it's even more colorful which he didn't think was possible. While crossing the street, he negotiates a banged up pickup truck alongside oxen pulling a fish cart.

At the market, he notices most of the vendors are women. Some are wearing the classic Tehuana tops generally worn for special occasions; the vibrant embroidered flowers are works of art. Frida Kahlo adopted this style from her Zapotec mother. As well, long flowered cotton skirts set off polyester tops and yellow aprons. The place buzzes in Zapotec and Spanish.

The aroma of fried fish and corn cakes speaks directly to Enrique's stomach and leads him to an elderly woman stirring a caldo de pescado, a pot of fish soup. She's robust, with two braids down her back, and has beautiful bronze-brown skin. Enrique realizes he hasn't eaten in twenty-four hours and orders enough for two. He doesn't barter; instead, he pays more than what she asks and is rewarded with a gold-toothed smile. Enrique takes his plates and finds a bench under a palm tree. As he breathes in the scents and colors, something fills up in him slaking a thirst he can't name. He feels like singing but his mouth is too full of fish and cornmeal.

He notices one of the vendors across the way who's selling papayas and limes. She's wearing an embroidered top cut close to the shoulders and flaunts graceful defined arms. This vendor's face is clearly made up even from this distance. This scene would make a beautiful picture, Enrique thinks, maybe something Gregorio would want to paint. Engrossed in this sensual carnival, Enrique doesn't realize a young man has come to sit at the end of his bench.

"He's a beautiful muxe, no?" Enrique looks over at this man, looks towards the vendor he's pointing out and nods, not wanting to reveal his ignorance. It's the same person Enrique had noticed, lithe and muscular yet fine-boned and looking more than anything like a striking young woman. I wonder if I should refer to him as he or she? Again, afraid to appear the rube, Enrique leaves his question unasked. The young man looks at the food in Enrique's lap.

"Two plates. You must be hungry, yes?" Enrique nods and swallows. "I was famished."

"You aren't from here, from Juchitán, no?" Enrique looks at him more carefully, a man yes, but gay? Possibly.

"No, this is my first trip to the Isthmus."

"Welcome then, my name is Marcos. I grew up here. I lived in Vera Cruz for two years, did some fishing, some carpentry but came back. I missed it too much. The vendor next to the beautiful muxe, she's my mother, Angelina. I help her out, but I'm done for the day." He extends his hand and Enrique shakes it. Did he let it linger? Enrique notices the mermaid tattoo on his bicep. Marcos is medium tall and clearly works out. His eyes are black as onyx and his smile radiant, his best feature. "Where are you from?"

"Oaxaca, well near Oaxaca, a small pueblo called Santa Ana del Valle."

"Qué lindo. I've heard of it. What kind of work do you do?"

"I'm a part-time mechanic, and I DJ at a restaurant that turns into a nightclub on weekends where I give salsa classes."

"So, you can give me lessons, yes? We are always dancing here. Would you like to have a drink after your meal?" Enrique can't figure out if this guy is coming onto him, or just being friendly, and does everyone here end their sentences with a question?

"I know a restaurant close by with excellent rum and the biggest palm trees in the country. Come. Or maybe you don't drink. That's fine too."

"Is this a gay bar?" Enrique asks, then feels embarrassed. Raquel's always telling him he's too impulsive.

Marcos looks surprised. "Why? Do you have a problem with gays?"

"Oh, no, no." Enrique shrugs and opens his arms. "I mean, of course not."

Marcos laughs. "Good. There's no need for gay bars here. For the most part, muxes, straights and gays socialize together. Welcome to Juchitán!" Marco stands up and extends his hand.

Enrique lets himself be pulled up by this stranger and an edge of distrust transforms into giddiness. Is it this easy here? He accepts a hand up, and they walk across the plaza and through el Jardín Juárez. Enrique is enchanted with the vibrant marketplace, the smiling faces of the Isthmus people, and the warm breaths of ocean air on the back of his neck. He knows, in the future, he'll conjure up this memory when needing a reminder of moments worth living for.

Marcos and Enrique sit on the patio of La Ronda and order rum with pineapple juice. Salsa and meringue music play over speakers. Enrique looks up at the huge tree trunks and sees these are indeed the biggest palm trees he's ever seen. Notes from a nearby marimba band float along the Isthmus breeze.

"The air here is so balmy. In the Sierra Madres, it's drier and can get really cold at night. We have huge fireplaces in our houses."

"Yes, that's because we're on an isthmus open to water on both sides. But the wind can get totally crazy, and same as in most of Oaxaca, we get our share of earthquakes."

"I can imagine," Enrique says, feeling an undercurrent of excitement and danger. He suddenly realizes he and Gregorio have never discussed monogamy. Enrique assumed it was a given, but now he's thinking again. After all, Gregorio's been distant lately and is now at home in Guanajuato where his ex-boyfriend lives. And he didn't invite Enrique to meet his family like he's been saying he would since last Christmas. It's hurtful, but Enrique's been trying to accept what's happening with Gregorio as relationship bumps, like one of the hundreds of topes, or speed bumps, at Oaxacan crossroads, unavoidable, but not life-threatening.

"You are distracted, yes?"

"No. Maybe. Well, yes, somewhat. I have a lot on my mind."

Marco laughs good-naturedly. "Come to my house for dinner. Forget your problems. My mother's a great cook. After we can go in town and find some dancing. You're a dance teacher, no? You can show me some moves."

"Sure." Feeling that excitement/danger duo again, Enrique's not sure he should have so readily agreed. When Marcos lifts his arm to signal the waiter, Enrique sees that his other tattoos say *"loyalty"* and *"family"* which gives him some assurance about Marcos's character. That leads him to wonder what Marcos looks like without his shirt on.

"Great tattoos. I've always wanted one."

"Thank you. From the best artist in Juchitán, Xierveto. She may be at the club I have in mind. There'll be other friends there too. There's a vela in two days, you know, a festival with a procession. They're preparing for it, so they'll be talking about it. You should really think about staying for the vela."

"Maybe. I'm here for a few days."

"Great! And the amazing one, La Vela de las Auténticas Intrépidas Buscadoras del Peligro, (The Festival of the Authentic, Intrepid Searchers of Danger) is in November. If you like this vela, you'll have to come back for that one. It's something you'll never forget."

Enrique's just finished his third rum y piña. When one of his favorite salsa numbers begins playing, he jumps up. "Come!"

Already dancing, he extends his hand to Marcos whose surprise is brief. They sashay their way to the open part of the patio and dance the salsa with sexy hip action and dizzying turns. A few customers begin to clap and soon others join them on the dance floor. After a few songs, sweaty and grinning, they decide to take a break. This is so much fun Enrique thinks. Moments later, though, like hearing a singer hit the wrong note, he realizes he and Gregorio have never danced together.

Marcos says, "I hope you'll come to dinner."

"Your mother will be okay with your bringing home a stranger?"

"Of course. My mother's used to that. She loves people."

"So, she has no problem with different lifestyles?"

"Ah, if you mean gay, like me, no. Gay is okay with most people here. And, a lot of mothers actually wish for a muxe since they usually don't marry. That way they never leave home and can take care of their parents when they get older. They're a pretty industrious group. A lot of muxes are stylists or seamstresses. You'll meet some tonight. My mom probably secretly wishes I were one, but she loves me anyway." He grins.

Enrique nods his head. "Wow! I wish your mother could talk to my father. Is your father accepting too?"

"Ah, my father died when I was ten, but I think he would have been. He wasn't un machista. Some men here are. You just have to stay clear of them. Juchitán is great, but no place is perfect."

Enrique looks around as if scanning the crowd for any machistas, then satisfied, says, "Let's go back to el mercado so I can buy your mother some flowers."

***

"These tamales are delicious," Enrique says between bites. Angelina is chatty even after her workday at the market and is making him feel at home. They eat in the courtyard of their small adobe home, a fifteen-minute walk from the center. Enrique excuses himself to use the bathroom. The window above the toilet is open to the courtyard, and he inadvertently overhears their conversation.

"Yes, he wants a tattoo, but I don't know about getting his hair colored."

"Perfect. Xierveto's trying to save for her niece's fifteenth birthday, her quinceañera. We can talk him into salon work later. Regina will be generous with our cut. We've sent four customers in two weeks."

"I'll try, but I really like Enrique. I'm not pushing."

"You can like people and still make money, mijo."

"True."

"Son of a bitch," Enrique mouths. He flushes the toilet and takes a long time washing his hands to calm down and stop feeling like a sucker. At least he said he likes me, Enrique thinks, which seemed sincere, and we did have fun dancing. It all makes sense now, and what did I expect? You never get something for nothing. Then it hits him that he does the same thing with foreign tourists in Oaxaca. He's done it for years. That's how his friendship with Francesca began. Enrique wets his hands and slicks back his hair. His enthusiasm for being here in Juchitán is not diminished, in fact, it's making him feel a bit randy.

Chapter Thirty-One

TALKING PARROTS

It's been five days since the earthquake and Frankie wakes to the distant thrum of jackhammers and cement grinders rebuilding the city. She moved into La Casa de Isabel yesterday morning. Walking two doors down the hall, she knocks on Paula's door.

"Are you ready for breakfast?"

"Come in. Just gelling my hair." Frankie has always coveted Paula's straight black hair, cut short in little spikes framing her heart-shaped face.

Frankie stands in the doorway with her arms crossed. "I wish my mom would go home now. She's like ubiquitous. That's the word, right?"

"Yes, like she's everywhere."

"Exactly. Like she's in this room now even though she isn't."

"She's just concerned about you."

Frankie isn't listening. "She's incessant. 'Where's Raoul? What happened to the other dancers? Are they okay? What about the program? Will the show go on?' She's a broken fucking record."

"But what do you expect, Frankie? The earthquake was a big shock, and she came all the way down here to see you. I think she deserves to know what's going on."

Frankie sits on Paula's bed. "I know, but she has a way of peering like she's boring into my soul. It's emotional forensics. As a teen, I hid in the bathroom."

"Well, now you're an adult, so let's go eat. I'm sure she's waiting for us. And don't forget who's always in the front seat on the first night of your performances with a gorgeous bouquet in her lap?"

"You?" Paula gives her a serious look.

"Fine. You're right. She's always been there for me. She can't help it her daughter's a liar."

Paula puts her arm through Frankie's. "Come. No more sitting on the pity pot. Time for the truth."

***

Tricia is sitting at a table in a corner of the courtyard. "It's a buffet, girls, so let's get some food before it's gone." As they fill their plates, two large green parrots perched in the lobby keep the guests amused. One randomly yells, "Hola, hola!" and after every fifth or sixth "Hola", the other screams, "Cállate!"

Frankie laughs. "One is saying hello and the other is saying shut up. It would be annoying if it weren't so funny." They sit down, and after Frankie orders a soul-strengthening mimosa, her cell phone rings. She spent all afternoon yesterday in line at the AT&T store to replace the one destroyed in the earthquake. Thank God she has a good memory for numbers.

Raoul's name lights up and before she can flip the phone over, Tricia says. "Oh Raoul! Finally! Tell him hello for me." Frankie shuts off the ringer and sips her drink.

"Later."

"But honey, I thought you've been waiting to talk with Raoul?" Tricia emphasizes with open palms, then does her peering thing. Frankie tries to stares back, but between the earthquake, Mac, and her unsolved dilemma, her personal armor crumbles and she starts to cry. At that moment, one parrot yells, "Hola, hola!" and when the other yells, "Cállate!" Frankie starts to giggle, but it quickly reverts into full-blown crying. Tricia looks at Paula, the empath, who is of course tearing up.

"My God, what's going on? Maybe it's all the stress from the earthquake and the upcoming performance?"

"No, Mom. It's something I need to tell you. I'm not here with the company. Raoul is calling from New York. I'm here alone on a break."

Paula nods and urges Frankie on. "Yes, that's true."

"So, *you* knew? Why didn't *I* know?" Tricia leans forward and peers and Frankie soldiers on.

"I'm considering leaving NYC Moves if I decide to become a mother."

"You what?" Tricia's voice is so loud, heads turn and the parrot yells, "Cállate!" Tricia yells back, "You shut up!"

Now the other patrons are really listening. Tricia drops her voice. "After all you've put into this, how could you possibly? I mean, I don't understand." Her mother puts her hands to her chest in a beseeching way so unlike her.

"Mom, you're so invested in me as a dancer, you can't even see it. I need to figure this out on my own. Ever since I started to dance, it was all tied up with pleasing: first you, then my teachers, Raoul, then the audience. And I do love an audience, but I want to be a mom too!"

"Okay. But you've always said you love dance and you're so good at it. Why are you putting this on me?"

"Geez mom, that's a great response!"

"Well, I feel like I'm being blamed here for something!"

Paula puts a hand on each of their arms. "Tricia, I don't think Frankie's blaming you for anything. She's just confused. I know she really appreciates all you've done for her dance career. She's always said that."

Frankie nods. "Of course."

"Then why am I hearing it from Paula?"

"Mom, of course I appreciate you."

"Really Frankie, I've put my heart and soul into being a supportive mother."

Frankie puts her face in her hands and rubs her forehead.

"Mom, two years ago, I was pregnant and got an abortion. I didn't tell David until it was over and that's why we broke up. I'm sorry I lied about that too."

Tricia looks at Paula and sees she already knows this too. "Well, this is just stunning! And frankly hurtful."

"Look, I love you mom, but you know how you are. You would have convinced me to keep the baby and marry David, or get an abortion and marry the dance company. I don't know which, but I can't do this part of my life with interference."

"Oh, so paying for lessons and taking you to classes was *interference*?"

"No, I'm sorry. Involvement's a better word, but you always wanted this as much as me, or more. I don't know. I can't separate things." As if on cue, everyone sits back in their chairs.

Moments later, Tricia sits up tall. "Why does it have to be an either-or situation? I think being a perfectionist is getting in your way. Personally, I don't think it's the best way to go through life, although it does help if you're an artist. And I for one, am glad I'm not. Have you ever thought you could perform *and* have a family? I had you and worked, even when my mother didn't approve of me doing both. At least that was our last conversation."

"What? No Mom, your parents were dead by then, so you can't use that line however you were going to."

"I used the word *dead* metaphorically."

"Well, this is getting interesting," Paula says trying to lighten things.

Frankie crosses her arms. She's dying to bite her nails but won't give her mom the satisfaction of telling her to stop. "So how is death by cancer and a heart attack metaphorical?"

"I meant they were dead to me." One parrot screams, "Hola!" Tricia suddenly pushes her chair back and looks at

Frankie. "Let's get out of here before I make those stupid birds never talk again."

Paula can't help giggling. "I'll see you two later. I'm going upstairs to meditate and then shop for presents to bring home." Frankie gives her a weak smile. Paula gives each of them a hug. Frankie, trying to absorb the news that her grandparents may be alive, doesn't move until her mother gets up, touches her arm and says, "Let's go, Francesca. We could both use a walk."

***

Walking in silence, they pass blue, yellow and orange walls of cafés as patio umbrellas are unfurled by waitstaff with hair still wet from their morning showers.

Frankie breaks the silence. "Why don't we walk up El Cerro De Fortín? It's a beautiful hike up to a park and the entrance off Calle Crespo is only a block away."

Tricia links arms with her daughter. "That sounds lovely, my dear." Honeysuckle scents the path as they begin a leisurely climb. "Let's not keep secrets from each other anymore."

They walk around a curve in the path and Tricia begins. "My story is complicated, so I thought it best, certainly when you were a child, just to say your grandparents were dead. The truth is, your grandmother is alive and cranky in a nursing home, a very high-end one I might add."

Frankie stops mid-path and stares at her mother, who continues. "We weren't middle class. My parents were filthy rich. I grew up with nannies and maids and hardly ever ate dinner with my parents. That's how they lived, distant and self-absorbed. My mother drank a lot and flirted endlessly with the help. Who knows what happened behind closed doors. She wasn't a very nice mother. My dad was a workaholic whom I barely saw. He earned money off the backs of factory workers in the U.S. and abroad. He died when you were a teenager." Knowing she'll never get a word in, Frankie doesn't try.

"Now, a lot of what I told you is true. I was a hippie and rebelled against my parents and what they stood for. A lot of young people rebelled in those days, but for most it was temporary. Now that I'm older and a mother, I realize how mercilessly judgmental I was. I'm sure they weren't total monsters, but at the time all I could see was their greed and wealth. On the other hand, I didn't see my own hypocrisy in living off their trust fund and sharing it with my friends in the Village. I was a free-spirit, especially with *their* money."

Tricia pauses for the first time and sighs. "So, then came the Jamaican man, your father. Everyone just called him 'the player' so that might tell you something. He had dreads, a harmonica and a beautiful voice, but all we had together was a two-night stand. And you came nine months later. I'm so sorry I can't tell you more about him. I don't remember." Tricia stops walking and squeezes Frankie's arm. "I've always felt terrible about your not having a father. It's why I never wanted to talk about it."

They slow their pace as the path gets steeper. "When I got pregnant, my parents only found out because they were paying for my medical bills which went to their address. My parents wanted it all hush-hush of course. I was to come live with them during the pregnancy then give you up for adoption." Frankie feels a jolt thinking about her abortion. "When they threatened to cut me out of the trust fund unless I came home, I thought they were bluffing, but when I told them the father was Jamaican, they went over the edge. Racist and moneyed, but not cultured, is how I think of them, ignorant really. We disowned each other and I grew up fast, scraping by with various daycare jobs. It's why we moved so much. But once I owned my own daycare, life wasn't just about survival."

As she hears her own history rewritten, Frankie thinks about Mac discovering his roots so late in life. "I was so young when I had you, I did defer a lot of my dreams. I wanted so much for you, but you became a dancing star on your own: all that hard work and determination. And your perfectionism, that's when you put it to good use."

There's a long pause. "Are you done?"

"I am."

Frankie sees a bench. "Let's sit for a minute." As they sit watching three pale-yellow butterflies dancing in jagged circles, Frankie's surprised by her mom's sustained quiet.

"Mom, I was horribly depressed after the abortion and what happened with David. To think clearly about my future, I had to get out of New York. It just took me a few years."

"But maybe you didn't give David or me enough credit, honey, to confide in us."

"I'm not proud of how I handled things."

Tricia looks sympathetic. "Well, maybe you *did* have to get away to figure things out."

"Wow. I didn't expect you to come around so quickly. Thank you." Frankie puts her hand over Tricia's.

"I'm not an ogre, dear, and sometimes you shut me out so I don't know what you're thinking."

"Well, I can share one thing I'm clear about. The feeling I had, lying in the hospital unsure if my legs were working, was my message in a bottle. It said, *you have to keep performing.* I just wish Raoul were fond of children and more supportive that way. It would make considering both dance and motherhood more of a possibility."

"Raoul? No, he loves you and a child wouldn't be his responsibility. Why would he care?"

"Because the dance company is *his* baby. He'd have to be convinced I could still be there one-hundred percent for NYC Moves."

"Couldn't you wait a few more years until you're completely finished with performing? I'm just asking now. I don't have an agenda."

"Full disclosure, Mom. There's a little girl and boy at Los Niños de Amor I've gotten attached to. The girl is six, the boy is three and they're so loveable. I've been thinking more about adoption since volunteering. I'm trying to figure out if I can perform and be a mother. I wouldn't have considered it before, but being down here has given me a different perspective."

Tricia does her peering thing and Frankie can see she's using her every ounce of self-restraint. "*Very* big decision, Francesca."

Frankie looks at her and laughs. "That's it? No really, Mom. I do want to know what you think."

Tricia smiles. "If I've learned anything from being a mother and working with kids all my life, it's that you've got to put the child first. Their needs are the parents' North Star. And six? That's pretty old. Does she have any trauma? What does this little girl need to feel safe and secure? And the boy, what's his story? And two at once? Have you read much about foreign adoption and adoption of older kids? Are you okay with me asking all these questions?"

"Yes, they're all good ones. I know my next step is researching international adoption, but Mom, if I adopt, will you help me out?"

"Of course, I'll help out, but you'll still be their mother."

"Maybe Leonel could go to your daycare?"

"You'd move back to Brooklyn? That'd be quite a commute to the studio."

"Just considering options. But let's not talk about this anymore."

"Okay, sweetie. But can I remind you that you just said you don't want to give up performing. You said that, not me." Frankie nods. Tricia squeezes Frankie's arm. "I'm just saying."

Chapter Thirty-Two

BROADWAY AT LOS NIÑOS

Frankie sees Paula and Tricia off at the airport Wednesday morning, then gets on the bus to Xoxocotlán. She considered packing up and heading home with them. The earthquake has really rattled her, but she can't just up and leave the kids, especially with the upcoming dance performance and fundraiser. One of *The Four Agreements* guides her: *Do Your Best.*

She'd also like to see Mac. She really misses spending time with him. After Deanna's visit, they've kept in touch via text only and neither have suggested getting together. Mac offered to help out weeks ago with the fundraiser before the La Olla debacle and the seismic earth shift, but he hasn't brought it up since. This makes Frankie sad, but she understands it's probably for the best.

They had also discussed spending El Día de los Muertos, The Day of the Dead, together and going to the cemetery in Xoxocotlán, but that too is up in the air like the balloons floating over the zócalo. Frankie knows if she sees Mac, she won't be able to turn off her attraction, and she's not sure she wants to. It's been years since she's felt this delicious energy and it makes her feel, well, hungry, but it doesn't mean anything has to happen.

***

Frankie gets off the bus and walks the dirt driveway from the highway to NNAA. She arrives by eleven. There's plenty of time to rehearse between now and the dance recital in two weeks. Yesterday, the doctor removed her cast which the kids decorated with autographs, so she's saving it as a memento. The doctor said she can go back to the gym tomorrow but will have to take it easy with any lifting. Her cuts have almost fully healed, her bruises now a light gray-green, and her hair is growing back in reddish tufts above her ear, nothing she can't hide in one of her scarves. Today, it's a calming turquoise silk, like the Caribbean.

She sees Enrique's father's truck parked out front and is surprised to see Raquel at the front desk rather than Enrique. She figured Enrique was there to fix a pipe or repair a wall or desk. There's always something that needs fixing. Frankie's aware from helping with administrative tasks that there isn't much money coming in, and she wonders how they survive from month to month. This is one of the reasons she offered to help with fundraising efforts.

"Buenas días, Raquel."

They hug briefly, but Raquel is uncharacteristically distracted. "Have you seen my thoughtless brother?" she asks as she rifles through papers on her Uncle's desk. "I'm looking for any sign of him."

"I saw him last night at El Saguaro. He just got back."

"Well, thank God! Where the hell has he been?"

"We didn't talk about that. It was Paula and my mom's last night in town, so he waited on us. I was hoping he'd be here this morning."

"Well, he apparently left town weeks ago and hasn't been answering phone calls. I've been staying in Oaxaca with one of my cousins to be closer to the University because I'm trying to get my father and Abuela used to me not being there, but then when I do go home, my father tells me Enrique left and took Abuela with him! That makes no sense! Enrique's supposed to be keeping an eye on them. My father refused to talk about it. I asked Uncle Pepe to talk to Papá to see what's going on. I hope Enrique doesn't ruin everything for me. He can be so unpredictable. Who's going to help my father and Abuela when they need it? I'm not moving back right now. No way."

"Well, Enrique's around. He's working shifts at the restaurant." Frankie's never seen Raquel go on like this and feels badly for Enrique. He wants to spread his wings the same as she does. The same as everyone.

"Well, I'm relieved thanks to you. Abuela is the mystery. What in God's name did he do with our eighty-year-old grandmother?"

"I'm sure she's okay, and I don't think Enrique will ever go too far from Miguel."

"Oh, by the way, I went to Lachatao a few weeks ago with Mac to meet La Curandera and learn about her midwifery herbs. She's so knowledgeable, truly amazing."

"Sounds great." Frankie turns away thinking, oh God why do I care? I'm so messed up.

"Mac's learning so much about herbs and even some Zapotec. He actually knew *nayeli* means 'I love you.'"

Frankie lets that fact roil around for an annoying moment. "Well, off to see the kids. Time to start teaching them some dance steps."

"I'm sure they'll love it. I'm leaving and hopefully Tío Pepe will be back soon. And promise me if you hear anything from my aggravating brother, you'll call."

Frankie smiles and says, "No problema," even though she knows she won't. Right now, her faux novio is her BFF in Oaxaca and where her loyalties lie.

When Frankie goes out to the playground to round up the kids, Esme crashes into her, flinging chubby arms around her waist. "I thought I heard you and ran all the way." She's breathless, looking up and not letting go an inch. Frankie gives her a hug.

"Well, I'm happy to see you too, and right now we're going to learn some really fun dance moves with cool music, so lead the way."

"Yay, yay!" Esme squeals and jumps up and down, surprisingly reminding Frankie of Enrique which makes her chuckle.

From the office window, Raquel watches them go off hand in hand. She hopes Frankie doesn't break Esme's heart or vice versa.

***

Raquel surprises Enrique at El Saguaro that evening at the end of his shift. She leaves her annoyance behind. There's too much to be done. They sit at a table away from the bar.

"Enrique, please tell me where you've been and what's going on at home?"

Enrique explains his father's ultimatum, his escape from their house with Abuela, Teresa's generosity, and his week in Juchitán.

"Wow! I'm sorry Papá kicked you out. If Mamá were alive, he wouldn't have dared, but I have an idea." Enrique is leery. "Why not have Teresa, Esteban and Miguel move in with Papá? And Abuela move back of course. Our house is bigger and he needs help with the sheep and farming, and he would love to have Miguel around. Teresa could rent out her place and help Abuela with the household."

"Great idea, hermana. One major problema. What about me? I know you're going off to medical school, but I still live here. Right now, I'm staying with a friend in Oaxaca, not Gregorio. He's still in Guanajuato, but my living situation is temporary."

Raquel is embarrassed. "Ah, well, I assumed you'd be living with Gregorio." She pauses. "Wait. I know! Maybe you could live in Teresa's house. Then you'd be close to

Miguel. I could talk to Papá. Tell him Miguel can't live there unless you can come around."

"Good luck with that. Then again, you've always been su favorita. Maybe he'll listen."

Raquel kicks him lightly under the table. "Come on, hermano. I'm trying to help us both."

Chapter Thirty-Three

CRUSHED TO DUST

Mac returns to Hospital La Reforma the day after his first visit, but Frankie's been released and there's no information as to where she is. NNAA is his only hope of finding her, but Abuela's expecting him this morning so he packs up for Lachatao.

The drive on Camino Real is no longer white-knuckled, giving Mac plenty of time to reflect. On his last visit, he and Abuela trekked to a clearing in the forest. They sat across from each other, and as Abuela kept beat on a small drum like Xanu does, they journeyed to their animal guides seeking counsel: Abuela for her patients and Mac for his personal questions. Later, they worked in a small outbuilding next to Abuela's healing room, grinding and mixing herbs for specific ailments and storing them in small glass bottles.

Mac imagines maybe this is how Deanna feels in her lab and wonders how her grant is coming along. Has she been considering adoption? Is she feeling more comfortable about their situation since her trip, or was it too strange and off-putting, especially her conversation with Abuela? Mac's already purchased his ticket to depart two days before Thanksgiving and hopes that will give Deanna some solace.

Then he thinks of Frankie, their dinners and walks and conversations and can't imagine not ever seeing her again. He told her he'd help with the fundraiser, and he wants to help, to give back to NNAA and to her, but he doesn't have the courage to reach out just yet. Guilt's got him stuck halfway on a suspended bridge. Guilt for not staying in Oaxaca and finding Frankie after she left the hospital, and guilt about his marriage. Even though he didn't cross any lines with Frankie, he wanted to. Frankie makes him come alive. He loves her laugh, and Mac's never seen a woman eat so much; it makes him jealous and smile at the same time. He's also moved by her deep caring about the kids at NNAA.

Mac starts humming a melody he's been working on this past week, but he's too distracted by the turmoil in his life. He then turns on the news channel, but the rapid delivery is an annoying blur of sounds. Frustrated, he shuts the radio off and is soon humming again. Then the anthropologist in him takes over wondering if humming is a universal human trait like singing. Did humans hum before they spoke or sang? Do any other animals hum or create music? Birds of course. Yes, thank God for music!

Mac finally stops thinking long enough to string together a few notes to add to the new melody. The more he hums, the less he thinks, and the less he thinks, the more he recognizes the sheer brilliance of the day. And then there he is, once again in Lachatao.

***

As he approaches the front door, Mac counts the number of times he's been to see Abuela this past month. He can't believe it's his seventh. Frankie hasn't joined him lately, but language has become less of a barrier. Abuela, in a long black cotton skirt, sky-blue blouse and yellow-flowered apron, sits on the porch. As he approaches, she smiles.

"Hola hijo. Venga." He kisses her cheek and she leads him into the living room where she has spread Mac's notes over the table and counters. On separate sheets next to each page are the translations into Spanish and Zapotec that her granddaughters have completed. Mac's drawings accompany the notes. Among the drawings are verbena, lavender, eucalyptus, basil, and wild mushrooms. In Mac's mind, they evoke the forest's damp earthy smells and the slow careful movements of Abuela's skillful harvesting. The legendary Abuela.

By now, he's heard many stories from his aunt and nieces about patients she's cured, some with very challenging cases. Mac, too, is in awe of his grandmother and loves her, but finds her at times irritating. It's her way or the highway. Perhaps she's earned it, but he senses she was born like this. Focused and strong, but at times unyielding, like her steely refusal to think finding his mother is a good idea.

"Abuela, I'm still not sure exactly what to do with this information in the States."

"I will send you to Sage Mountain in Vermont. The healers there will help to publish the book, and I could still train you, niño. You could to be un curandero."

Mac balks, not for the first time. "I would like to learn more, yes, but Abuela, you know that teaching and music, these are the central pieces of my life."

"Do you think teaching people is more important than healing them?" Mac is suddenly tired. He wonders if Deanna is right in thinking Abuela is obsessed with him.

"It's my life's work. I'm a teacher like you are a curandera. I want to learn more about shamanism, but it's not my life's path, certainly not right now."

She looks at him for a long time. "Maybe."

"*Maybe?*" Mac asks, annoyed.

She doesn't even smile. "Let's sit together again later in the clearing. We'll journey for guidance, okay?"

"No, Abuela, I don't need guidance about this. You have to trust me. I feel light-headed even thinking about blood and really sick people."

Abuela shakes her head, "Maybe you have more of your mother in you."

"Is that so bad? Do you realize you've never said one good word about her?" Mac rubs his shoulder that's feeling tense.

"Okay, I speak again de Rosario for you. When una niña, she helped with the herbs, to dry them and make teas y los remedíos. She is so good. She help with los temazcals.

Todo. At age nine she helps too with the births. But she is not here. So, what nice thing do you want for me to say?"

"Maybe it wasn't her destiny."

"Of course, es su destino. She mija! Pero no, she go to D.F. and Díos knows what she does." Mac thinks, you don't know only because you never took the time to find out, but he's not going to fuel her anger.

Abuela retrieves her cane from the back of her chair. "No more talking. Come, let's walk outside. An old woman needs ejercicios. You know you must to keep moving."

Mac shakes his head. "Yes, use it or lose it, but I think you're in better shape than me."

Mac and Abuela head down the driveway towards the road. With her cane in one hand, she hooks her other hand through Mac's arm. She leads him down the road to a wooden bridge they start to cross, but Abuela stops in the middle and leans on the railing. It's the dry season, yet a shallow stream finds its way over speckled rocks.

"Will you come back after you visit home for your holiday, niño?" As Mac watches the irrevocable pull of water by gravity, it stirs in him a sense of the passage of time. Midlife, was he there yet? Would time erode his chance of fatherhood? He realizes Abuela's waiting for his answer.

"I'm planning to come back, Abuela, but I'll go to D.F. first to look for Rosario."

Abuela takes that in as she keeps her eyes on the stream. When she begins to speak, her voice is so soft that Mac has to lean his head in, almost touching hers.

"Is possible I will not to see you again, mijo. The thing is, I don't have much time here. Maybe that's why I so strong about to teach you."

All sounds in the forest pause. "What? What do you mean, Abuela?" Mac's stomach drops.

"I try todas mis hierbas y I see un médico, your kind, but some cancers are too strong, muy destructivos, before you can name them. I have a big life and soon I can rest in the forest con mis hierbas and the trees."

"No, Abuela, listen. I could bring you to the States. You could see the best doctors in the world. Really, there are so many things they can do with cancer these days."

"I think there is no time for that. The Great Spirit is coming soon." She pats him on his hand. "I tell you now because you have the herbal knowledge to bring to Los Estados Unidos. Nayeli can teach here in the pueblos with our book, but we need other people to know the herbs and healing." She puts her hand on his arm with force. "This why the spirit guides make us together at this time. And I hope you will stay here and I pass on the curandera work to you, but I see now you teacher first, maybe healer later. You Professor Mac." Smiling, she looks up at him and lovingly squeezes his arm.

With that acknowledgment, Mac feels like crying, and the lurch in his stomach is now an ache. If only I could rewind to this morning before this conversation. Am I really going to lose mi Abuela so soon and the major connection to my birth mother? He stares at the water feeling a bit ill, fighting the full gravitas of the situation. He becomes aware of her hand on his arm and can't believe he's only thinking of himself.

"I will help, Abuela. I'll do whatever you need."

"I know Mac. You be a loyal man. I know you will finish the book."

"I promise." Mac puts his hands on his heart. "Even if I have to self-publish, I'll do it." Mac puts his arm around her shoulder and holds her.

She sighs. "Another thing. I think my cancer is from Rosario."

Mac is incredulous. "No, Abuela, you don't really blame Rosario for your cancer, do you?"

"No, mijo. Es culpa mía. I so bitter, so eat up with anger. I cannot to forgive. I pray, I cleanse, I try, pero es imposible. But now with little time left, I see I do still love her."

"Abuela, I don't think you can blame yourself for getting cancer."

She grins at him. "So now you the healer. You know this thing?" She laughs. "It no matter niño. It is what is. But I ask you for one more thing. I know you will find Rosario. Tell her I should have been looking for her years ago." She withdraws her hand from Mac's arm, folds her hands, and stares at the stream. "Tell Rosario, mija, I am so sorry." Then she looks into Mac's eyes. "Tell her I love her."

As they stand on the bridge, the stream pools and flows, crows caw to one another and a light wind wraps around them. Abuela looks peaceful, but Mac feels empty, the happiness he had in coming to Lachatao has been crushed to dust.

Chapter Thirty-Four

ESTÚPIDA

Frankie, on her second week of rehearsals at Los Niños de Amor, is on her lunch break. She strolls into the woods behind the buildings, finds a patch of sunlight amid the pine trees and sits on the soft needles. She takes out a chicken sandwich and thermos of lemonade, then leans back to bask in the warmth. But, after only a few seconds, Frankie hears footsteps and there is Esme plopping down next to her.

"Whew! I ran all the way!"

"I'm happy to see you, Señorita Esmeralda, but does anyone know you're this far from the playground?"

Esme smiles coyly, "Maybe."

Frankie gathers her lunch. "Let's go back. You can keep me company at the picnic table." Esme literally runs circles around Frankie as they head back.

Once Frankie's seated, Esme twirls around and drops flat on the grass moving her arms like she's making a snow angel. "Frankie, are you married?"

Frankie didn't see this one coming. "Ah, no."

"Do you have any kids?"

Frankie hides her surprise. "No, Esme, I don't."

"Do you want kids?" A bite of the chicken sandwich gets stuck in Frankie's throat. She knows this is as close as Esme will come to asking her if she'd be her mother. Frankie reads it in the warmth and worry of those beautiful brown eyes. She manages to swallow her bite.

"Someday I might want children." After the abortion and losing David, and taking leave from the dance company, Frankie's become afraid of making a wrong move. Her self-doubts, once whispery little things, even as she danced on the international stage, have turned up the volume. Now a precious little girl is involved.

Their attention is diverted toward screeches and thwacks of balls as more kids come out to play. Leonel comes barreling over. The moment Frankie finishes her sandwich, Esme jumps up and touches her thigh.

"Tagged!" says Esme, grinning and ready for the chase.

Leonel follows Esme's lead screaming, "Chase me!" She runs after both and tags each back.

Leo yells, "Lift me up to the sky, Frankie." Frankie lifts him and swirls him around. He screeches with joy.

The second he's on the ground, Esme pulls on Frankie's arm. "Me too. Lift me more high!" Esme is short and stocky. Leonel is thin and small boned. Frankie's not sure she can even lift Esme, never mind over her head. And her forearm is healed but needs strengthening. Plus, she can't chance throwing out her back or anything else, especially if she's to perform in the spring. She can't explain all this to Esme who may be sensitive about her weight.

Moments hang between them, brown eyes to hazel until Esme runs off and pushes Leonel hard out of her way. He lands on packed earth, scrapes his knees and bumps his nose on a root so hard it starts to bleed. His knees have tiny rocks embedded in the skin. As soon as he sees blood, he begins to wail. Frankie grabs a napkin from the picnic table and holds it up to Leo's nose as she carries him into the cafeteria. She spots Esme watching from behind a tree.

"It's okay Leo. It's just a little blood. You're okay." Frankie shows him how to pinch the top of his nose. She cleans up his knees with warm water and soap. "You're being very brave." His wailing has subsided to a whimper. "Try sitting up a little more, sweetie. The bleeding's stopped. We'll rest and then go back to the playground, okay?" Leonel nods.

She kisses her fingers and plants them on his cheeks. He giggles. Frankie sees Esme watching through the window. When she catches Frankie's eye, she runs off. Leading Leo by the hand, Frankie takes him outside where he joins a group of younger boys.

Frankie finds Esme hiding behind a tree.

Esme peeks around the trunk. "Go away!" A stick flies at Frankie brushing her ankle. Esme's voice is now high-pitched. "Go away!" Frankie wonders how deep this resentment and neediness runs.

"Esme, you need to apologize to Leonel. Pushing isn't okay. You hurt him. And I'm sorry I didn't lift you, but I need to get my arm stronger. I'm sorry I hurt your feelings."

Esme mimics, "I'm sorry I hurt your feelings."

Frankie ignores that and waits for her to come out of hiding. And waits.

"Okay, come see me when you're ready to talk. I'm not mad. I just want to talk to you."

As Frankie turns to go back to the office, she hears a muttered, "Estúpida."

Oh boy, Frankie thinks. Tough cookie. I wish I could take a week off from this place, hike in San Felipe and think things through. She quickly realizes, though, Esme could easily interpret that as rejection. Since both of them know she's available for adoption, Frankie feels like she's walking a tender tightrope. She's trying to keep her balance, trying not to fall, to fail.

***

Later that day, Mac arrives at NNAA. He sheepishly watches the dance rehearsal out on the playground from behind the safety of the office windows. He had called ahead and spoken to Uncle Pepe, so he knew Frankie would be there, but now realizes he should have spoken to her. He stands in the exact place he stood his first day almost two months ago. Hearing Frankie laugh fills him with alternating relief and anxiety, and he starts to hum.

He half-hopes she'll see him looking out the window so he could wave as if he's just popping by, a casual hello, something a friend would do. And that's what they have to be really because he's committed to seeing things through with Deanna, whichever way it goes. Mac watches Frankie show the kids a dance move. He recognizes most of the kids from his visits to play with them.

He's thinking, maybe I should just leave a note when he notices an iridescent green and black hummingbird shimmering at the feeder just outside the window. What's that line.... something about hope is a feathered thing? Or hope is the thing with feathers? Or the feathered thing that flies with hope? Inspired by his versions of the poem and this tiniest of aerial creatures, Mac steps quickly out the door. He holds his Red Sox baseball cap in hand and strides over to Frankie and the kids, having no idea what he's going to say.

Frankie hears the office door shut and turns, putting a hand above her eyes to block the sun. When she recognizes Mac, she lights up. He sees it's her first and honest reaction, but then her face changes.

"Hello, Mac. We're rehearsing for the fundraiser."

"I can see that, and you guys look amazing! Muy bueno! Magnífico!" He gives a thumbs up and looks at Frankie. "Do you need any help?"

Frankie hesitates. "I have to say, I was hoping to hear from you a while ago." Her resentment is clear. "The fundraiser's next week."

Mac puts on his cap. "I'm sorry." He shuffles his feet like a misbehaved schoolboy as the kids look on, their presence pulling at Frankie.

"We have to get back to rehearsing."

A motorcycle whine interrupts, growing louder as dust clouds appears on the road fanning out in all directions. Enrique passes the parking lot and heads straight onto the playground towards the kids who start to scream and scatter. Then he makes an abrupt turn and drives around in a big circle. The kids clap with delight. With a dramatic U-turn flourish, he stops dead in front of Mac and Frankie while the kids chant, "Rique! Rique! Rique!"

Frankie exclaims, "Quite an entrance!" He gets off the bike, waves his helmet to the kids and bows. She turns to the kids. "Okay, breaktime. Take ten." The kids scatter and Enrique gives Frankie a big hug. He's about to give her a kiss on the lips but she whispers, "Stop. Mac saw you kissing Gregorio."

Enrique pulls back and looks at Mac. "It's true. I'm a homosexual. And I'm not only gay, I'm happy!" Enrique beams.

Frankie laughs. "Oh my God, Enrique, you're out! I guess this means we've broken up?"

"Yes, I'm so sorry, mi amor." He grabs her hand with fake remorse. "Juchitán, on the Isthmus, is what freed me up. I've spoken to Uncle Pepe and I had already told Teresa. They're both cool but mi papá remains fanatically homophobic. But, that's okay. I'm free."

"Way to go," Mac encourages.

Enrique's wearing a tight white t-shirt, and Frankie notices a tattoo of a motorcycle with wings on his bicep. "Great tattoo!! Did you get that in Juchitán too?"

"Yes, great place! I'm going back in late November for La Vela de Las Intrépidas Buscadoras del Peligro."

"Wow! Sounds potentially decadent! I can't wait to hear your stories, but I've got to get back to the kids. The fundraiser's next week."

"Yes, I know. Uncle Pepe asked me to build the dance platform and figure out the lighting. He said you were short of help." He looks at Mac who looks sheepish. "I could use some help. Do you have the time?"

"Yes, I would love to help." He looks at Frankie.

"We need all the help we can get." Mac's relieved she wants his help, but he's still not detecting a lot of warmth.

Frankie turns to Enrique. "Hey, have you spoken to your sister? She's been trying to find you."

"Yes, but that's another story."

Frankie takes hold of Enrique's arm. "I can't wait to hear. Let's meet for a drink soon, but after the fundraiser." Mac envies their open affection.

"Yes, we'll make a date. You too, Mac?"

He looks at Frankie who finally smiles and says, "Sounds like a plan to me." Inside Mac dances like a kid.

As Enrique and Mac head to the office, Mac looks back once hoping to catch Frankie's eye and wave, but she's gathering the kids to show them their next dance move. God, she's something, Mac thinks without meaning to.

Chapter Thirty-Five

A CHANGE OF PLANS

It's been several days since Mac's learned the sad news about Abuela's health. He's eating Chinese take-out, hunkered down and miserable in his B&B. He'd rather get a root canal than tell Deanna he won't be home for Thanksgiving. She deserves better, but he doesn't know what else to do. He'll tell her about his visit last night to Santo Domingo where he lit candles and prayed for Abuela's health. He hopes it will impress her. He also prayed deeply for Deanna's understanding.

Mac decides to first speak to his parents. His mom picks up on the first ring.

"Sweetie, I was just thinking about you as I was making a cup of tea. I bumped into Charlene's mom the other day."

"You mean, Charlene my high school girlfriend?"

"Yes, of course, and she asked about you. So, I explained the whole thing. How you're in Mexico meeting up with your birth family. I'm just doing it, Mac. I don't care what people think anymore. After being dishonest with you, never again with the lies."

"Wow! That's so good, Mom. I'm touched, really."

"We are so looking forward to seeing you. What is it? A little over a month?"

"Well, that's why I'm calling." Mac rubs his cheek. "I know this will be hard to hear, but I can't come. Abuela just told me she has cancer and only a short time to live. It's her pancreas. The doctors here have done what they can and her herbs help, but she's resigned herself that barring a miracle, she's not going to get better. It could be a month or two or three. I really don't know, but I don't want to lose what little time I have left with her, and in February I'll need to start teaching again." He can practically hear his mother's excitement deflating and feels awful.

Sophia's voice is soft. "Oh Mac, we'll miss you, but I understand. You can't just leave her now. Goodness, that's so sad it's making me cry. Now I know we'll never meet her." Mac hears her blow her nose. "I'll tell dad when he gets back from his bowling league. He left right after dinner. He'll understand too."

"Thanks, Mom. Look, could you do me a favor? I'll call Deanna soon, but she may need some support from you guys. Things have been a little rocky lately. She's not comfortable with my shamanic experiences, and I never told you this, but Deanna doesn't want children. That *was* okay with me, but being in Oaxaca's made me think I may want to be a father, so there's a lot of tension."

"I'm sorry for the tension, but bless you. That makes me so happy. If I were there, I'd give you a big hug.

I never asked either of you about children because it's so personal and those questions were always painful for me. But I've often thought you'd make a great father, and of course I'd love a grandchild. Given my personal history though, I'm the last person in the world to put that pressure on anyone. And if it's going to cost you your marriage, that's a whole other thing."

"I know, Mom, and I never brought it up because I hoped Deanna would change her mind. I'm still hoping."

"Oh Mac, everything was fine before this whole adoption thing and Oaxaca. You two were so happy. I feel terrible."

"It's not your fault, Mom. It's not just about having a child, and we're working on things. Can I let her know she can call you?"

"Of course. We'll invite her for dinner. But staying to be with Abuela is something she should understand on her own."

"Ideally, but just try to cheer her up, okay?"

"Of course. Oh Mac, I'm so happy to help you in any way. It makes me feel just a little bit less awful for waiting so long to tell you the truth."

"Thanks, Mom." Mac doesn't share that he'll also soon be looking for his biological mother. They chat for a few more minutes about each other's health and the rest of the family. He learns his younger cousin is engaged to be married at the end of the summer on Cape Cod.

"Mom, thanks for helping with Deanna and give my love to dad. And you know, Mom, no matter what, you and dad will always be the only real parents I have."

"Oh, now I'm going to cry again. Thank you for saying that sweetie. We love you too, to the moon and back."

"Bye, Mom."

"Bye, sweetie. Good luck with Abuela. Give her our love."

Mac flops back on the couch and sighs. In his mind, he sends his mom a huge hug. When he thinks of Deanna, though, the phone becomes radioactive. He grabs a beer from the fridge and takes his lo mein and General Tao's chicken out to the patio. The beer helps the so-so food and his nerves, as does sitting quietly under the stars. The constellations are different here. He can't find the Big Dipper or the North Star, and unlike in placid Montague, the canine call-and-response chorus has begun. It prompts him to go inside where he's well aware of the cell phone thrumming in impatience.

It rings and he jumps. "Hi, Mac. I called your mom about a chicken recipe and she just told me about Abuela. I'm so sorry! Of course, you'll need to spend time with her. You must be really sad." Mac's so relieved, he starts to tear up. He's noticed he gets more emotional this far from home.

"I'm so glad you understand, Deanna. I'm grateful I've gotten to know her at all, but I can't wrap my brain around the fact she's dying so soon after we've met. I'm kind of numb. I want to still learn from her and be with her. But, enough of the sad stuff. How's everything going there?"

"Well, the grant approval was an unusually quick turnaround, so now we're hiring a few lab assistants."

"That's great. And what about Thanksgiving? Will you still go to my parents?"

"Hmm… since you won't be home, maybe I'll go to my folks. It only takes about six hours to get to Pennsylvania." Mac wants to ask if she's been thinking more about adoption, but he's afraid. Like she's a mind reader, Deanna says, "I have been thinking about what we talked about. I wanted to let you know that, but I've also been really busy with other things."

"Okay," Mac says, but feels disappointed she doesn't say more. He wonders how much influence his mother had in Deanna's being so accepting of his staying in Oaxaca. "Thanks again for being understanding, Deanna."

"Of course, Mac. I've got to head back to the lab now, but I'll call you tomorrow night. Love you."

"Love you more."

Chapter Thirty-Six

CHAMPAGNE

A few days after the successful fundraiser, Enrique, Frankie and Mac have their promised rendezvous at a small cozy restaurant in one corner of the zócalo. Mac is a few minutes late, and there's already a bottle of champagne opened and poured into three glasses.

"Just in time, Mac!" Frankie raises her glass. "Salud! To the $65,000! Half of which came from the ex-Pat volunteers. Salud to those with big hearts and deep pockets!" As they sip champagne, Mac is drawn once again to Frankie's energy. It's emotional physics, he thinks, as binding as any chemical compound.

Enrique adds, eyes sparkling, "And to Frankie! You did a great job with outreach, and the dance performance was clearly the highlight. This year, it wasn't about feeling sorry for the kids but appreciating them."

"That's true. I can still see Esme swirling in her red-spangled dress and Julio doing his hip-hop moves. What a talented kid!" She looks at Mac then Enrique. "Couldn't have done it without my crew."

"Yes, and Uncle Pepe's *over the top*. Ha! I just learned that idiom, and *top me up*, too," Enrique says, while pouring more champagne into each glass. After several toasts, Enrique tells his tale of Marcos and Juchitán. Mac then tells them about Abuela's cancer.

"I'm so sorry about Abuela." Frankie touches Mac lightly on the arm. "That's awful."

"Yeah man, that is too sad. You're just getting to know her." Enrique places his hand on Mac's shoulder.

"Thanks." Mac, not wanting to bring down the mood, says no more.

After another pour of champagne, Frankie asks Enrique about Gregorio. "I thought he might come with you."

"He's still in Guanajuato. He says it's to be with his dad, but I wonder. He's not texting as much or calling. I know his old boyfriend lives there."

"Is that a problem?" Frankie tilts her head, and Mac notices how lovely her profile is.

"It depends on what happens. I don't know. Maybe being separated like this for a while is a good test." Enrique stretches his arms over his head. "Mac, how is it for you being so far away from your wife?"

"Oh, I miss her of course, but I'm busy here." He pauses. "We've been together for ten years." Mac stumbles through a non-answer. He focuses on the table to avoid looking at Frankie, and when he looks up, she's found something fascinating in her champagne flute.

Enrique says, "Well, let's not be too serious. We're celebrating. Salud!" They raise their glasses. Frankie downs hers so fast the bubbles come up and out of her nose and she begins to giggle. When Mac thinks even that's cute, he knows he's in trouble.

Frankie looks at them both. "I know, right? Exquisite table manners for a professional New York City dancer." Just hearing that makes Mac want to look at her legs. Tonight, she's wearing a short, gold sparkly dress.

Enrique laughs. "I don't think champagne is meant for chugging, mi amor."

Frankie smiles. "You're so right, but I know what is." She waves her hand at the waiter.

Chapter Thirty-Seven

El DÍA DE LOS MUERTOS (THE DAY OF THE DEAD)

It's the last day of October. In New York City, Frankie would be wearing a fall jacket, but here, she tosses her thin sweater over one shoulder, revelling in the spring-like air. She's on her way back from the gym to La Casa de Isabel and stops at Café Campeche to buy coffee and a pastry, a treat after her grueling core, strengthening, and balance workout. She's now also renting an exercise room at the gym where she practices some of the company's dance routines and creates her own choreography.

Once back at the hotel, Frankie settles in the courtyard with the chatty parrots to write Paula a letter. She explains that she and Mac will explore the cemetery in Xoxocotlán tomorrow night, November 1st, the first day of El Día de los Muertos. She adds that Esme asked to come, so the three will go.

Hopefully, Paula won't rebuke her about spending so much time with Mac. She doesn't want to be judged, but working with him at the fundraiser has brought them closer. And it's not that she doesn't respect the sanctity of marriage, but being with Mac is hard to resist, like opening a box of chocolates. Plus, it's his marriage, she rationalizes, his responsibility, and she feels she's doing the best she can with her own struggles. Frankie seals the envelope, and as much as she values Paula's take on things, knows the letter will arrive after the facts, whatever they will be.

****

Esme walks between Mac and Frankie holding their hands. "Uno, dos, tres," says Mac as he and Frankie swoop Esme, squealing, up into the air. It's evening and they're standing in front of the entrance to El Panteón, the cemetery in Xoxocotlán where candles are glowing like dancing sprites up and over the hillside of graves.

Frankie says, "Once we enter, no more squealing. Okay? We need to respect the dead and their families." Esme nods. They walk between gravesites where family members greet the dead with basketfuls of orange, yellow and white marigolds to adorn their graves. The flowers glow amid the thousands of lit candles. Someone plays a guitar nearby.

Starting at midnight on October 31st, when the spirit and physical worlds are closer than usual, deceased children return to visit their families. Then on November 1st, Catholic All Souls' Day, deceased adults visit. Families surround the graves of their loved ones with their favorite food and drink to lure them back for one more night with their families. They light copal incense to cleanse the offerings and help draw the spirits earthward. Frankie notices cigarettes and liquor are common gifts as the living and dead celebrate together.

Mac looks mesmerized. "You know the tradition of these offerings comes from pre-Colombian Mesoamerica. The Nahuas believed the offerings helped the deceased as they moved through the nine challenging levels of the afterlife to the final resting place of Mictlan."

"Wow, that's really interesting, Professor." Frankie smiles at him. "Seriously."

After a few moments, Mac suddenly puts his hand on Frankie's arm to steady himself. "Whoa! That whiff of copal just sent me back to the playing field in Tikal. Remember that experience I told you about?"

"Of course. Are you okay?"

"Yes, just give me a minute to breathe and ground myself. Abuela taught me about that as part of her shamanic lessons."

As Mac is breathing, Esme looks worried and pulls at his sleeve. "Are you okay, Mac?"

"I'm absolutely fine, niña. I just got distracted for a minute."

Frankie says, "Look at all the photos around the graves. How moving."

Esme grabs Frankie's hand. "In school today, we got smiling skeleton heads and skeleton sugar candies."

They continue to walk by families camped out and eating alongside their dead loved ones. Some people are singing, some weeping. Frankie realizes she was wrong. Esme could shriek and run all she wanted and no one would notice or be offended. Death here in Mexico is neither fearsome nor silent. With that thought, she's happy to let Esme skip ahead. She keeps an eye on her, and when Frankie turns towards Mac, he's gazing at her.

"Did you do something different with your hair?"

"Not so much." Frankie lies. Ha! She spent fifteen minutes trying to get it to twist artfully around her scarf.

"It looks nice."

Definitely worth it, she thinks. Mac's eyes are shining. Is it the candles? Esme? "This attitude towards death feels so much healthier than in the U.S."

"Agreed, the afterlife here is very much alive. I bet most families have altars for their deceased loved ones at home too."

Esme skips back and they hear music starting up. Esme jumps up and down at Mac's feet. "Could you give me a piggyback?" Without hesitation, he stoops down and lets her climb onto his back, her arms circling his neck. Heading in the direction of the song, they come upon a makeshift stage in front of a grave festooned with orange marigolds. Upbeat music plays from speakers as two kids dance onstage.

Frankie looks at Mac. "Wow! I just heard someone say they're dancing for their grandparents. And, it's literally on their graves." Esme asks to get down and does her own little dance on the path. Mac and Frankie look at each other and smile. Is this what parenting is like? Frankie wonders. At least on a good day? With a partner?

By eleven o'clock Esme's tuckered out, so they drive back to NNAA. Frankie brings her to the girls' dorm and waits while Esme changes into her pajamas and brushes her teeth. She gives her a hug good night and waves from the doorway.

Mac waits in the darkened office, humming and looking through the window at the night sky. When Frankie taps him on the back, he turns, surprised, and Frankie feels suddenly awkward being so close in the dark. She backs up, but realizes she doesn't want Mac to leave right away.

"I think there's some wine in the fridge left over from the fundraiser. Should I open a bottle?"

"I'd love some." They look at each other for a few seconds and without thinking, Frankie leans towards him and kisses him lightly on the cheek.

She spins around. "Be right back."

***

Mac continues to stare at the night sky. He's not sure what the kiss meant. It was a quick peck on the cheek, the kind he'd give his mother, but the softness and warmth of her lips linger.

They go outside and sit next to each other at the picnic table sipping wine and taking in the quiet of the night. Frankie can feel Mac's body radiating heat, and the inexpensive chardonnay goes right to her head. Mac feels Frankie's electric energy like a low hum between them.

"Oh Mac, you've got to hear this song. Adele just came out with it. It's beautiful. Should I play it?"

Mac nods knowing he should probably say "no" and be getting home. Frankie opens the music app on her phone and they listen for a minute. "That's beautiful." Mac wants to say *and so are you,* but he doesn't.

Frankie turns to face Mac. "Would you dance with me? Just once?"

"Frankie, I'm not a very good dancer, and you're a professional."

"Just one dance. That's all." Between the music, wine, and a hefty dose of denial, Frankie's blissfully stopped thinking.

Mac doesn't know how to refuse her eyes or extended hand.

They hold each other and sway to the rhythm of the sensual sad song, and Frankie can't believe how good it feels to be held after all these years.

Mac, taken with her scent, pulls her close feeling the sinewy strength of the body he's so often admired.

Frankie's surprised at the strength of his arms and can feel his muscular thighs against hers.

To Mac, Frankie feels light and magical.

Frankie is in romance heaven: dancing on a starlit night in the arms of an attractive man, Mac's arms. She rests her head on his shoulder, and his hand caresses her back and moves up to her neck cupping her close. She gets goosebumps and feels like she's sixteen again.

The song ends but their embrace continues. Mac kisses her, lightly at first with just his lips, then deeply, with his tongue; he kisses her neck and ears, suddenly ravenous.

Frankie matches him, and they're off, lost in sensations as the world drops away.

"Hey!" A frantic voice topples them. They pull apart and Esme, barefoot and indignant, stands in front of them. "I want to give Mac a hug good night too!"

"Ah, okay Esme." Frankie, beyond annoyed, steps back thinking, wow! I see someone besides me needs attention. This little girl is not easy.

Mac, annoyed as well, stoops down and gives Esme a slap-me-five as he's trying to catch his breath. "That's the cool way I hug goodnight." Esme looks satisfied.

Frankie keeps her voice calm but it's stern. "You should be sleeping, Esme. It's way past your bed time." Esme, grabbing one of Frankie's hands, swings it a bit too hard and runs back to the dorm.

Frankie looks at Mac. "I'm going to make sure she's in bed and will stay there."

While Frankie's gone, Mac pours more wine and wills himself not to think. When she returns and says, "Come with me," he takes her hand.

***

Frankie leads Mac silently into the woods to the circle of pines where she likes to eat her lunch. The instant they stop,

Mac silences the gathering voices in his head by pulling Frankie close and pressing his body to hers. As they kiss and caress, continuing what Esme interrupted, Frankie wraps one leg around Mac pulling him closer.

They move to the ground undressing each other until it's skin on skin, alternating warmth and goosebumps. Mac wants to take his time with every nuance of her body, and Frankie wants to revel in discovering his, but their sex is urgent. He's on top, then underneath, as pine needles press crazy tattoos into their skin, and in their wild coupling, they sense the ripples of animal energy around them.

After, they lay together with only the blanket of night as a cover. With Frankie's head on Mac's chest, he reaches over and runs his hand through her hair and kisses the top of her head. Frankie surprises herself with tears. Release? Relief? Sadness? Mac lies spent and satisfied, ignoring the tsunami of guilt gathering on the horizon. Frankie, too, keeps her focus on the present: the smell of Mac's skin and his beautiful brown chest rising and falling under her hand.

Chapter Thirty-Eight

LA VELA DE LAS INTRÉPIDAS

A few weeks into November, Enrique heads back to Juchitán and is over the top, as he likes to say, about the annual Vela de las Intrépidas Festival and visiting Marcos and his mom. He goes straight to their house where Marcos told him to make himself at home until he and his mother get back from their workday at the market. Enrique, beat from his long bike trip, climbs into the courtyard hammock and falls asleep, waking to the smell of frying peppers and Marcos laughing at something his mother said.

After dinner, he and Marcos take a walk in the streets full of preening muxes, hoping to be this year's queen. Marcos provides a running commentary on the history of the festival and specific people they pass. Enrique notices Marcos often touches him when they speak, on the arm or elbow or shoulder and wonders if he's like that with everyone. It's such a thrill to be out walking in a city with a heart big enough to include gays, bisexuals, muxes… anyone really. Juchitán, its arms wide open.

That night Enrique can barely sleep. He recalls the artistry in the faces he witnessed that evening and is also wondering if anything is going on between Marcos and him. He's glad Marcos didn't make a move because he's not sure how he'd respond. There so much to take in, and he's not really sure what he wants, and then there's Gregorio.

At the breakfast table the next morning, Enrique says, "I wish the rest of Mexico was as accepting as Juchitán."

Marcos stirs the eggs while Angelina braids her hair and says, "It's wonderful, yes, but not everyone is accepting. I know a few muxes who had it tough at home; they weren't welcome and had to get out and make their own way. But, a lot of mothers do love to have at least one muxe to stay home and help them in their old age." She looks at Marcos and smiles. "Oh well."

As Enrique watches their closeness, he misses his own mother. "I learned that muxes have been part of the culture here for a long time. I have a friend from the U.S., a professor of pre-Columbian history, who told me some of the Aztec priests cross-dressed and some of the Mayan gods were both male and female."

"Well tonight, my dear Enrique, the gala fiesta will be full of goddesses," Marcos says while spooning eggs onto plates. He's more interested in breakfast than history. "Each contestant, yearning for the coronation, will have their own banners and sections. My cousin, Kazandra, is in the running. Wait 'til you see her! We can sit in her section. All you need to be admitted is a case of beer."

"Great. I'll buy three cases for us. You two have been so generous."

"No problema, amigo. And remember, if you need hairstyling, Izmelda is great."

"Actually, I do. I've been considering a new cut and some color. And I'll tell Xervieto that I get compliments on my tattoos all the time."

"We'll set you up, papí. No problema."

After breakfast, Marcos and Enrique go to the Muxe Mass in honor of San Vincente de Ferrer, the Patron Saint of Juchitán. Later that afternoon, Angelina finishes up early at the market and joins Enrique and Marcos to watch the parade. Nothing has prepared Enrique for this spectacle. Floats full of muxes and paper-mache animals and human-sized fronds pass by. The contestants are dressed in lavishly-embroidered blouses and skirts of the traditional Tehuanas, as well as gorgeous clingy dresses, like models on a catwalk. They throw candy and fruit to the crowds along with kisses.

Marcos, to be heard above the marching bands' horns and drums, yells into Enrique's ear, "Last year there were 10,000 people! Looks like more today."

Mesmerized by all these beautiful men who look like beautiful women, Enrique yells, "Maravilloso!" He takes a video on his cell phone and sends it to Frankie and Mac.

At the tented venue, they claim seats in Kazandra's section. The mothers of the muxes serve dishes of grilled mojarra, garnachas, chicken empanadas, tamales and Isthmus seafood specialties. Angelina, Enrique and Marcos fill their plates, and like everyone at the event, drink countless Coronitas as they watch the promenade. Cousins, aunts and uncles, and friends join them in Kazandra's section. They stand and applaud as she struts her stuff in an emerald sequined ball gown, slit up one side; a pink hibiscus headdress festooning her hair; and eyelashes longer than God's. Confetti-filled balloons pop and spray color into a night already filled with fireworks. The place throbs with live music and bodies.

Marcos grabs Enrique's hand. "Let go dance with Kazandra and her friends." Coronitas in the other hand, they move through the crowd, dancing. Marcos points to a group of dancers. "That's Kazandra's brother-in-law and his friends."

Enrique watches them move to the music and has given up trying to figure out gay male from straight from muxe. He and Marcos dance closely, and then Marcos turns to dance with a woman next to Kazandra.

Enrique finds himself dancing with a beautiful muxe. He's never seen such elaborate makeup or glittery fingernails. Her nails gently graze his shoulders as they spin. Her eyes are a golden-brown in a face with high hollowed cheekbones and bronze taut arms. In her thrall, Enrique pulls her closer and she laughs and bats her eyelashes, teasing him. She smells like jasmine and her hair, a glossy black, swings and shines as she turns. Enrique wants to kiss her but is not sure if she wants him to. When the dance ends, he keeps her hand in his, leading her to a table where they each grab another Coronita.

"My name's Enrique. What's yours?"

She leans towards him as she speaks. "Anayeli. People call me Yeli. Is this your first year at la Vela?"

"Yes, I'm visiting Marcos." Enrique points across the room.

"Marcos, si? I work with Kazandra at a club in downtown Juchitán. It's called Pájaros, probably because we're all such beautiful birds who work there." She laughs.

"What do you do there?"

Yeli smiles and runs her fingernail down his chest. "Many things." She pauses. "What about you, besides being such a sexy dancer?" Enrique is getting turned on.

"I work as a DJ at a club where I teach dance." Yeli's attention is suddenly diverted. She holds her finger up in a 'wait' gesture to a man across the room.

"Ah Enrique, mi amor, I have to run, but tomorrow night, come to Pájaros. We'll have a good time." As if she has wings, Yeli flits off, turning back once with a flirty wave. Enrique watches her and downs another Coronita. His intoxicating winged creature, his pájaro, has disappeared.

Slightly bereft, he watches the unfolding extravaganza before him. Enrique continues to dance and drink until 3 a.m., but Yeli's taken a ray of disco light with her.

***

The next morning, Enrique is nudged awake by kitchen sounds and aromas. Marcos yells, "Rise and shine, Enrique! Out of the hammock! Come slice avocados and pineapple."

Enrique groans as he gets up, yelling back, "I didn't realize you could get so hungover from beer." He shuffles his way into the kitchen.

Marcos pats him affectionately on the shoulder. "Nothing a shower and coffee won't remedy." Marcos is heating up tamales and gestures towards the coffee pot. "Help yourself. What time is your appointment with Izmelda?"

"Three."

"I'm so pleased. You're going to love her work. Have you decided on colors yet?"

"No, I'll ask her what she thinks." Enrique's resentment is long gone from when he realized Marcos and Angelina were first interested in him to make money. Enrique understands, given his own side gigs in Oaxaca. His Juchitán hosts have been nothing but good to him. He and Marcos even joke about it now, and he tells Marcos if he gets a good cut from Izmelda, he should split it with him. Enrique admires his skills as a salesman.

They sit down to a feast of warm tamales, black beans, avocado and pineapple. Between bites, Enrique talks. "Marcos, do you know Yeli very well? She invited me to Pájaros tonight. She says Kazandra works there too."

Marcos puts down his coffee cup. "Kazandra's a bartender, but Anayeli does more than that, if you know what I mean."

"What? She's a prostitute?"

Marcos shrugs, "Sometimes. She also dances and waits on tables. Muxes work hard to look beautiful, but their lives aren't always pretty. Take Yeli, for example. Her father beat her and kicked her out when she was sixteen. Kazandra's family took her in for a while, and after the father died, she moved back home. Now she supports her mother and a grandmother who's sick, so she does what she has to, to take care of them. Mi mamá was right."

"But I thought there was plenty of work, you know, as stylists and seamstresses and cooks?"

"Not everyone can do those things. You need talent and training, and sometimes muxes get held back by the culture here."

"That's so sad about Anayeli. She is *so* beautiful, like the perfect mix of a man and a woman."

Marcos nods as he bites into a chunk of pineapple. Enrique can't tell if Marcos feels the same or just loves pineapple. Breakfast done, Enrique picks up the plates and washes them in the sink. Marcos takes a shower, then leaves for el mercado. The men hug goodbye, and Enrique feels Marcos linger for a moment in his arms.

Enrique will head to Santa Ana right after his appointment at the salon, so before he leaves the house, he fills a vase with fresh white calla lilies he bought for Angelina. He writes Marcos a note, inviting him to Santa Ana and gives him Teresa's address. He figures they could safely stay at her house where he's been living. He's afraid his dad might take a machete to any male friend he brings home, or to the place that he called home.

Enrique feels good about his developing friendship with Marcos. He came thinking he might have wild random sex with someone at la Vela, but not being sure how Marcos would feel, he chose not to jeopardize their relationship. He feels his partnership with Gregorio is already in jeopardy, but isn't yet ready to give up on it.

He wonders what sex would have been like with Anayeli and gets a shiver. Juchitán has stirred in him many desires. He'd like to travel more, see more of Mexico, and maybe Miami and New York. He could DJ anywhere. But then, of course, there's Miguel. There's a lot to think about on the ride home, and he *so* hopes Marcos will visit.

***

Izmelda is dressed in red satin pants, a black blouse and high heels. Everything about her is sleek, and her smile lights up the salon. She seems genuinely happy to have Enrique as a customer.

"I was hoping you'd have some suggestions for a style and coloring."

Circling the chair, Izmelda takes in all of him. "I think we should go shorter on the sides and longer on the top with some bangs that can swoop over your eyes. Kind of a sexy look. And maybe create some blonde streaks to highlight your beautiful coloring."

As Izmelda washes his hair and massages his scalp, Enrique lets the tension drain from his body. She cuts, shapes and then sections pieces she wants to make blonde. "I'm going to put a solution that has bleach on the sections, but I won't go super close to your scalp, and then I'll wrap them in foil."

Izmelda is about three-quarters of the way through when Enrique's phone rings. "Sorry, but this is my sister." She nods patiently comb in hand as he takes the call.

By the time Enrique says good-bye, he's gone completely still. Izmelda waits for him to speak. "Mi papá's in the hospital. It's a stroke. Mi abuela found him on the kitchen floor this morning."

"Oh, my God! Do they think he'll be okay?"

"I don't know. They're doing tests, but I don't know if I should go see him. He kicked me out of the house, and I'm afraid if he sees me, he might have a heart attack, or another stroke!"

"Oh dear. Enrique, I think you should go, and now. If you don't at least try, you might regret it. But, Dios mío! Your hair! In a half-hour, you'll need to rinse that stuff out. Promise me you'll find a bathroom someplace, and call me tomorrow."

Enrique nods and sees she's trying not to look too panicked. "Go now, I hope your papá is okay. And don't forget to stop! Send me a selfie when you've rinsed it out."

Enrique reaches into his wallet and gives her much more than she expected. "You're a friend of Marcos, so please, take it." Touched, she kisses him on the cheek and ushers him out as he takes one last glance in the mirror. This should be good, he thinks.

As he revs his bike, he realizes he's shaking. He hopes he makes it back before anything worse happens.

Chapter Thirty-Nine

AUNTIE

Frankie walks from La Casa de Isabel to El Llano, the park in her old neighborhood. It's only a twenty-minute walk, and El Llano is not as crowded as the main zócalo. She loves to sit on the wrought-iron benches under jacaranda and palm trees and people-watch. Young, Indigenous and Mestizo men with black slicked-back hair, work boots, and cowboy hats arrive on bicycles every few days to sweep the park with handmade brooms. She watches Indigenous women in traditional clothes cross paths with women on cell phones clicking by in high heels. Her usual enjoyment is today tinged by an edgy feeling as she calls her friend.

"So, Paula. There's something I want your opinion on. It could be amazing, but it's also terrifying."

"Is this about Mac? Do you really want to break up a marriage?"

"Whoa! I haven't even seen him since El Día de los Muertos, and trust me, we won't be having sex again. I felt way too vulnerable after that. Not to mention, I came here to get clarity, no matter how adorable, sweet, sexy and smart he is."

"You're not really convincing me, Frankie."

"It's true, though. I can't help it my timing with men is so majorly fucked up, but I do want to stay connected to Mac. I just can't stay *that* connected."

"Well, now that I'm in a serious relationship, I think I'd be devastated if someone came along and slept with Sasha. That's why I reacted like that."

"Well, I didn't *force* Mac to have sex, and clearly he's not one-hundred-percent happy in his marriage," Frankie says defensively. "Plus, this isn't even about Mac."

"Sorry, Frankie. I guess I'm getting anxious about moving in with someone. I've lived alone for fifteen years."

"But, from everything you've said, Sasha seems like a loyal guy, and you two have so much in common."

"Yeah, yeah. It's not him; it's like pre-nuptial jitters."

"You're getting *married*?"

"No, that was just an expression. I'll be okay."

"I've never heard you sound like this. Doesn't your Buddhist practice help?"

"With everything else, yes. Anyhow, what's terrifying you if not a guy?"

Frankie gets up and starts walking around the park. "Potential motherhood. It's Esme. We've gotten really close. I love Leonel too, but I don't think I can handle two kids alone."

"Oh my God, so you're seriously thinking of adopting Esme?"

"That's why I'm calling. I don't know what to do and you know me better than anyone. I'm thinking maybe I could bring Esme home with me at Christmas for a few weeks to see if she's comfortable there. I know I'd have to figure out the legal stuff with Uncle Pepe, but if it works, then I was wondering if you and my mom could help out during the spring while I'm performing?"

"You mean you'd continue performing?"

"That was the message in the bottle. My legs were spared in the earthquake. That's like some kind of divine intervention. Don't you think?"

"But Frankie, if you're going to bring Esme home, you can't just jet off to Paris for a show. She'll need you around close to her. Imagine the adjustment she'll be going through."

Frankie sucks air through her teeth. "But you're like family and my mother is family. Like here, the whole village helps raise the children."

"But Frankie, I live in Brooklyn and work full-time and I'm moving in with Sasha. The logistics alone would be a nightmare. And your mother? I'm sure she'd help out with Esme, but she'd take over raising her. Is that what you want so you can dance?"

"Wow! That's pretty harsh. I thought you'd be happy for me."

"I'm helping you be realistic. Have you done any research on international adoptions?" Frankie sits down on the nearest bench. "Frankie?"

"Yeah, I'm here, and my mom suggested the same thing, so yes, I've started researching."

"Look, I'm totally in for being an Auntie, like sometimes we can go to Serendipity's for frozen hot chocolate and the Natural History Museum, but I can't be on a schedule."

"Okay, Paula. I get it. You're right. I've got to go now." Frankie never lies to Paula, but she suddenly feels like she doesn't have a second to lose.

Back in her room across town, she once again googles "adopting older children" and "international adoptions," but this time, sits and reads article after article for hours, taking notes. Frankie learns that adopted children experience trauma when they lose their biological parent(s), and each new placement is another loss. Frankie winces when she thinks of all the foster children that are moved from home to home, sometimes never finding a family. She reads about the possibility of attachment issues where the child struggles with trusting their adoptive family enough to fully connect emotionally. Frankie can see why it's easier for infants than older children. And, as with any international adoption of an older child, Esme would bring her own cultural experiences and first language. Esme's already lost her parents and grandmother. No wonder she craves attention and acts out sometimes, Frankie thinks. And now I would be asking her to face losing her family at NNAA. Frankie, feeling daunted, closes down the computer and decides to talk a walk around the zócalo to clear her head.

That night she has a dream of performing a jazz solo in Berlin. In a moment of kinesthetic perfection, her arms elongate to the music within the music, with perfect pace, like perfect pitch. As she turns with exquisite control of her core muscles, Frankie creates spin after spin in gravity-defying symmetry. But then she notices the audience is walking out in pairs until there's only one person left in the theatre. Raoul rushes on stage, yelling, "Stop! I'm so sorry." Frankie stops. "Your mother's dead."

"No Raoul, look at the front row, at the woman with flowers. That's my mother."

"Frankie, can't you see she's not moving?"

Frankie wakes up with her heart pounding and a sick feeling inside. It's 3 a.m. in Oaxaca and 2 a.m. in New York. She doesn't want to startle Tricia by calling in the middle of the night, so she waits until 6 a.m., her mom's time, knowing she gets up at 5. They chat casually and Frankie decides not to mention the dream. Hearing Tricia's voice is enough, and Frankie understands her dream, like most, is about more than what it seems.

Chapter Forty

DISTRITO FEDERAL (D.F.)

Mac, on an evening flight to the capital of Mexico, El Distrito Federal, imagines being home in the States today. He'd be at his parents with Deanna, celebrating his favorite holiday with turkey, homemade cranberry sauce and his famous chocolate pecan pie. He feels a mix of longing and guilt. His parents will be alone for Thanksgiving and Deanna has a long drive to Pennsylvania. It's too early for blizzards, but the highways will be packed with holiday drivers.

Another kind of longing and guilt accompanies him. Images of Frankie persist, even when he longs for a nap; they come unbidden with an energy and urgency he can't deny: dancing under the stars; making love in the woods, her scent, her hair. No matter what he feels for Frankie, Mac has promised his parents and Deanna that he'll be home for Christmas. He prays Abuela won't be on her deathbed because if he doesn't come home, it could be the death of his marriage although Deanna assures him each time they talk that she loves him.

***

After tossing and turning all night, he leaves his hotel at 8 a.m. the next morning to find his way to an apartment building on the corner of Campeche and Tonalá. He's been to Mexico City before but never to this neighborhood, the Roma section in the Cuauhtémoc borough. The wide streets are beautiful with overarching ancient trees and small parks every few blocks. He stops to appreciate a street duo, a trumpeter and saxophonist, their notes reaching above the tropical flora and drifting over outdoor cafes and juice stands. God, how he misses performing. The rhythm stays with him as he pauses to take in an art deco mural of a tiger's head on the side of a building. He researched well, wanting to learn as much about his mother's environment as possible before making his grand entrance, but the images on the internet didn't capture its unique ambience.

Mac is hyper-aware that Rosario may not be happy to see him. With thirty-seven years of not trying to find him, she could quite possibly slam the door in his face.

His adoptive mother, Sophia, comes to mind and he feels a surge of love, then a twinge of guilt. He knows his searching makes her nervous, even though he's tried to allay her fears of being replaced, or that he might find another home in his birth country. Sophia feels remorseful enough for the years of subterfuge, which still gnaw at him, but he knows he could never replace his mom. He loves her dearly and deeply. He wonders why he isn't just as angry at his father. He really should be. He's been holding back from both of them lately. Is it revenge? Self-protection? A sense of propriety? Words come to him from a song the lead guitarist in his band wrote. “There’s a ruckus in my brain.” That’s for sure, he thinks, and starts humming the tune.

Mac wonders for the nth time how in heaven his biological mother has been so easy to find. There she was on an old Facebook account. Just like that. Under her real name: Rosario Alexandra Cocijo. No digging. She’s been hiding in plain sight, but he hadn’t known to look.

Why had no one in the family tried to find her, or she to find them, or more importantly, him? Why did Rosario leave him with strangers at an orphanage instead of the loving arms of his Aunt Consuela and Abuela. Is she a monster? Oh, there’s that ruckus again in my brain, he thinks. The truth, whatever it is, will at least free me from it.

He returns to the present moment to step aside for an oncoming mom pushing a stroller, a spotted dog trotting beside her. Mac notices all the twenty-somethings, freshly showered and purposeful, with backpacks and notebooks, many with sketch pads under their arms probably off to Arts Vita Studio, a nearby art school. The neighborhood has an old-world feel with gracious four-story buildings, but a youthful vibe. Black wrought-iron balconies frame billowing curtains and blood-red geraniums. Could it really be that his biological mother is somewhere in this enclave? After further investigation, which too was not complex, Mac found her address. There has been no obituary, no change of address, no reason to believe she has moved. Yet, as he’s learned, anything is possible.

With envy, he sees patrons enjoying breakfast at sidewalk cafes, the morning sun warming their backs. The smell of coffee almost brings him to his knees. He hasn't eaten since yesterday afternoon, trading eating for sleeping and waking up so nervous, he didn't want breakfast. Mac breathes deeply for the last few blocks, and when he finally arrives at her apartment building, number 240, he's humming like a swarm of bees.

She hopefully still resides in apartment 201. He enters the vestibule, the marble walls discolored but still dignified. Among the crossed-out names on mailboxes, he sees hers standing out in royal blue calligraphy surrounded by delicate brown feathers. He wills the butterflies in his stomach to stay this side of nausea. Mac presses her buzzer and waits. He takes off his Red Sox cap, fluffs up his hair and looks down at his walking shoes.

Seconds later, he looks up into a face searching his through the glass. She opens the door and steps lightly into the vestibule. Rosario, if that's who she is, is five-foot three at most with strong features and coffee-colored skin. Her dark brown hair cut in a bob frames her face, and she wears black jeans and a paint-splattered t-shirt. Her only makeup is black eyeliner and the depths of her brown eyes startles him. He notices wrinkles at the corners and violet shadows underneath.

Rosario speaks in Spanish, "Are you delivering photos from Juanita? I'm Rosario Cocijo." Her voice sends a shock up Mac's spine. Rosario scans him up and down while he's trying to figure out what she just asked. He can't think. Her eyes rest on the baseball cap in his hand. She furrows her brow and speaks in English. "Do you speak English?"

"Yes."

"Oh boy. I guess this means you're not the delivery person?"

"No, I'm not." Everything he's rehearsed escapes his brain, like he accidentally hit the delete button.

She steps back slightly wary. "Can I help you with something?"

A voice comes from the stair landing above and behind her. "Rosario, someone called your cell and I have to go. Do you have your keys?"

"Si, Helena." She looks at Mac like the stranger he is. "We have an automatic lock system."

Oh God, Mac thinks, she's afraid of me. "I mean no harm. I want to speak with you."

"You're American, aren't you?"

"I'm American, but not by birth." His heart is pumping overtime and his breath so shallow he can barely speak. "You, more than anyone would know that."

Rosario blinks a few times and her hand comes up unbidden to her mouth. She steps back, brown eyes snapping. "Who are you? How old are you?"

"Thirty-seven." Rosario tilts her head studying the angles of his face like she's going to sketch him. "I can't believe this! Let me see your ankle."

"You don't need to see it, Rosario. The birthmark's still there, a small turtle above my right ankle bone."

She backs up and pulls a pack of cigarettes from her shirt pocket. "Jesus Christ," she intones. She lights up and inhales while shaking out the match. Is this anger, Mac wonders, or anguish. He can't tell. She hasn't taken her eyes off him. There are certainly no tears.

She hugs one arm around her waist as she drags on the cigarette and leans against the wall. "For years I've tried to quit." She blows the smoke out slowly. "How did you find me?"

This cool reception lodges like a stone in Mac's throat. "Your Facebook account."

"But how did you know who to look for? Your adoption records were sealed."

"The rules changed a while ago. I'm glad to see you too!" Incendiary rage threatens to blow this whole trip up. He fights an instinct to flee. "I'm not sure which planet you're from, but it's everyone's birthright to know how the hell they got here."

Rosario throws her cigarette down, stamps it out, and picks up the butt to deposit it in a stand-up ashtray. She pulls both arms tight around her waist and stares at him. Mac gets trapped in her bottomless brown eyes, a mirror reflection of his. If there's any warmth, he's not sensing it.

She shakes her head. "You have to forgive me. I'm in shock. I made sure this day would never come, but here it is. The hospital wasn't supposed to say where I brought you, and the father never knew I was pregnant."

"The visiting professor? Abuela said you came here to live with him, well, to be kept by him because he had another family."

"You've met my mother? Dear God, that was never supposed to happen, and that's what she told you?" Rosario lights another cigarette.

"She said you were crazy in love and he didn't want the baby, so you gave me up for him and a ticket to Mexico City."

Rosario cringes and gives him a sharp look. "I need to sit down." She leads Mac out the door and they sit on the top step of the building. "My mother often says things she shouldn't, that she doesn't know about." They hear footsteps coming down the stairs and into the foyer. Rosario takes his arm briefly, the first time he's ever been touched by his biological mother, but it's calculated and furtive.

"Don't say anything now. Please."

Helena comes through the door. She's big-boned with blonde cropped hair and looks German or northern European. "Bye, my sweet. I'll see you at dinner." She bends down and kisses Rosario on the lips then stands back and looks at Mac.

"Are you delivering the photos?"

Rosario intervenes, "No, he's looking for someone in the building. I'm helping him."

"Okay, bye. I hope the photos arrive." Helena looks younger than Rosario by a good decade. They watch as she unlocks her bike in front of the building and rides off.

"She doesn't know about you. No one does."

"You've made that clear." Mac's never felt this uncomfortable in his life. "Well, I'm sorry to have bothered you." He starts to get up.

Rosario reaches out to stop him. "Wait! Please! Don't go. It wasn't the professor I was crazy in love with. Look, I have to work this morning. I'm on a deadline, but can you come back at noon and we can go to a cafe?" She stands up. "Please? You've come all this way." She looks at him closely. She reaches out to touch his arm again, but he pulls back. Her face registers pain. Ah, he thinks, she can feel. "You are right about your birthright, to know how you came to be." Mac stares and puts on his cap. Her black eyebrows furrow. "Will I see you here at noon?" He nods and heads down the stairs.

"Hey! Wait a minute!" Mac looks back. Rosario, one hand over her mouth, lets it drop and asks, "What's your name?"

***

Mac walks towards the public garden he saw on the map, Jardín Ramón Lopez Velarde. He's feeling light-headed and empty, like he's in a trance. He walks three blocks and finds the broad stone-paved path and enters a tropical garden oasis. Breathing in the damp fertile earth, he closes his eyes and is back in the forest in Lachatao with Abuela. He says a prayer for her health like he does whenever he thinks of her.

Mac approaches a fountain pulsing water twenty feet into the air. The spray catches on the wind and sun just right and beads of prismatic stars streak overhead. He closes his eyes and feels the sunlight warm his lids. Mac lets himself relax for the first time since the beginning of this trip. Soon, he's almost asleep on his feet, and it dawns on him how stressful unearthing the truth is. There are reasons for secrets and keeping them so.

His stomach growls and Mac imagines himself propped up in his hotel queen-sized bed, eating huevos rancheros with freshly-squeezed orange juice. Like a dog on a leash, his appetite leads him back to the hotel where he devours his breakfast and collapses back on the pillows.

***

After sleeping for two hours, Mac showers and then takes a cab to Rosario's apartment. She's waiting on the top step. The only thing that's different is she's changed her spattered t-shirt for a lovely blue silk blouse. He's not nauseous-nervous now that he's met his mother, but his insides are still churning with everything he doesn't know.

They walk side by side in her neighborhood until they come to a corner restaurant. As they order lunch, life goes on around them, but Mac feels like he and Rosario are in a bubble. He clings to every nuance: the way she tucks her hair behind her ears, the timbre of her voice.

"By the time we moved to Oaxaca for my high school scholarship, Abuela and I had been at each other's throats for years. She wanted me to carry on the curandera tradition, apprentice to her and live my life in Lachatao. It was out of the question. I am an artist through and through and I knew it. She knew it too. I drew and painted every spare moment. I studied every art book in the Oaxacan library and went to all the museums. As amazing as Abuela is as a healer, she was a domineering mother and didn't value what I wanted. She said as her daughter, herbs and healing were my destiny. She never questioned that. My scholarship was my ticket to escape, and I was horrified when the family decided to move to Oaxaca with me."

"But she said they did it for you, that it was a sacrifice and she didn't want to leave Lachatao."

"Ha! Yes, to indebt me more to her so maybe I'd change my mind, but I wasn't having it. I lived with them only in body. My spirit was at school where I could learn. Everything excited me then. I lived in my head and my art. I still do." Mac listens and watches Rosario picking at her food.

"What about you, Mac? What makes you get up in the morning?"

"I'm a professor of pre-Columbian art and culture, so my students get me out of bed."

She looks at his ring. "I see you're married, yes? Children?"

"My wife, Deanna, is a scientist and no, no children. Not yet. But that's complicated." Rosario tilts her head in question, but Mac has no interest in talking about himself.

"Let's go back a bit. You didn't completely live in your head. I mean you did get pregnant."

Rosario looks startled. "Touché, Mac." She shifts in her seat and bites her thumbnail for a moment. "Okay, part two of my story. I did get pregnant. Your biological father is Frederico Velasquez, the older brother of my friend Magdelena. She was sixteen like me at the same high school, and it was her I was madly in love with. If I could have run off with her, I would have been truly happy, but she didn't notice me that way. All I knew was I had to get as close to Magdelena as possible, and I used Frederico. He became my novio. They were very close, so the three of us always did things together. I often ate dinner at their house, and we went out dancing and to parties, the three of us. She was my knife-edged obsession, a dangerous game. I don't think she was gay or understood my torment although she must have known I was taken with her. It was agonizing and pathetic really." Mac has been deeply attentive, and Rosario pauses like she's waiting for a reaction, but he remains motionless, absorbed. "I'm sure I'm not the mother you were expecting."

Mac leans forward. "I didn't know what to expect. Look, it's your story, so it's my story too. This is what I came to hear." Rosario looks relieved.

"Thank you. One night we were all drinking and I danced so closely with Magdelena I thought I would faint. I took that fire back to Frederico all the while thinking of his sister. This became a pattern. I spent my young lesbian libido on her brother, and then I found out I was pregnant.

You would think the daughter of a midwife would have been smarter, but my head was in the clouds, and it was quite a shock. I was already two months along and there were three months until graduation so I hid it with big blouses and smocks. Not even Abuela noticed until the middle of the summer."

Mac is struck by the irony that his adoptive mother, Sophia, also engaged in a charade, but pretending she was pregnant, not hiding it. "I'm sorry to say this to you, but this was a dark time for me. In Spanish we say "dar a la luz," to give light, when a child is born, but I knew this was death for me and Magdelena. I slowly dragged myself away from being around her and Frederico, fearing one of them would notice my body changing, and then my life would be ruined. I would be expected to marry him. I made up all sorts of excuses. I was in anguish. Frederico had a harder time with the separation than Magdelena, making it even more painful for me."

"But why does Abuela think it was the professor who was the father?"

"Because, during this time, I was getting close to this visiting professor from D.F., Professor Almoneda. His confidence in me is why I'm here, doing my art, and making a living at it. There was never anything romantic between us. He took me under his wing and said he could find me work in the city with a graphic design company. He was my mentor, and his timing couldn't have been better. He didn't know I was pregnant. I never told anyone other than Abuela and Consuela when they confronted me."

"All this time Abuela has thought you were a "kept woman" and that you gave me up to be with the professor."

"I knew that's what she probably thought, but I wasn't about to tell her the truth. I had you one month early at the end of the summer and then moved to D.F. If I had stayed in Oaxaca, I would have been a kept woman, but by Abuela. There's no half-way with her. That's why I've stayed away. I've missed Consuela, I really have, but I chose not to ask her to meet in secret behind our mother's back because that would have been an awful burden. Abuela had a hold on me. She still does in some ways. None of this has been easy."

Mac again notices the shadows under her eyes. "I'm sorry."

Rosario looks away and back at him. "I'm sorry too for any pain I've caused you, but it wasn't just the situation with Magdelena. I knew I wouldn't be a good mother. My art has always been my priority. It's healing and uniquely truthful for me in ways nothing else is, but my commitment to my work doesn't mean I didn't want the best for you. I just couldn't give that to you, so I took steps to make sure you'd have the best life possible. Looking at you, I think I made the right choice."

"That could be true, but when you're the child, it's hard to accept your mother doesn't want to keep you, no matter what the reason is."

"I'm sure. And I'm sorry I couldn't be your mother." Rosario pauses, "Maybe we could get to know each other and be friends?"

The suggestion stuns and feels all wrong. It is *something*, Mac thinks, but is it something I want? He shrugs noncommittally. "Why didn't you leave me with your family? Abuela and Consuela would have been very loving."

"I was afraid if they had you, I wouldn't be able to leave. I would be tied to them and you without the strength to stay away. I was seventeen and selfish, but that is the one regret I have. I should have left you with them."

"So instead, you cut yourself off completely."

"Yes, but I never hid, and I figured if they wanted to find me, they could."

"Yes, and I figured if you wanted to find me, you would."

Rosario's eyes well up. She reaches into her bag for a cigarette, holds it up and looks at Mac. "Do you mind?" He shakes his head in the negative and she lights up. "Mac, I've thought of you a million times. I wondered where you lived and what you looked like. Did you like dogs better or cats? Blue or yellow? Were you smart in math or science or languages? I asked NNAA to be in touch with me when you were adopted, so I knew your parents were Americans, but I didn't want to know more. It hurt too much and was a reminder of my failings. I assumed you were headed for a better life. At that point, the documents were sealed and I let you go with all the blessings and naivete of a young girl. The haunting came later."

But Mac understands without asking, given the chance, she wouldn't have done anything differently. He thrums his hands on the table.

"You're not going to believe this. But I didn't even know I was adopted until five months ago."

"What? They never told you? How did that work? I mean, are they Latinos?"

"No, but my mom's Sicilian with olive skin and dark eyes, and I do look like some of my cousins. Now that I know I'm Mexican, it's more obvious."

"So, all of those decades I was worried you felt abandoned, you didn't even know you were adopted?"

Mac shrugs. "Life can be funny like that."

"Wow. I'll say." Rosario gestures for the check. "Well, I'm grateful you didn't have all those years of wondering. Will you come back with me to the apartment? You're in some of my art work, not in a way you'd recognize, but there is one sketch I made of you as a newborn. I want you to have it."

Mac is touched, then remembers Helena. "But what about your partner? I'm not going to pretend to be someone else."

She inhales her cigarette, closes her eyes and slowly opens them. "I'll take care of Helena." Mac's not sure what that means, but he wants to see her apartment and take in as much of her life as possible in this short, and quite possibly, only visit.

"I'll come back with you, but I want you to consider something. Abuela's very sick now, close to death. And she asked me when I found you, to say that she should have looked for you years ago, and she's sorry. She said to tell you she loves you. Maybe this is a chance to reconcile?"

Rosario looks as if he's just grown horns. "That's what she said? I don't think you understand."

"I'm just asking you to consider it. For my sake. To have the three of us together once before she passes; I think it could be healing for everyone."

Rosario lets out a moan then laughs. "I think seeing me would kill her on the spot. Why on her deathbed would she suddenly be understanding and forgiving? I'm a lesbian artist who deprived her of her only grandson. Because she said she should have looked for me doesn't mean she's forgiven me. She stopped speaking to one of her sisters when her sister was twenty over some misunderstanding. I don't trust it."

"But what about Consuelo? And your nieces?"

Rosario gets up from the table. "Let's go see your sketch."

***

Mac is surprised at how orderly the apartment is, Rosario's studio especially. Every paint tube and brush is in its place. Sun shines on the hardwood floors and two paintings in progress are propped on easels. They are striking edgy modern paintings in purples and greens and black. Rosario is able to lay her hands on the sketch in seconds. She hands Mac the envelope.

He looks at the drawing trying to feel grateful, but the conversation about Abuela has been disappointing and disturbing. Suddenly everything feels strange. This woman, the apartment, this whole trip. He feels no connection between the infant in the sketch and himself as a man, or this woman in front of him who is his biological mother.

He puts the sketch back in the envelope. "Thanks Rosario. I've got to go now. Thanks for meeting me, for the story." He smiles. "For my birthright."

Rosario sighs. "Come, please sit in the living room. Just for a minute." She leads him to the couch, a deep green with a glass-topped table in front. The room has a minimalist style, sleek with only touches of color. They sit side by side. It's a comfort to him that his biological mother excels at something and is giving her art to the world, even if she couldn't and can't be his mother.

"I know at first, Mac, I seemed unwelcoming. I was shocked. But now that we've met, I would love to get to know you better."

"I don't know. I mean, I live in the U.S. and you live here. It's a long way." He pauses. "And I have a family there. A mother and father and a wife."

Rosario blinks a few times. "I see. But there is the phone and email. We could stay in touch."

Mac shrugs, confused and suppressing anger. "I guess. I hadn't thought that part through. I was so intent on finding you, especially before Abuela died." Quiet follows, punctuated by car horns and a bus engine. They hear footsteps in the hallway and suddenly Helena's in the room. She looks surprised to see Mac and looks at Rosario who gets up to greet her.

Helena kisses Rosario on the cheek. "Hi, Rosa." She looks at Mac. "I'm Helena. Weren't you here this morning looking for someone in the building?" Rosario grabs Helena by the hand and leads her to Mac. "Si, mi amor, and it was me he was looking for." She gestures gently. "Helena, I'd like you to meet my son, Mac."

Chapter Forty-One

PAPÁ, CAN YOU HEAR ME?

By the time Enrique arrives at the hospital it's 9 p.m. He did as Izmelda instructed and found a gas station, took off the foils and rinsed what looked like a collection of unkempt skunk tails. He towel-dried his hair and covered it with a mauve knit cap he had in his side bag.

The nurse at the reception desk explains that his father's stroke was on the left side of his brain which controls speech and language. Hopefully, there will be a big improvement within the first three to six months with therapy. Right now, he's able to speak but slurs or jumbles some words. During the next few days, they'll be doing more tests and bloodwork.

Enrique steps quietly into the room. Hooked up to IV's and lying under the covers sleeping, his papá looks fragile. He reaches to take his hand but flashes on Abuela swiping the Bible off the table. In contrast to that moment, with the soft beeps and light snoring, it's peaceful here. Maybe this is as good as it'll get between us, Enrique thinks, falling into a chair, exhausted from the intense ride. He nods off, and when he wakes hours later, his father's watching him.

Enrique stands. "Papá, can you hear me?"

His father nods.

"Raquel said you wanted me to visit. Is that true?"

His father nods again. He licks his lips in preparation for speaking.

"I saw your mamá." His words are raspy and he elongates the "your" and has to search for the word "mamá". Enrique thinks, oh boy, is it the meds or the stroke that makes him think she's still alive?

"She said…" He points to Enrique. "Love your son like you love me." It takes time to puzzle out his meaning as the words are even more slurred through tears running down his father's face. Enrique reaches out to hold his hand.

But his father is shaking his head "no" and doesn't take Enrique's outstretched hand. "I'm sorry. I can not to do what your mamá ask."

Enrique doesn't know what to say. His father turns his head away and closes his eyes, shutting Enrique out even more.

Enrique sits down. His head is starting to sweat, but he's afraid to take the cap off and give his father another stroke. He wonders if his mother's spirit really did visit him and in case, thanks her for trying. But, why would his dad want to see him if he still can't accept who he is? Enrique longs for a loving goodbye, but at least his father is sorry rather than angry; either way, something's broken, and his father, who's usually so good at fixing things, has given up on him. Inertia and a sickening feeling set in.

Enrique finally tears himself from the room. On his way down the hospital corridor, he takes off his cap and shakes out his skunk tails. He gets on his bike and flies through the streets, revving the engine to drown out whispers of "maricón y abominación". Tears threaten to force him to pull over, but he drives on. By the time he's in Santa Ana, the whispers are screams and it's Enrique who's angry and yelling and his father who's una abominación, a shame.

***

After his marathon ride back from Juchitán and visit to the hospital, it takes Enrique a few days to recover. He continues to live in Teresa's house. He's working four days a week at the garage and still doing his DJ work on weekends. This weekend, though, he found a sub because Marcos invited him to Juchitán. He says the distraction will be good for him and Enrique agrees.

As he's packing his side bags, his cell rings and he's surprised to hear Gregorio's voice. "I'll be back tomorrow morning for the night shift at El Saguaro. My dad seems to be stable." Enrique thinks he sounds slightly drunk.

"Gregor, I'm glad about your dad, but this is the third time you've said you were coming back. And just so you know, my father had a stroke and is just coming out of rehab." As Enrique talks, he circles his motorcycle like a restless dog.

"Oh, dear God. Is he okay?"

"Yes, except for his incurable homophobia."

"Enrique, I explained about the other times. This hasn't been such an easy trip… There's a lot to talk about."

Enrique kicks at the dirt and looks at the sun gauging the time. "I gathered. The topic is old boyfriend, I'm sure."

"The thing with Ronaldo is over. It never really got started all that much."

"Well, I'm off to Juchitán again. I told you about my friend Marcos and going to see La Vela de las Intrépidas a few weeks ago."

"So, you won't be DJ'ing Saturday?"

"No, and I really have to get going. I want to get there before dark."

"The velas, all that fanfare. You don't find it overblown?" Enrique's silent, tired of these not-so-subtle put-downs.

He hears Gregorio take a sip of something before he speaks. "I guess I'll have to wait to see you when you get back. Will you come by El Saguaro's on Monday after the lunch rush so we can talk? I miss you Enrique."

"Yes, I'll see you then Gregor, but I've really got to go." They hang up and Enrique realizes it's the first time he hasn't told Gregorio he misses him too.

***

When Enrique arrives at Marcos's house, he's greeted with a big smile and a kiss on the cheek. He fluffs up Enrique's hair. "Oh my, I love the new hair style! Very creative." Marcos looks at his motorcycle.

"I have to say, I worry that you ride all the way down here on that thing. It's not exactly a Harley, is it? And there're so many accidents on the highway with crazy people driving and rockslides. My mother told me to stop being such a mother. Imagine that?"

Enrique, instead of getting annoyed like he would with Raquel, is touched. He shifts his helmet to his other hand. "Thanks man. You're like the brother I never had."

"Brother? Of course." Marcos drapes his arm over Enrique's shoulder as they walk into the house, giving it a little squeeze, and then kissing him on the cheek.

Chapter Forty-Two

BENEATH THE PINES

Mac sits cross-legged on the couch of his B&B trying to meditate, but he finds himself thinking about the leftover quesadilla in the fridge, and does his car have enough gas to make it to Lachatao, then he sees Rosario's face, and thoughts of Frankie emerge of another nature altogether. He's usually able to escape the chaos long enough to make meditating work, but not today. Today, it's all distraction and agitation. He gives into it, bowing his head and hoping the spirit that illuminates the universe will take a rain check on his devotion.

He gets up and rummages around the counter and tiny refrigerator. He grabs some cheese, a half-eaten bag of popcorn, pops open a Dos Equis and heads to the patio. Now that he's had some distance from his encounter with Rosario, he can see that getting the three of them together before Abuela passes on was a fantasy. There will be no reconciliation. He has to live with that, as much as he has to accept his own biological mother can only be his friend. Do I want to be her friend, he wonders. He takes a long draught of beer. He hears children playing in the street and is aware of water running somewhere in the building, everyday sounds that make him wonder if his life will ever have normal and natural rhythms again.

He's about to call Deanna when he sees a text from Frankie. She's checking in to say hi and see how he is. She's friendly enough in her texts, but neither she nor Mac have suggested getting together since the night of El Día de los Muertos. He knows it's silly, but he likes looking at her name in his contacts, having some part of her with him. It's already early December and he'd like to see Frankie at least once before they each return to the States. While things are unresolved with Deanna, he knows he won't sleep with her again, but given the number of times he's replayed the scene in his mind, he may as well have.

Mac calls Deanna to say he has tickets to fly out of Oaxaca on December 23rd but gets her voicemail. Deanna's texts have become increasingly cryptic since the Thanksgiving change of plans, but they always end with "I love you." The last one included just one more word, "thinking". He's on a seesaw of confusion and hope.

It's all so frustrating! Mac throws the cell phone from the patio to the couch. He's relieved to see it settle on the cushion rather than splintering on the unforgiving tiles. When he retrieves it, he sees Deanna's left a voice message.

***

The next day, Friday, December 13th by 10 a.m., Mac is hiking up the familiar road to Abuela's. They plan to journey together on the hill behind the house in the sacred clearing. Abuela's probably already there burning copal and a bundle of basil, rosemary and piru leaves to purify it. Later, Mac will collect the final pages for the book.

He hums a song he's been composing. Every evening he goes to the zócalo to hear his favorite band with two sets of marimbas, a guitarist and several drummers. He lets the tones and rhythms wash over him and knows if he listens long enough, their music style will naturally infuse itself into his composing. As he nears the house, Mac can't believe how enjoyable this trek to Lachatao is, compared to the first time when he was so out of breath he had to sit and rest. He wishes Frankie could see what shape he's in. He wonders if she will ever agree to see him again. Shouldering a backpack is now easy as he shifts its weight and hears a clink-clink. He's brought the family's favorites: jars of chocolate-covered peanuts and a popular Oaxacan snack, chapulines, or fried grasshoppers. He imagines the smile on Abuela's face when she opens the bag.

He rounds the last curve and the house comes into view, but it's eerily silent, like a shadow suddenly darkening your path. Mac stops humming. Even the birds and air are still. It's only when he gets closer that he hears a low-keened wailing. He sinks down on the steps like a giant fist has punched the wind out of him. Leaning forward, he tries to breathe while a "no, not yet" reverberates in his head.

And then the rains come. Mac can't remember ever breaking down like this. The sobs originate deep in his solar plexus and force him to submit. He cries for Abuela and Rosario and for the years lost in not knowing this family and not having a family of his own. After he's cried out, the door opens behind him and he feels a hand on his bowed head. He looks up into the sympathetic eyes of Consuelo.

***

They've dressed Abuela in a white cotton dress embroidered with delicate flowers and birds. She lies in her bed surrounded by candles and calla lilies and bowls of her favorite herbs, lavender and verbena. Consuela, Francisco, Nayeli and Inda Jani sit in chairs in a semi-circle and chant prayers in Zapotec. Mac slips in to join them. Abuela looks like she's sleeping peacefully with her hair braided neatly and woven through with red and blue ribbons circled on top of her head like a halo.

Francisco is the first to speak. "We found her this morning, just a few hours ago, up in the clearing. She must have gone out before dawn."

Mac's heart sinks. "Abuela and I had plans to journey together there this morning."

Francisco says, "Yes, that's where she passed over. There were herbs and copal smoldering next to her. She must have decided it was her time." This is the most Mac's ever heard him speak.

Consuela and her daughters exchange glances. Consuela says, "Now I understand." She looks at Mac. "Yesterday she said the next time she would see you is when you journeyed to your guides. I thought she meant this morning, but clearly, she meant later, in spirit."

"You mean, she took her own life?"

Consuelo adds, "She knows the herbs that heal and those that destroy. She spoke with us a few days ago to let us know she was ready. She was feeling very sick, too weak to gather herbs, almost too weak to walk. She was in a lot of pain and suffering. She said to me, 'The book is done. I am done. Time to return to the clouds.'" Mac feels goosebumps on his neck and a brush of air along his cheek. His eyes fill but he's cried out.

Nayeli touches Mac's arm and speaks. "A few days ago, Abuela woke from a nap and made me promise to tell you this. 'Tell Mac, I see children around him. More than one.' Then she smiled and fell back asleep." Now Mac *is* crying again.

After supper, he gets up from the fire to take a walk in the evening air and look at the stars. He finds himself walking up to the clearing. Following the scent of rosemary and copal, he sits next to it and stays there for a long time.

***

By midday the next day, the entire village knows of Abuela's passing. Mac and the family sat by the casket all night in the main room praying and chanting and burning copal. Mac is washing up in the stream when he hears the

Lachatao brass band coming up the road. He rushes back to the house, and as he's dressing in the best shirt he's brought, the band arrives.

A dirge of horns and drums leads the march from Abuela's house to the church. Mac, Francisco and four neighbors carry the casket. The women of the family and pueblo follow in a line, many with gray shawls draped over their heads and some carrying fronds and flowers. They head towards the church for Mass, then on to the cemetery at the south side of the village. A huge cross of flowers waits there, adorning her grave under the sheltering pine trees.

Walking back from the cemetery, Mac wonders when he might be here again. He knows he'll come back at some point, but with Abuela gone, he's lost his touchstone. He was a worker bee to his Queen. As they near the town plaza, the dark-green trees begin to feel oppressive instead of majestic, the road is too dusty, and the cerulean blue sky mocks his darkened mood. He wishes the band would stop playing. It's grating and out of tune, and Mac is suddenly and horribly homesick.

Chapter Forty-Three

WROUGHT IRON

At La Casa de Isabel, Frankie opens her computer at the small wooden desk next to the balcony. She continues to educate herself about adoption. The current article focuses on potential learning challenges. Frankie recalls a dancer, Sandra, who left NYC Moves during Frankie's first year with the company. She was in the process of adopting two boys from Russia. Frankie emails Raoul for her phone number, not explaining why, and calls.

"I won't sugarcoat it, Frankie," Sandra says in her heavy New Jersey accent. "There will be bumps. None of the agencies tell you just how much support you'll need; otherwise, no one would adopt. But don't get me wrong. Can't imagine life without my boys."

"How did they adjust to school?"

"Oh, just assume your kid will need an IEP."

"A what?"

"An individual education plan. How old is she?"

"She'll be seven."

"Oh God, yeah. And you're saying maybe two kids, wow! Definitely. Coming to the U.S. at that age. But, it's not a bad thing, an IEP; everyone wants one now. I mean everyone. And, can I ask, do you have a partner?"

"No."

"Okay, so doing this solo. Hmm. You're just going to have to get support. I have a husband, a good one, and some days I was ready to tear out my expensively colored hair. It's a labor of love for sure, any kid is, biological or not. My boys came here when they were three, and now they're young men. I'm so proud of them."

"I bet you are. Thanks Sandra. You've been really helpful. I have one last question. How was it leaving the company?"

"Ugh! Like losing a leg. I won't kid you there either. It was terrible until we brought the kids home, and then there was no time to even think. I don't know if you remember, but my knees were really going at that point. I'd already had one replacement at thirty-three and the other was heading south. I knew I'd never be at the top of my game again, but it was still a tough decision. But I don't do the looking back thing. Life's too short. Believe me though, there was grief. If you've got more dance years left in you, think carefully. Those, you will never get back."

"Thanks again, Sandra."

"Oh my God, I'm always happy to help anyone thinking about adoption. Let me know what you decide, okay? Call any time. You take care now."

"Thanks. Will do." Frankie, feeling like a verbal semi has run over her, clicks off her phone. Staring through the wrought iron bars of the balcony, she mulls over everything

Sandra said. She sits there until the earth, shifting on its axis, takes the light with it and brings on a chill.

***

That next morning, a Monday, her cell rings at 7 a.m. Frankie gropes for the phone and sees Raoul's number. She sits up, heart racing. Raoul doesn't usually make it to the studio until 10, and then needs three cups of coffee before he can even speak.

"Are you okay, Raoul?"

"Yes and no, La Francesca Bella. Tina took a spill on black ice yesterday; she's got a concussion and broken vertebrae. I need to fill her part and you did this number, *Doves,* two years ago, a duet with Russell. Remember? It's a very long piece." Frankie's standing by the bed. She doesn't remember getting up.

"Of course, I remember, Raoul."

"Maya's the understudy, but I wanted to give you right of first refusal. Frankly, it would make life easier for me because you and Russell nailed it, but I know I promised you until the end of the month. The thing is, I need to know now, or close to now. You understand my position."

"Yes, Raoul, of course. Can you give me ten minutes?"

"Sure. Take fifteen. I'll be here." Frankie paces around the small room. It's too early to call Paula. She won't call her mom and Mac is on her "not to do" list. Frankie notices Esme's music box and Leonel's sneakers, Christmas presents she bought for them on the floor by her bed. She picks up the music box, winds it and watches the ballerina in her pink tutu turn around and around and around.

***

Frankie spends the rest of her day packing and settles up her bill at La Casa de Isabel. She calls Uncle Pepe early in the afternoon to explain her situation and let him know she'll come that evening to say good-bye. Around 6 p.m., she takes the bus along the familiar route to NNAA. Her stomach is in knots, not knowing how she'll explain herself to Leonel and Esme when she can't explain this decision to herself; all she knows is she's thrilled she'll be performing again.

She finds Uncle Pepe in the office and he escorts her to the dining hall. Everyone yells, "Sorpresa!" under giant loops of purple and pink crepe paper. There's a cake decorated with "Adios!" on it and fruit punch on the table. The kids are gathered with Enrique, Raquel, Uncle Pepe and some of the other volunteers, and then Frankie sees Mac walking across the room. It's all too much. She wants to be in New York already, but knows she owes it to everyone here, including herself, to go through this sad, prickly turmoil of good-byes as graciously as possible.

"Wow! Oh my God! I'm so surprised! Thank you!" Frankie says while scanning the faces for Esme but not seeing her. She's happy to see Leonel sitting at the end of a table. Frankie smiles and blinks a lot to stop her tears and sits down with the kids to eat cake.

After a few minutes, Julio approaches Frankie and everyone else quiets down. "We have a surprise for you. Close your eyes." The kids tiptoe to the middle of the floor in even lines. When they're set, Julio yells, "Open your eyes!"

The music starts and the kids perform a dance routine they've made up, the older ones knowing the steps and the younger ones improvising. It's so heartfelt that by the time they're done, Frankie can no longer hold back her tears. She rises and gives them a standing ovation.

Leo runs over and grabs her thigh. "Leonel, hello sweetie." Esme's absence is gnawing at her. "Where's Esme?"

"She's in her room. She doesn't feel good."

"Oh no, is she sick?"

"Right before you came, she got a stomachache." Frankie looks towards the girls' dorm and wants desperately to go find Esme but is afraid of making things worse.

Mac approaches Frankie and Leo grabs his hand. "Hola, Leonel!" He looks at Frankie. "I didn't know you were leaving until Raquel texted me today about the party." Frankie's happy he sounds sad rather than angry.

"I'm sorry, Mac. My head's spinning. It just happened this morning. Raoul, the Director of the dance company called and said they need someone immediately. A dancer's injured and I've done this particular piece in the past."

Leo chimes in, "Yeah, Frankie has to dance. On a big stage and she's going to send us a video."

"Yes, I promised and I will."

Mac lightly takes a hold of Frankie's arm. "Frankie, I came to say a quick good bye. I'm heading back to Montague myself in a week, in time for Christmas. Could we be in touch?"

"Yes, I would like that. I'll be in New York. I'd love to hear how everything turns out."

Mac looks at her for a long moment. "Me as well." He kneels down next to Leo. "Leo my friend, I'll be back tomorrow. I hope Esme's better because we're going on a field trip to El Museo Infantil de Oaxaca, the children's museum."

"I know!" He slaps Mac five and runs off.

Mac kisses Frankie on the cheek and leaves. She watches him walk out through the office, the same place they met a short, long few months ago. Shit, she thinks, this is really hard. Leo runs back and grabs Frankie's hand.

"Leo, I promise I'll come visit next year right after the spring performance. Please tell Esme that. And I'll teach you both a new dance. Oh, and I left a present for each of you with Uncle Pepe, but ask him in the morning in private. Okay? Promise?" Leo nods, eyes sparkling. "I'm going to walk around and say good-bye to everyone." She gives him a long hug and he runs off to play.

"Frankie." She turns to see Raquel, looking lovely but tired with Enrique right behind her.

"So dancing is calling you home?"

"Yes, it's all very sudden. One of the dancers is injured. I'm so glad you're both here tonight. I can't imagine what living in Oaxaca would have been like if we hadn't connected. I want to thank you both."

Enrique puts his arm around her shoulder. "You will be missed mi amor."

Raquel nods. "Yes, you will, and I want to thank you for all your help with the children and fundraiser and wish you good luck. I hope it's hasta luego, until the next time, not good-bye."

"Yes, I'll be back in the spring. I promised the kids. And, mi casa in New York es tu casa. I mean that, for both of you. Enrique you could bring Gregorio if you want, anyone really."

"We broke up a week ago, but that's a story for later. It's okay, really; it's better. I have my friend Marcos in Juchitán and I think there may be something special there. Vamos a ver, we'll see."

"I'm happy for you. And Raquel, do you think you'll be starting med school next year?"

"I'm applying for next fall, si."

"Good luck to both of you." Frankie takes each of their hands, then looks around. "Do either of you know how Esme is? She hasn't come out of her room."

Enrique puts a hand on her arm. "Uncle Pepe said she had a bit of a meltdown when he told the kids you were leaving."

Frankie feels sick at heart. "Oh God, do you think I should go to her and explain what happened?"

Raquel is quick to add, "I don't think so, because whatever you say, you're still leaving. I'd just leave it alone. This isn't the first time she's been through something like this."

"I hope I haven't really messed her up. I hope there's been more good than bad."

Raquel puts her arm around her shoulder. "Oh yes, I think so, Frankie. But please make good on your promise to come back in the spring if that's what you told them. Kids never forget."

"I know. I will."

Enrique shifts his weight clearly ready to move on. "I've got to go because I work at the garage in the morning and I'm giving Raquel a ride home." They hug good-bye and Enrique throws Frankie dramatic kisses on the way out.

Frankie goes around the tables saying her last good-byes and heads to the office for her sweater. As she's putting her arm into one sleeve, there's a tug at her back. She turns and sees Esme in her pajamas scurrying back through the door. On the floor is an envelope. Frankie picks it up and reads, "Open on el aeroplano." She turns it over and sees a circle of tiny butterflies and hearts and in the middle is a stick figure with a big smile and a cast on her arm. Frankie is so relieved she wants to run and grab Esme and twirl her around, but she keeps her feet planted in a strong dancer's landing. No good will come of an extended good-bye, no matter how wonderful a hug would feel right now.

***

The next morning, Frankie's packed and waiting for a taxi to take her to the airport. She's carefully wrapped all the presents for everyone in the dance company and said goodbye to the owners of the hotel.

The first thing Frankie does once settled on the plane is open Esme's card. On the front she's drawn a woman holding a little girl's hand; both are smiling. Inside the card, balloons float in the background and the same smiling stick figure has spokes sticking out of her curly hair pointing to words: FUNN, GOOD DANZER, MY FREN, SO NICE TO ME. The countless colorful tiny hearts become a blur. Frankie turns towards the window and lets her tears fall into the wide empty blue sky. On the way down, she had hoped for a parachute to land her in a better place. She didn't know it would be in a little girl's heart.

Chapter Forty-Four

SNOWED IN

Mac, bone-tired, arrives in Montague at 9 p.m. in the middle of a snowstorm. He landed in Hartford, Connecticut and rented a car. What would normally be a two-hour drive has taken him four. Adrenaline keeps him awake as he anticipates Deanna's surprise at his arrival a day earlier than expected.

Mac's humming volubly to keep notes of dread at bay. In over two months, Deanna hasn't clarified where she stands on adoption, not one word. He wishes he could hold her close, not discuss anything, and have everything feel like it did a year ago. He's hoping for a Christmas miracle.

Mac pulls into the driveway, so familiar he takes no note of it, but looking beyond the swirling flakes, he gets a jolt. The house is a dark outline. What, no Christmas lights? No house lights? Mac puts on the cell phone flashlight to see while he trudges through six inches of snow with his stuffed backpack and another bag weighing him down. It's frigid inside, the propane heater on just low enough to keep the pipes from freezing. Mac doesn't bother to yell for Deanna, and if Pumpkin were home, he'd already be at Mac's feet. He crouches before the woodstove in the study, rolls old newspapers into balls, tops them with kindling and starts a fire.

There's not one sign of Christmas, and Deanna loves Christmas, decorating the house with twinkle lights and pine boughs, and baking Christmas cookies. Panic grips him by the chest and Mac begins to shiver. A desolate homecoming; there's nothing like it to make you face the music and its dissonance.

Mac looks out towards the stream, barely visible through the thick silver-dollar snowflakes. Deanna's absence is more articulate than any conversation he imagined. This is it, he thinks. The finality pulls him up short, like when a beloved, sick for a long time, finally dies. Before that moment, there's a pulse, a possibility, however weak or frayed.

Mac goes to the kitchen and puts the kettle on for tea. The click of the burner sounds like a "tsk." He yells out loud, "Merry fucking Christmas!" The kettle starts to make a high-pitched screech. She could have at least stayed to see things through, he thinks. He silences the screaming kettle and swipes the box of teabags across the room. They scatter like old love letters. Mac realizes the weird groaning noises are coming from him and not the pinewood floor he's pacing.

After mindlessly staring out the kitchen window, Mac returns to the study and adds logs to the woodstove. He flops onto the couch, closes his eyes and has a visceral anticipation of Pumpkin jumping up and kneading his paws on Mac's belly. He senses the snowflakes gathering around the house, normally a peaceful sensation like being wrapped in a giant comforter, but now he feels a chilly claustrophobia. It makes him imagine how Deanna must have felt being left alone in this house for three months. Her not being here is teaching him a lesson. His life turning upside down, turned hers as well. Clearly, I expected too much, he thinks, and I was distracted by Frankie.

Mac approaches his beloved keyboard, but even the thought of music is no comfort. He puts his hands in his pockets and walks to the window. Maybe Deanna's absence is a strange dark kind of Christmas present. Maybe I should be grateful for the clarity. Mac then wonders if Deanna's told his parents she's leaving him. More dread. Tidings of shame and failure ring inside his head, their only son, childless, and now soon to be divorced.

He moves closer to the window and watches as the snowflakes, like whirling dervishes, spin and land on the field, their separate forms melding to become something unified, like words in a poem seeking connection.

In the study with his back turned, Mac doesn't hear the front door opening and startles when Pumpkin meows at his feet. Mac bends down, picks him up and clutches him to his chest. Deanna's in the dining room doorway watching. He puts his head down and cries into Pumpkin's fur. In seconds, Deanna's arms are around him.

"Sweetie, are you okay?"

"Yes, now that you're here. But who would be okay coming home to a cold empty house?"

"But I thought you were coming back tomorrow?"

Mac shrugs. "I wanted to surprise you, but with the dark house and no decorations and Pumpkin gone, I was sure you were too." Mac puts Pumpkin down and they hold each other.

"I wouldn't leave you that way."

Mac pulls back. "Are you leaving me another way?"

"Oh Mac, I'm not the one who first left."

"So, you *are* leaving?"

Deanna says, "One minute, Mac." She takes off her coat and boots and puts them away. She comes back and takes Mac's hand and leads him to the couch. "I didn't want it to be like this. I was going to cook dinner for us tomorrow so we could sit down and talk."

"Well, let's do it now, Deanna. Whatever it is, I'm getting the feeling it's not something I'll have an appetite for."

Deanna takes a deep breath. "You're right, Mac. I don't have the stomach for last meals either if that's what it would be, but that depends on you." They sit down on the couch and Deanna tucks her legs up under her and faces Mac. "Look, I've given motherhood so much thought since we talked. I've spoken with friends, your parents, my parents, the priest at my church." Deanna tears up. "I'd be an ambivalent mother at best, and that's not fair to a child. And it seems we're growing apart in other ways. The main point is, I love you too much to keep you from being a father, if that's what you really want."

Mac takes her hands in both of his. He chokes up. "I didn't realize how lonely this place could feel until I came home and you were gone. I'm so sorry."

"That's why I left. I've been at Alice's for a week, and I didn't have the Christmas spirit to decorate alone." Pumpkin jumps up next to Mac's thigh, and he lovingly brushes the familiar fur.

He looks up and realizes Deanna's bravely waiting to hear if he's going to end their marriage. His gut is tighter than a wrench. "I'm sorry, Deanna, but I can't let go of wanting to be a father. It's something I'll regret not doing. This desire, it's in here." He raps his fist on his chest. "But you're in here too." They reach their arms out for each other and hug, and rock, and cry.

Chapter Forty-Five

A WALK ON THE HUDSON

Frankie's back living in her East Village apartment, but she's hardly been home, rehearsing and performing, day and night. It's been so consuming she's had no time to reflect on or feel anything about Oaxaca or Mac or NNAA. Was she really there for three months?

Their last performance was this evening, Sunday, December 23rd. After hugging everyone good-bye and wishing them happy holidays, on the cab ride home, Frankie realizes everything and everyone in her family of dancers is the same as when she left in September. That's an odd effect of travel. You cherish the experiences that have changed you, but no one else can see them: morning light on the cathedral; bumpy bus rides as the one gringa; the first bite of an enchilada mole; Esme's hand around your neck; Mac's soft brown eyes.

After this final performance, Frankie feels life can finally begin to slow down. She pours herself some wine and sits cross-legged on the couch. She thinks about Mac and the fact she hasn't texted him since she's been back. Maybe I should at least wish him a Merry Christmas. He's probably home by now, and I wonder how things are going with

Deanna. Frankie decides it's better to wait for him to get in touch.

Frankie sleeps through most of the next day and goes to Paula's on Christmas Eve to have dinner with her and Sasha. Frankie doesn't look forward to Christmas Day, going out to dinner with her mother and her friends and their husbands.

Waking up on Christmas morning in the solitude of her apartment, Frankie finds herself reminiscing about Oaxaca. It makes her melancholy and she's physically exhausted, so rather than get out of bed, she snuggles more deeply under the covers. David's gone. Mac's gone. Paula will soon move in with Sasha, but there's something more, something else.

Frankie calls her mom. "Mom, I'm so sorry, but I have an awful migraine. I can't possibly make it to dinner." Frankie listens. "No, don't come over. Talking just makes it worse. Yes, I'll call you later this evening. Yes, I know it's Christmas. Merry Christmas, Mom. I love you too. I know, I'm sorry you're disappointed."

Frankie hangs up, showers and makes a strong cup of Mexican coffee laced with chocolate and cream. Her lethargy has morphed into restlessness and she paces the apartment. She puts on her deep-red winter coat, black boots, and hat and gloves as white and soft as snowflakes. The water is drawing her.

Frankie heads towards the Hudson River, striding the forty-minute walk in bracing air laced with a few half-hearted snowflakes. She walks to the docks and heads north registering the abandoned boats and listening to the quiet of a city that never sleeps, only on this one peace-filled day. No street dogs bay across the river, no fireworks bloom, no brass bands play proudly to God. Frankie stops and faces the water, the wind both numbing and invigorating. A tugboat, towing a rusty barge, sounds its foghorn. The solitary note pierces Frankie, breaks something apart inside her that crumbles and spreads through her body and soul. On a second note, just as piercing, she turns and heads home.

Frankie enters her apartment, and without taking off her coat still damp from the Hudson, goes straight for her cell phone. "Hola, Tío Pepe. It's Frankie."

Chapter Forty-Six

Four Months Later – April, New York City

HOT CHOCOLATE

It takes Mac three trips back and forth from the hotel bathroom to the bedroom to get up the courage to press her number. Frankie and Mac haven't texted or called for months.

"Hello, Frankie?"

"I'll go get her." The little girl's voice is jarringly familiar.

"Esme, is that you?"

"Yes, it is! Mac, is that you?"

"Yes, is Frankie in Oaxaca?"

"No, silly Mac! We're in New York. This is my new house. Well, really, it's an apartment and I'm going to get a dog! We've been looking on the Internet. Where are you, Mac?" Mac has to sit down on the hotel bed.

He hears Frankie's voice in the background. "Esme honey, I've asked you to please let my phone go to voicemail when I'm busy."

"But it's Mac. Don't you want to talk to Mac?" There's not the slightest pause.

"Hi Mac!" Frankie's voice is alive and happy.

"Congratulations! You're a mom?"

"Yes, for about three months now." Frankie looks at Esme. "Wait a sec Mac, please. Esme would you go get my sweater off the bed? Thanks." Esme skips off and Frankie speaks softly. "I'm sorry I didn't tell you sooner. Honestly, I didn't know myself until I came back to New York and realized I didn't want one more thing to regret in my life."

"So, you figured it out. Good for you!"

"Hmm…yes, and then it was more like a leap of faith." Esme returns with her sweater. Frankie smiles and gives her a thumbs up.

"Wow! I'm so happy for you, Frankie. I really am. So, are you still with NYC Moves?"

"Well, that's the thing, I am. I finally got smart and hired a nanny, a lovely young woman, Niza, from Santa Ana. She's a friend of Raquel's and now lives here with us. In March, both she and Esme came to Europe with me for a month when we performed, and I hired a tutor for Esme." Esme, bored with adult talk, skips off down the hallway. "Life is completely berserk, but we're happy most days. So, what's going on with you?"

Mac looks out the fifth-floor window at the skyline and sighs. "It didn't work out with Deanna. It's been really hard. There's still a lot of love there, but I do want a family and she just couldn't come around. But, you've inspired me Frankie with what you've done, adopting on your own."

"It's something anyone can do if you want it enough and plan for it."

Mac turns away from the window. "I keep thinking of Leonel, but then I get overwhelmed."

"We should definitely talk, Mac."

Esme flies back into the room with lipstick smeared on her face. "I want to talk to Mac too!"

"Oh my God Esme! Is that my lipstick? You look like a clown!" Mac laughs so loud that Esme hears him.

Esme puts her hand on her hip. "Mac thinks it's funny."

"Well, I don't. Go wash it off and then I'll let you talk to Mac." Esme flies back down the hall and Frankie hears her turn on the faucet.

"Actually, I'm in town doing some archival research, and I'd love to see both of you. Could you meet for coffee?"

"You're in New York? Oh my God, where?"

"I'm at a hotel in Washington Square Park."

"No way! I can practically see the park from here. Sure. When?"

"What are you doing now?"

"One minute, Mac." Mac can hear Frankie yell to Esme.

"Esme, want to go meet Mac? He's here in New York." Esme flies back into the living room with half the lipstick washed off, puts her hand out to her mom for the cell phone and gives her a pleading look. Frankie put her cell on speaker and hands it over.

"I'm so excited Mac. Will you buy me a hot chocolate?"

Mac laughs and say, "Of course."

"Now go and wash the rest off so we can go." Esme races away again.

"By the way, Esme and I are going to NNAA right after the last spring performance at the end of May. I promised Leonel we'd visit. That's something to think about."

Mac doesn't know how to respond, but is happy to hear what sounds like an invitation. "We can talk about that, but first, let's meet for coffee, and hot chocolate of course."

"Sure. What hotel are you in?"

"The Washington Square Hotel."

"Great! We'll see you in the lobby in fifteen minutes."

Esme comes back into the living room with a clean face, wearing a yellow spring coat and red rubber boots. Frankie puts Esme's beautiful heart-shaped face between her hands, the most tender and loving of gestures, and says, "That's my girl. Ready for an adventure?"

GLOSSARY

abuela - grandmother

alebrijes - brightly colored Mexican folk art sculptures of fantastical creatures

aquí - here

borracho (a) - drunk

boca grande - big mouth

bueñas tardes - good afternoon; **bueñas días** - good day

calle - street

cálmate - calm down

casa - house

cerveza - beer

chapulines - fried grasshoppers

cojones - testicles, nerve

comedor - small restaurant, dining room

comida - food

cómo no - of course

con - with

curandera - healer

de nada - you're welcome

de veras - really

Díos - God

directo - straight ahead

esposo - husband; **esposa** - wife

fouetté (French) - in ballet, a turn with one leg extended
frijoles - beans
guapo - handsome
hasta luego - see you later
hermano - brother; **hermana** - sister; **hermanita** - little sister
hija - daughter; **hijo** - son
iglesia - church
igualmente - likewise
jardín - garden
jeté (grand) (French) - a broad, high leap in ballet;
jeté (tour) - a high, turning leap
leche - milk
limpia - spiritual, energetic cleansing
mancomunados - jointly responsible
maricon - offensive term for a homosexual
Maya - an Indigenous people living in Mesoamerica (Mexico and Central America) Before the Spanish conquest, the Maya possessed one of the most advanced civilizations of the Western Hemisphere.
muchacha - girl
médico - doctor
mercado - market
mijo - my son
molinillo - a wooden whisk used for frothing
montañas - mountains
mucha gente - many people
mucho gusto - nice to meet you

muxe (moo-shay) - a Zapotec word based on the Spanish mujer (woman), for males who, from boyhood, have felt themselves drawn to living as a woman and identify as female, or as neither male nor female but a third sex

muy bueno - very good; **qué bueno** - that's nice

naturaleza - nature

nieto - grandson

niño - boy; **niña** - girl

pliés (French) - in ballet, deep knee bends

noche - night

pobresita - poor thing

por favor - please

primos - cousins

qué linda - how pretty

rebozo - shawl

ropa típica - traditional clothing

sagrado - sacred

seguro – sure

sí - yes

sobrino - nephew; **sobrina** - niece

solamente - only

tía - aunt

tienda - small store

tío - uncle

todo - all

topes - speed bumps

vámonos - let's go

vela - candle, festival

venga - come

vida - life

Zapotec - an Indigenous pre-Columbian culture living in and around Oaxaca, Mexico whose culture originated 2,500 years ago

zócalo - central plaza of a city or town

AUTHOR'S NOTES

My connection and love for Latin America began when I was twenty-three and went to Antigua, Guatemala to visit my friend, Emily. I stayed for two months studying Spanish, and then we spent two more months traveling by bus through Central America to Colombia and Ecuador. With no selfies, I lived wholly in the adventure of the moment: walking black volcanic beaches in El Salvador, sleeping in hammocks with pigs grazing underneath, and drinking corn liquor with Ecuadorian Indians.

In the winter of 1993, I taught and did a homestay in San Cristobal de las Casas in Chiapas, Mexico as part of a Master's degree in TESOL. (Teaching English to Speakers of Other Languages). That summer I went back to Guatemala to work on my thesis project studying the Mam language in Todos Santos.

On February 9, 2000 my husband, Gary, and I flew to Guatemala City to meet our infant son, Nicolas, a moment that sparkles forever. When Nicolas was six, in the fall of 2005, Gary and I decided having a Latin American adventure would be good for the whole family, especially Nick. The three of us and our aptly named dog, Rio, climbed into a green Honda Odyssey and made the ten-day trek south to Oaxaca, Mexico. The seed for this book, planted decades earlier, blossomed and thrived in magical Oaxaca. We rented a house in San Felipe del Agua nestled in the foothills of the Sierra Madres and visited pueblos every weekend. We made many ex-Pat and Mexican friends, ate tons of enchiladas, drove over thousands of topes (speedbumps), attended posadas, and soaked in the colors and textures. We also volunteered at a Children's Center and for Libros para Pueblos.

My mother, in her eighties at that time, had diabetic retinopathy and could no longer read, so every two weeks I sent her tapes describing our journey so she could feel she was with us. When we returned, I transcribed the tapes which became the source for many of the descriptions in this book. LuciaPress is named for her, a lifelong reader and amazing mother. She died on August 25, 2006.

ACKNOWLEGEMENTS

It takes a village…

To Gary, my loving, adventurous husband who has been patient, kind and extremely helpful with my zillion questions during the writing of this novel. He deserves a medal.

Nick, my son, mijo, whose Latin roots entwine my heart and without whom, we never would have lived in Oaxaca. He's made my heart, big, big, bigger than the sky.

My brother, Roger, who is most definitely still gay in heaven and inspires me still.

My parents, Lucille and Harold, long departed, but never gone.

Thanks to my gigantic extended family who all promised to buy the book before even knowing what it was about.

Special thanks to my editors: Meghan Flaherty and Amy Calkins for their honesty, expertise and encouragement. They were water to a thirsty writer. Megan counselled wisely on many aspects, including use of a second language and gave me confidence the manuscript had "good bones". Amy, the comma queen and stickler for clarity, was a steady source of support and humor as we slogged through lines. She also lent her expertise with the book cover design.

I am so grateful to my readers for their thoughtfulness and guidance: Lisa Limont, Rick Fentin who wants to date

Frankie; Toni Fentin, Joy Harris, Linda Holder, Colleen McGrory, Diana Kinch, who's been encouraging from the beginning; and Linda Hewitt who kept my feet to the fire and hands on the keyboard. Diana and Linda are part of my Kitchen Table Writers Group. (KTW) To them as well – a bevy of supportive women who love to listen, write, and encourage in the most loving of ways: Marie Murphy, Susan Prindeville, Nancy Hewitt, Cindy Liepman, Deirdre Whelan, Joan Kovach, Fran Araujo, Jane Widiger, Jane Zimmerman, Marion Reed, Melissa Boynton, Susan Albiero, Deborah Mary Higgins, and Leni Gross Young who is still with us in spirit.

I am grateful for publishing counsel from Sam Kafrissen, Brian Shillue, April Eberhardt, Linda Carbone, Sandra Miller and Mary Rowen.

Big hugs to my gym/coffee klatch for listening to me throughout this entire process and providing me with encouragement, caffeine, and helping me come up with a new book title every other day: Janice Rohlf, Liz Sumorok, Marie Burack, Diane Crowley, Rong Tilney, and Martha Craumer.

Because of everyone's support, my dream, *Weaving Dreams in Oaxaca* was realized.

ABOUT THE AUTHOR

Karen Samuelson is a career/life coach and writer. She has written three screenplays, a play, several dramatic scripts for Sunburst Productions in NY, and the Teacher's Guide for episodes of Degrassi Jr. High. She was a quarter-finalist in the Cynosure Screenwriting competition in 2015 and 2016 for her screenplay, *Sanctuary*. In 1987, she received a Certificate of Recognition from the City of Boston for producing *City Roots*, a documentary about high school dropouts. In 2018, Arlington Friends of the Drama stage-produced her play, *Circling Back*. She lives with her husband, son, and dog outside of Boston and spends quiet time in Vermont.

Made in the USA
Middletown, DE
12 December 2023

44372116R00208